T0274619

CUTLER

**Published with support from the
Fremantle Press Champions of Literature**

David Whish-Wilson is the author of ten novels and three creative non-fiction books. He was born in Newcastle, NSW but raised in Singapore, Victoria and Western Australia. At eighteen, he left Australia to live for a decade in Europe, Africa and Asia, where he worked as a barman, actor, streetseller, petty criminal, labourer, exterminator, factory worker, gardener, clerk, travel agent, teacher and drug trial guinea pig.

David is the author of four novels in the Frank Swann crime series and two in the Lee Southern series, two of which have been shortlisted for Ned Kelly Awards. David wrote the Perth book in the NewSouth Books city series, which was shortlisted for a WA Premier's Book Award.

He currently lives in Fremantle, WA, with his partner and three kids, and teaches creative writing at Curtin University.

CUTLER
DAVID WHISH-WILSON

FREMANTLE PRESS

First published 2024 by
FREMANTLE PRESS

Fremantle Press Inc. trading as Fremantle Press
PO Box 158, North Fremantle, Western Australia, 6159
fremantlepress.com.au

Copyright © David Whish-Wilson, 2024

The moral rights of the author have been asserted.

This book is copyright. Apart from any fair dealing for the purpose
of private study, research, criticism or review, as permitted under the
Copyright Act, no part may be reproduced by any process without
written permission. Every reasonable effort has been made to seek
permission for quotations contained herein. Please address any
enquiries to the publisher.

Cover image: Fishboat vessel fishing in a rough sea, istockphoto.com
Designed by Nada Backovic, nadabackovic.com
Printed and bound by IPG

 A catalogue record for this
book is available from the
National Library of Australia

ISBN 9781760993252 (paperback)
ISBN 9781760993269 (ebook)

Fremantle Press is supported by the State Government through the
Department of Local Government, Sport and Cultural Industries.

Fremantle Press respectfully acknowledges the Whadjuk people of
the Noongar nation as the Traditional Owners and Custodians of the
land where we work in Walyalup.

This book is dedicated to ocean defenders
And to Simon and Jeremy, for the deepwater meditations

Processus cum figures, figurae in processu.
(The process is made by those who are made by the process.)
−Ernst Bloch

List of Abbreviations

ACIC	Australian Criminal Intelligence Commission
AFP	Australian Federal Police
AIS	automatic identification systems
EEZ	Exclusive Economic Zone
EPIRB	Emergency Position-Indicating Radio Beacon
FAD	fish aggregating device
FFA	Forum Fisheries Agency
GPS	global positioning system
INTERFET	Inter(national) F(orce) E(ast) T(imor)
PNA	Parties to the Nauru Agreement

Prologue

The seven men removed jackets, belts and bandanas, which they used to wrap their knuckles. Framed by the headlights that enveloped them in a milky corona, their boots were at Cutler's eye level, down in the dust, and he knew the owner of every one of them.

Cutler struggled a final time with his restraints, then gave up. He swore through his gag, an oil-stained rag from the clubhouse. His cursing made no sense because the men wouldn't remove the gag. If he challenged them one on one, or all together, their sense of honour would demand that they let him fight, but they had seen him fight, and they wouldn't risk it.

He was in the forest clearing to be murdered with fists, boots, tyre iron and pickaxe handle.

Cutler would never know how they'd learned. This was not a movie, where the details of his mistake would be made clear. He had lived among the men for fifteen weeks, and he knew each of them well – their wives and girlfriends, children and grandchildren. But they were not murdering Cutler. They were killing the man they knew as Hennessy, a smurf who cleaned their cash and made it real. Soon they would learn that the encryption app they communicated on, introduced to them by Cutler, had been corrupted. Even their cleaned cash, the property owned in blind trusts, would be taken from them.

This meant nothing to Cutler, giddy with fumes and concussed to the point that if he weren't about to die, if he wasn't already in pain, might close his eyes and sleep. He felt no satisfaction at the thought that his killers would soon be arrested, and likely imprisoned. They would never be charged with Cutler's murder, because his body would never be found, four hundred kilometres west of Sydney, deep in a national park.

Dex, the sergeant-at-arms, sucked on his glass pipe before tipping spent crystals into the wild oats beneath him. He stepped toward Cutler and stretched his arms, cracked his neck. Because of the looming forest at the edge of the circle, his steps appeared large and distorted, like those of a giant.

Dex would strike the first blow, as was his right. Dex, who Cutler had seen using a needle, which was against club rules, and who added sugar to his Milo, despite his diabetes. Who liked to do a cryptic crossword every morning, in his long johns by the fire. Who was now so emaciated and strung-out that he wasn't strong enough to handle his giant Harley CVO Softail, couldn't support its weight at traffic lights.

Dex took another step and cracked his wrists, hoisted his jeans. A whoop behind made him flinch, as Midget emptied his pipe and stamped toward Cutler, skirting Dex's arm that missed its mark, failed to hold him back.

That was the problem with the club – nobody took the hierarchy seriously. Cutler had gained access to the organisation via Midget, who was a lean six foot five, for the offer of a shave on the percentage Cutler took of every transaction.

Midget was a proper sadist, and he buried his boot deep in

Cutler's belly, began to circle, stamping on his ankles, his knees, looking for a breaking point. Cutler could move a little, just enough to take some of the blows on the meat of his legs, but then Dex joined in, began stomping his ribcage, placed a boot on his throat to hold him still.

'Do it,' Cutler said through the gag, and with his eyes – crush my throat and be done with it. The older man shifted his weight and dragged the sole of his boot over Cutler's face, slowly and with force. Another joined the circle, grunting with his exertions, the sharp spears of pain strobing from Cutler's body, barely illuminating his dulling mind, in shock now, feeling the paddling of the pickaxe handle on his spine, his forearms, longing for the bottom of the freshly dug grave behind him, the smothering of earth.

'Aw fuck,' someone yelled, from away by the cars – might as well have been from another valley, another forest, another life. Behind his eyelids Cutler watched an orange fountain spray the darkness. He opened his eyes to the grassfire, whipped by its own wind, climbing the sides of the open jerry cans placed behind the men, there to burn his body into rubble, spurting fire in gouts, yawing geysers of odd colours, the men jumping, ant-bitten, flames catching on their greasy jeans, patting themselves down, racing for the cars as the fire began to speak its guttural whispers to them, chasing them to the rim-line of forest trees. There the fire paused to dance among the smaller saplings which began to crackle, speaking in whip-cracks and vibrato drones as the cars sped across the blackening hillside and down the track, an honour guard of flaming branches lighting their way. The wind swirled in the clearing as the forest raged smoke into the spaces between the flames. Cutler began to roll, felt the heat on his skin and clothes and hair, rolling over his mashed arms, tasting the dirt and smoke and blood in his mouth. He reached the lip of his grave and breached the edge, sliding headfirst down into the six-foot hole, birthing a cloud of dust as he watched the flames lick at the edges of his sanctuary before passing above, the sound of its eerie whispers and banshee laughter as Cutler lifted his legs and bent his body in two, passing his wrists beneath his feet and freeing his hands. The grave was deep and cool and when the fire was gone he would follow it, a ghoul of cinders and ash, until he met the angelic men and women in fluoro yellow, who would cleanse him and make the call to his handler.

I.

The room Whelan organised for Cutler was on the second floor of a besser-brick apartment block overlooking the Suva docks. The apartment was rented by the American company whose vessel Cutler would be riding to the fishing grounds, until they located the *Shuen Ching 666*, and Cutler was transferred. The apartment was empty most of the year and smelled of ashtrays, damp curtains and the black mould that covered the bathroom ceiling. It had a kitchenette, and a hot shower and toilet. The main room contained a bed and a couch with a view over the port, where two American purse seiners were undergoing repairs. Cutler didn't know where the captain and mates of those vessels were billeted, but he assumed in a hotel downtown, past the municipal market where he'd bought himself some supplies, including three jars of peanut butter, two bags of brown sugar, three boxes of muesli bars and a coconut that he drank on the sweaty walk back to his apartment. The trade winds were blowing from the east and the temperature was mild, but humidity was high, and he'd arrived at his door lathered in sweat.

He didn't bother unpacking. His passport and cash were laid across his bed in the money belt he'd bought at Perth Airport. The bag contained the clothing he'd thought necessary for the six-week job, with a few last-minute purchases, including wet-weather gear and a waterproof puffer jacket, a heavy woollen beanie and a pair of polarised sunglasses. The idea was to look like an inexperienced but enthusiastic fisheries nerd, embarking on his first employment aboard a commercial vessel as a licensed PNA observer.

Whelan had told him to buy large at the Australian duty-free, and so Cutler had bought his allowance of litre bottles of Johnny Walker Red Label, and six cartons of cigarettes, to ingratiate himself with the captain and crew. Whelan would supply everything else.

Cutler checked his watch and pulled the sliding doors that led to the balcony. He lit a cigarette and watched the creamy-blue waters swirl behind an antique lugger approaching the wharf, kestrels riding the winds above in wafting circles, diving into the ocean to spear baitfish. The lugger turned into the docks, nudging plastic rubbish and parting petrochemical rainbows that glazed the surface waters. The men aboard the lugger wore shorts and tee-shirts draped around their heads. Their skin was purple-black and their bodies lean with hard work. A boy among them leapt to the dock with a rope between his teeth that he hitched to the nearest mooring. Two others slipped tyre-fenders down the side of the clinkered hull, the boat shuddering on impact before jerking at its leash, and settling.

The satellite phone behind Cutler trilled. He re-entered the room and saw a large shadow cross the front window. Instinct caught him hard, and he felt dizzy, staggered as he leaned to the phone. The man at the door knocked, and the trilling died.

Whelan was dressed for the tropics, in board shorts and a beige shirt from a camping store. If the shirt was designed to wick moisture away from the skin, it wasn't working. As Cutler waved the older man into the room, he could smell the sourness on him, could see the beads of sweat on the back of his neck. His boaters creaked in the silence of the room, and his shirt stuck to his body as he collapsed onto the couch.

Whelan looked at Cutler and frowned. 'You're a smoker?'

'You want one?'

Whelan sniffed, shook his head. 'My wife, Deb, died of lung cancer five years ago. Not a nice way to go.'

Cutler paid it no mind. 'You come straight from the airport?'

'Yeah, the driver's waiting outside, with the ... materials.'

'I'd offer you a beer, but I've only got water.'

'Had a few ... too many on the plane. Free bar, of course.'

Whelan had flown from Perth to Suva direct, bypassing the international airport at Nadi, in the private jet of a mate – one of the world's biggest retailers of luxury pearls. Back in Australia, he'd talked about their weekend trips from Perth to Greece just to dine at a particular Cretan restaurant. Whelan was filthy rich, too, although he didn't talk or dress like a man worth sixty million dollars. He was the CEO and main shareholder of one of Australia's largest commercial fishing operations, with licences to take toothfish in the Antarctic, and tuna just about everywhere else.

Cutler had done his due diligence on Whelan, who'd started out the old way, working as a deckhand on his father's southern-bluefin fleet, before the vast migratory shoals were thinned out. He then managed tuna ranches off Lincoln, where juveniles were dragged from the open ocean in giant enclosures to fatten them up, before that too became unviable. Whelan was his father's son, had manifested the business into a behemoth, following what he called the Australian principles of efficiency, investment, technology and constant adaptation. They were pretty words, and Cutler had little idea of their veracity, and cared even less, because the nature of Whelan's business wasn't the reason the two men were there, in a badly painted hotbox overlooking a sleepy port.

Whelan stared at the balcony, his expression forlorn, helpless as only the parent of a missing child can be. He seemed unable to speak, and Cutler didn't fill the silence. If Whelan's fishing operation wasn't the reason they were there, his attitude toward the industry certainly was. Cutler had asked around. Whelan's outfit was distinctive because of its obedience to the laws, and his determination to be a good actor in an industry plagued with organised crime, ruthless multinational cartels, cowboy operators and the soft-power projections of the rival Chinese and Taiwanese fleets. Being a good actor meant sticking to quotas, carrying shipboard observers, having his ships flagged to Australia, maintaining MSC certifications, reporting data accurately for the purposes of stock conservation, allowing his ships to be electronically monitored and, increasingly and controversially, giving money and resources to conservation entities and fisheries agencies aimed at bringing the rest of the world's major operators into line. The pun had been intended when it was described to Cutler as Whelan's turning the massive ship of his business away from fisheries science – whose entities he saw as suspect and industry-captured – toward fisheries conservation, when the two approaches had existed at loggerheads for decades. The move had won Whelan many friends in the conservation movement but many enemies among his fellow fishermen, and among the bureaucrats and merchants whose livelihoods depended on a growing supply of fish, whatever its provenance.

'Do you want to go for a walk?' Cutler asked, when it looked like Whelan was on the verge of collapse. He was a big man, toned for his age, with boyish looks and a natural head of sandy hair. Whelan's socials were full of him mountain biking and road racing, scuba diving and spearfishing. Astride a large-frame racing bike, Whelan looked like he was mounted on a tricycle, so large were his limbs.

'No thanks. Too hot. I don't feel right.'

The man before Cutler hadn't shrunk, exactly – he still commanded the room with his bulk – but his once-tanned skin was now pale, and his eyes were sunken, and his cheeks sagged on his otherwise youthful face.

'If you don't mind me saying, you look like you need to eat. Or sleep. Something.'

Whelan sighed, put his face into his hands. His shoulders trembled. He wept. Cutler left him alone, went to the balcony and smoked a cigarette, watching the shift-change on the docks, men in orange jumpsuits and high-vis greeting one another as they departed and arrived through the main gates – no security that Cutler could see.

Cutler heard the front door open, and when Whelan returned, he had an impact-proof plastic suitcase, heavy in one hand. He placed it on the bed and fingered the combination locks, cracked the spine. He began to lay out the maps, the cone-shaped EPIRB, laptop and boxes of batteries and even more of medicine – antibiotics, disinfectants, painkillers, bandages – that Cutler had requested. When the suitcase was empty, Whelan sighed. He tensed as he firmed his resolve, peeled back the suitcase liner, removed the Glock pistol that he held like a piece of evidence – with a pinkie finger – and quickly dropped it onto the bed.

'First time I've handled a pistol. It's lighter than I expected.'

'Made of polymer, mostly. You don't carry weapons on your ships?'

Whelan took a deep breath, but it didn't refresh him, instead made him sag to one side, reaching for the wall to brace himself.

'Fucking vertigo. Yeah, sure, we always carry weapons. Every fishing boat does. Shotties, mostly, but that's always the first mate's job. I never went near 'em.'

'Not many pirates down there in the Southern Ocean.'

Whelan tried to laugh, but it didn't sound right. 'Not for *pirates*, mate. For fucking mutinous cretins, on the meth, or coming off the meth. Lots of sharp objects on a fishing boat. Once you've had a gaff swung at your head, or a filleting knife digging at you, a shotty in the wheelhouse seems a good idea.'

Some colour had returned to Whelan's face as the memories of conflict worked though his heart, his blood – the old male restorative.

While there was adrenalin in his system Cutler broached the question. 'What about Bevan? He ever dabble?'

The question made Whelan reel for the wall again. 'Seriously? Alright. I promised full disclosure. Bev wasn't into fast; he was more into slow. The odd party drug, plenty of ketamine, when he was younger – we did that together once at a festival. Turned me into a jellyfish, a blob on the grass. But Bev, he liked dancing, the floatiness, the out-of-body. We could always talk about that stuff. He tried heroin once, but it made him violently ill.'

'What about you?'

'Is that pertinent?'

'Full disclosure, right.'

Whelan gathered himself into a ball, leaned against the bed, his legs steady. 'I like a bit of coke, but who doesn't? Special occasions only. I get a bit greedy. My dad was a drinker. Addiction's in the family. What about you?'

The question was gently put, Whelan's pale eyes tentative, not expecting an answer.

Cutler shrugged. 'I take dexedrine to stay sharp. Valium to counter that, when I need to.'

'Nothing else? You must have been around a lot of drugs. Your line of work—'

Cutler held up his hand. 'You don't get to ask about that. What about the Taiwanese fleets – there a specific culture of using?'

Whelan thought about it. 'We're talking about fishermen. Long hours. Brutal hours. Robotic killing. Loneliness. Months at sea, sometimes years for the crew, the slaves I mean. *Yaba, kyethi, shabu*, horse pill, call it what you will. Some captains give the crew meth to keep them working. Saves feeding them too. They have their own ways to deal with the behaviour problems that result. You can imagine.'

'That'd be across all the fleets. What, specifically about the Taiwanese?'

'Nothing specific. *Worse things happen at sea*, you know the saying. We drug test, so do the Yanks, but not reliably. Fishing fleets, they're all ... hierarchical, the command structure. The captain and mates have total power. Outside of a few countries, the crew have no rights either, no union, no ...'

Whelan was flagging again. He slumped on the couch, put his head in his hands as the dizziness passed. Cutler spoke to the top of Whelan's head.

'Everything's on the laptop, as agreed? Bevan's logs, his blog, the GPS data, all that?'

Whelan nodded but didn't risk opening his eyes.

'Then I don't need you anymore,' Cutler said. 'I'll call when necessary. You've paid me for six weeks. This goes over, you make the same payment, the same way. Otherwise, I'll see you back in the Lucky Country.'

Whelan stood too quickly, groaned and covered his mouth. He panicked, looking for the bathroom. Cutler stood aside as the old man went and emptied himself, his retching noisy in the stifling little room.

—

During the night Cutler awoke to the sound of clanking from the port and the wind humming forlornly in masts and rigging, the curtains on his open window slapping the walls. He'd tried to drink himself to sleep on the duty-free, and had taken two valium to see him over, passing out on the old couch, the laptop splayed on his chest.

Cutler's eyes opened to the digital image of young Bevan Whelan, smiling beneath a purple bucket hat, his lips chapped, and his nose burned by a tropical sun. The photograph was a selfie, standing on the bow of a ship with a pod of dolphins riding the bow wave beneath him. His eyes were slitted due to the midday glare, but even so the warm blue of his father's eyes was unmistakable, as was the dimpled chin, the strong jaw and sandy-blond hair, shoulder-length on his reddened shoulders. The photograph headed a blogpost about a report he'd heard, aboard the American purse seiner, of fishing captains still setting their nets on migratory whale sharks, despite the practice being banned in the vast PNA fishery. The fishermen were doing this because juvenile tuna shoaled beneath the hulking whales, and below them, larger tuna congregated, much like how a FAD, a fish aggregating device, operated to attract fish in the middle of the big blue ocean. It was, Bevan said, almost as if the fish tried to form their own island, their own community, in the face of a volume of water that to a small fish must resemble the voids of interstellar space. His American captain, Rick O'Reardon, an old salt who'd fished the Pacific for decades, had admitted that setting a net on whale sharks was common practice when he was younger, as was the setting of nets on pods of dolphins, whose feeding attracted seabirds, visible for miles, for much the same reason. The whales and the dolphins inevitably drowned in the nets, part of the cost of doing business, but the blogpost was hopeful, Bevan said, because they were currently in a closed-to-fishing region of Palauan waters some 475,000 square kilometres in size. Despite the hundreds of thousands of dolphins that continued to perish in purse-seine nets, and the thousands of whales, that very day he'd seen the results of this conservation measure – dozens of whale sharks and pods of dolphins several thousand in number, free from the hand of a rapacious industry. He believed in the PNA mission, had seen with his own eyes how it was working.

The post was uploaded on 1 May 2024. Cutler slapped the laptop shut. Four weeks after that date, Bevan Whelan disappeared from the face of the earth.

2.

The noise in the port was the result of the *Monterey* unloading its cargo of frozen bigeye tuna, the hundred-kilo monsters chained at their tails and hoisted across from the hold, clanging three at a time into steel buckets, which were then forklifted into the back of waiting trucks. The frost on their skins smoked in the early morning humidity, their stunned eyes catching the first rays of sunlight that broke over the green hills behind the port.

Cutler passed through immigration without event, surprising considering his newly issued Papua New Guinean passport, organised by Whelan in a matter of days, during which time he'd schooled Cutler on the nature of the institutions and treaties that governed, or were supposed to govern, fisheries in the area Bevan had disappeared in. Fisheries observers in the Western Pacific were required to be citizens of the eight PNA states, or Parties to the Nauru Agreement, and while Fiji was party to the FFA, or the Forum Fisheries Agency, according to Whelan it wasn't officially part of the PNA cartel that controlled twenty-five percent of the world's tuna fishery. Captain O'Reardon and the *Monterey* operated out of Fiji and used a Fijian crew to fish in international waters north of PNG, but passed through PNA waters, where the fleets of Japan, China, Taiwan, Korea, the EU and the US operated alongside mostly illegal fishers from Indonesia and the Philippines.

Cutler's cover story was that he was the son of an Anglo-New Guinean coffee-plantation owner from the north, and therefore qualified as a citizen. The young Fijian woman stamped his passport without comment, her eyes friendly above a Covid face mask, sweat dampening the armpits of her blue shirt. Cutler was the only person leaving port, and he'd thanked her and collected his single duffel, and the plastic suitcase given to him by Whelan, heading across the puddled and broken tarmac toward the *Monterey*.

Cutler didn't know his way around fishing boats but had done his reading. The *Monterey* had the classic silhouette of the tuna purse seiner, with a high bridge at the front and a lowered stern, where a small skiff was chained. In the middle of the ship was a crow's nest, open to the elements, where a lookout kept an eye for feeding seabirds or surface dolphin activity. Behind that was an open deck piled with a net laced with orange floats. Above the net was a power block and heavy boom, connected, Cutler presumed, to a drum winch. It wasn't a pretty-looking boat, low in the water and rust-stained along its sides, and at around forty metres looked more like a destroyer than the fishing boats he was used to seeing back at home.

Cutler checked his watch. He was early, and so lit a cigarette and watched the final tuna winched off the boat, while the Fijian crew, dressed in dungarees, white singlets and gumboots carried frozen swordfish, Spanish mackerel and dolphinfish on their shoulders down a ramp to a waiting utility. There was no sign of Captain O'Reardon, who was supposed to meet him at 0600 hours sharp. O'Reardon was taking Cutler to the fishing grounds as a favour, and as an act of penance, according to Whelan. The American captain had initially taken on Bevan Whelan as an observer despite his lack of Pacifica citizenship, because Whelan was an investor in O'Reardon's fish processing plant outside Suva, employing and training locals in the processing and fishing game. The long-term plan was to revive a native Fijian fishing industry, which had struggled in the past decades.

O'Reardon's sin was that he'd allowed Bevan Whelan to transfer his observer position to another ship, a Taiwanese vessel, despite misgivings and without running it by Whelan Snr first. The transfer had happened, according to O'Reardon, because *he* followed the law, and so the young Bevan Whelan had become bored. He wanted to be an observer on a ship where he could make a difference. That ship, as it turned out, was the *Shuen Ching 666*, a tuna longliner whose previous observer had quit in fear of his life, returning to Kiribati after demanding to be taken to the nearest port in Honiara, spending all his savings on a plane ticket home. He was later interviewed by Whelan Snr, via Skype, and Cutler had watched a recording of their conversation. The man had made specific allegations against the captain and first mate, including attempted bribery, cruelty to his workers, breaking every fishing rule possible and eventually threatening murder when they demanded to see the man's computer, and read what he'd written there. But none of this was known to Captain O'Reardon, or Bevan Whelan either, when he'd climbed aboard the *Shuen* in international waters somewhere west of Nauru. The Kiribatian observer had advised Whelan Snr to hurry, if he planned on pursuing the Taiwanese captain, because it was near the end of season, and he would likely dump or swap out his crew, assuming he was complicit in Bevan Whelan's disappearance.

A woman around Cutler's age, twenty-five or so, walked confidently down the ramp and onto the dock. She waved at Cutler, and called him over, tying her hair in a ponytail with quick, whipping movements. She looked European until Cutler grew closer, saw the warmth of her skin and islander features, her calm brown eyes framed by long black hair. She wore shorts and bare feet, and a baggy singlet over a bikini top. She was as tall as Cutler, and every bit as athletic.

Cutler dropped his duffel, put out his hand, smiling, but caught the woman's eyes hardening as she looked into Cutler's own, as happened so often. She glanced at the scars on his wiry brown arms, put on a big smile and shook his proffered hand.

'I'm Casey. Captain's daughter. I'm also the first mate. Show you to your bunk?'

'Paul … Cutler. Sure, that'd be great.'

Cutler didn't know how much Captain O'Reardon had told his daughter about him, but in any case she'd read him truly: his service history, the jail time perhaps, there in his eyes and the scars he wore.

He followed her up the ramp, felt his tread soften as the boat shifted in the tide. She moved with assurance, not a wasted movement, and was clearly streetwise too, as he assumed every first mate on a fishing boat must be.

The sunlight was already harsh on the unpainted steel rails, the walkways and the white fibreglass walls, everything built to be blasted clean with wave and hose, the stainless-steel floor beside the hatch and chute bloodless and dry. A generator thumped somewhere, and the smell of diesel was strong near the engine room, whose door was open. Cutler followed Casey O'Reardon into a darkened chamber at the foot of the bridge, where stairs rose to the wheelhouse. Ahead was the kitchen and mess, where stacked crates of canned food and eskies containing vacuum-sealed meat beside sacks of onions, potatoes, waiting to be sorted and packed. A man was singing inside the kitchen in a language Cutler didn't recognise. He smelled coffee, and burnt toast, but Casey had already taken the stairs and was waiting for him on the next floor.

'You're in my room. I'll hot-bunk with Dad until we find your assigned ship.'

Cutler clambered up the ringing steps, the duffel and suitcase unwieldy in the small space. 'You sure? I can sleep anywhere,' Cutler lied, 'sleep like a baby once I'm out.'

There was something in the way she'd said 'assigned ship' that made Cutler realise that Captain O'Reardon hadn't shared the nature of Cutler's employment with this daughter. This was perfectly understandable, although it would make it awkward, involving some degree of deception when they were together, because she'd already sensed something of him, back there on the dock.

'Yeah, I'm sure. Dad and I usually swing twelve-hour shifts anyway, ships in the night and all that. I'll insist he showers before hitting the bunk, at the very least. Did you serve? You've got that look. My brother's in the marine corps.'

Cutler was relieved at the question. What she'd sensed of him on the dock, he hoped could be explained by his service. One less lie that Cutler would have to tell. 'Yes, but not for long. Basic training, one tour of Afghanistan, that's it.'

It was the truth, although not the whole truth, leaving out his subsequent shift into the AFP, and whatever you'd call his role since the beating and assumed murder, when he'd left the AFP and his undercover identity but also his real history, and started anew, a living ghost, which suited him fine, at least for the time being. When his AFP handler, Malik Khalil, had transferred to the ACIC, the Australian Criminal Intelligence Commission, a secretive organisation that ran human sources all over the globe, he'd been lured back with the promise of a choice of work and unlimited new identities. He wasn't on a salary and was instead paid according to his needs, and for the scalps he took. Unlike most ACIC human sources, Cutler wasn't being compelled to risk his life in exchange for a reduced sentence either – Khalil had nothing on him, and he could walk away at any time. It felt like freedom to Cutler, who'd lived and worked within institutions for the majority of his life.

Casey's room was as small and cluttered as he'd anticipated, although she'd made it homely, with a colourful doona and pillow, a shelf of books kept in place with a strap, and an open cupboard full of light summer clothes, with diving gear visible behind.

'I'll just grab that stuff.'

Cutler stepped into the corridor as she scooped into a case tampons, razors, a tube of roll-on deodorant and other toiletries, and a couple of packs of meds in plastic bottles. Sunlight glowed in the circular window, silhouetting her against the churning bay and green hills, which were dotted with squatters' camps and cassava fields.

She caught him watching. 'I'll give you the tour later, eh? Let you get settled in first.'

Cutler nodded, listened to her footsteps padding down the hall, the squawk of a heavy steel door. He tossed his duffel onto the bed and laid the suitcase on the bench-table, took out the laptop and opened the screen. It was a Whelan company laptop, but with a PNA logo on the keyboard and home screen. The laptop was fitted with hardware that allowed access to the satellites that Whelan's OceanFresh fleets used all over the world, in their nearly hundred vessels.

Cutler logged in using memorised details and was put instantly onto the OceanFresh website, which used an open-source global fishing map detailing information from AIS data, or the automatic identification systems that every ship carried. Every commercial vessel above a certain size was supposed to transmit AIS data 24/7, except that illegal fishers routinely turned their transponders off to avoid detection when engaged in pirate fishing, or turned on an alternative transponder, or swapped transponders with other vessels to confuse authorities. The map had been pre-programmed with the specific identification of the *Shuen Ching 666*, and Cutler walked his fingers on the screen, enlarging the map where the *Shuen* had last been seen, when he'd checked yesterday. There it was, a small rectangle that grew larger as Cutler enhanced the screen, its numbers typed in white font, remaining to the left of the speck that was Nauru. Whelan had showed him how to identify the movement of the vessel as indicative of its activity.

If it was stationary, and it was the only vessel in the area, it was likely drawing in its longline, which might stretch to some hundred kilometres of baited filament. This could take a significant amount of time. Because the PNA licence agreement was based on allowable fishing hours, and allowable fishing days, rather than using a quota system, the crews worked hard to strip the line of its catch before resetting it with fresh bait.

The *Shuen*, according to the AIS satellite map, was moving slowly in a north-westerly direction. There were no other vessels on the screen, even as Cutler shrunk down the map, with the nearest signals coming from a pair of what looked like large merchant vessels off the coast of the Solomon Islands, twelve hundred kilometres away. This was unusual, according to Whelan, because the Chinese, Taiwanese and Japanese fleets tended to work in similar areas, for reasons of safety, and on occasions to illegally tranship their catch to 'mother vessels' – huge freezer ships that returned to the mother country only when full, or to ports where they knew that the catch wouldn't be scrutinised for size, quota, species and other legal parameters.

Cutler stared at the screen for a few seconds, tried to picture the view from the *Shuen*'s bridge. Was the sea rough, as he feared it might be? Were the crew bent over cleaning tables, gutting, scaling, sorting while speaking among themselves, voices low? According to Bevan Whelan's log, the *Shuen*'s crew of five was made up of a mixed cast of young and older men from Burma, Indonesia, Malaysia and the Philippines. Their *lingua franca* was English, and scraps of Mandarin, sufficient at least to follow orders. Cutler wondered about the men, where they had come from, how long they'd been at sea. He had heard the stories. The common belief that the era of slavery was over failed to take into account the conditions aboard many distant-water fishing vessels. Men were trafficked, bought and sold like cattle, out of sight of any authority. *Worse things happen at sea.*

Cutler closed the laptop and took up the satellite phone. He dialled the number and heard the comforting ringtone, his connection to another life.

'Newtown Florists. How can I help?'

Cutler coughed, cleared his throat. 'Neve? It's me. Just checking in. Tell the boss I'm aboard and about to leave port.'

'Yeah? I'm pretty good thanks. Petunias are walking out the door. Don't ask me why. Must've been an article in some mag. Will pass that on. Stay safe. Ciao.'

Neve ended the call, leaving Cutler smiling. He had never met her, and likely never would. She was on the hook to his ACIC handler, Malik Khalil, for some indiscretion or other, and her job was all about plausible deniability, acting reluctantly as their go-between. Before Neve it'd been an older man who worked in a country bank, called himself 'the endangered species'. Cutler didn't know whether he'd died or had paid off his debt, but Cutler had been passed off to Neve sometime late last year. Intelligence Analyst Khalil wasn't much for going into detail, but he'd told Cutler one time that he bought flowers for his wife every Friday afternoon. She liked sunflowers, grew them herself, and when they weren't in season Khalil bought them for her. They sat on the kitchen benchtop and warmed the room with their relentless good cheer. When Khalil was on a job, as he often was, away from home for days and sometimes weeks, they were supposed to remind her of his smile. It sounded a bit cheesy to Cutler, but he supposed it made sense to have a go-between like Neve who Khalil contacted regularly anyway. Neve found it all a bit embarrassing – you could hear it in her voice. She didn't know who Cutler was, or even his name. He was known among the small group trusted by Khalil as the Asset, a title taken from a Jason Bourne film, which was embarrassing to both Cutler and Neve. When she greeted or asked after him, half-heartedly, she called him A, or sometimes A-plus, or sometimes A-hole if she was angry about something. She clearly didn't understand what some of her coded instructions meant, for the men that Cutler was living amongst, because if she did he'd hear it in her voice, as she began to worry.

Neve would never know it, but sometimes when things got sticky, when Cutler was wired with nerves and fearful that he'd been made, hearing her voice was like a small light at the end of the very dark tunnel – a marker of a normal person, living a mostly normal life.

On such occasions he found himself fantasising about what Neve looked like, behind the husky voice. He found himself daydreaming about meeting her, flirting with her, and there he stopped himself, because after all Neve was a florist, a civilian who sold pretty flowers, and Cutler was not a good person to know. He'd been undercover too long, to the point that he could no longer guarantee that his charm, his smile and sparkling eyes could ever be sincere, even for the right person.

Cutler's job was to get close to dangerous people, men and

women with hard-earned street smarts, and seduce them professionally, but most of all emotionally – to deceive and ultimately betray them.

Not many people could do his job. Cutler was good at it, maybe too good. He liked that he was good at it, even if he didn't always enjoy the work.

Cutler put the satphone in its canvas sleeve and tapped out a cigarette. The steel beneath his feet started to throb as the giant engine began to turn over. Journeying across the majesty of the ocean using an internal combustion engine seemed to him both a travesty and a metaphor for the anti-romantic reality of taking heavy-industry machines and putting them on the water. It was, he supposed, perfectly in keeping with the nature of industrial fishing, and the setting of hundred-kilometre fishing lines, each laden with tens of thousands of baited hooks.

3.

Captain Rick O'Reardon wasn't the Hemingway-esque figure that Cutler expected. He was clean-shaven, short and wiry, with black-framed Buddy Holly glasses under a faded LA Dodgers cap. Like his daughter he was barefoot. He wore blue jeans and a faded denim shirt, sleeves rolled to the wrist. The skin of his lined face was baked a deep brown, like a chocolate cake left in the oven too long, but the hairs on the backs of his scarred hands were bleached white. Cutler had seen those scars before, on old men and women after cancers had been cut out, and he assumed that the long-sleeve shirt and jeans was a matter of doctor's orders.

O'Reardon stood alongside Cutler as the purse seiner chugged out of Suva Harbour, aimed at the channel between two islands whose fringing reefs pulsed with surf. O'Reardon hadn't spoken since they left port. Cutler weighed the silence, and it was comfortable.

Finally, he spoke. 'Isn't Monterey where *Cannery Row* was set?'

Cutler met O'Reardon's cool blue eyes, red-rimmed with blepharitis or too much glare, and slightly enlarged behind the thick lens. The stare was friendly, however, until he broke and set his eyes back on the ocean. This was, Cutler presumed, how the captain had most of his conversations, side by side with others, speaking out of the side of his mouth.

'Yes, it was,' O'Reardon said. 'My ship's not that old, though. She was built in the seventies. Monterey was fished out by then. No more canneries now.'

'Didn't know that. Good novel though.'

'*Great* novel. You read *Travels with Charley*?'

Cutler shook his head, saw the captain watching him in the reflection off the bridge window. 'Was your father a fisherman?' Cutler asked.

'My father was a marine. I grew up all over. SoCal. Cuba. Hawaii. That was where I got the bug.'

'Casey, your daughter. She mentioned your son. Marines.'

O'Reardon nodded, turned the wheel a little to the left. 'Career soldier. He's an officer now. Stationed in Germany. All the shit with Russia at the moment ...'

'His father a fishing captain, I guess he grew up around leadership.'

'Nope. That was my second marriage. His stepfather was a marine. A better father than me.'

'So, Casey's a stepsister.'

The captain turned the wheel a little more, eased back on the power as the *Monterey* entered the channel, where humpbacked swells were lining up toward the horizon, crisscrossed with wavelets that jumped between the swells.

'Stepsister to five. Casey was my last. A happy accident. Her mother's from Guam. Still lives there. We're kinda together. It's a pretty casual arrangement.'

O'Reardon was silent for a long minute, Cutler content to watch the rolling swells and the sunlight shearing off the deeper blues. The silence didn't feel awkward, a product of O'Reardon revealing too much, or dwelling on past unhappiness. Instead it felt like he'd merely run out of words, or the need to form words.

But Cutler was wrong. O'Reardon's posture shifted, and his arms stiffened on the wheel. 'Where did you sit?' he asked, his voice hard.

'Where did I sit?'

O'Reardon's displeasure was visible in the glass, his jaw clenched.

'Where did you do time? You're an ex-con. I can pick it from a mile away.'

Now it was Cutler's turn to be silent. He thought about what he might say, what the captain's daughter had missed back there on the docks. He decided on the truth. 'Casuarina Prison, Western Australia.'

'What kind of prison is that?'

'Maximum security.'

O'Reardon nodded again, pleased at the honesty. 'Don't worry, son, I don't judge. I've had plenty of scrapes in my time.'

'You did time?'

'My second tour of Vietnam was cut short. I did two years in a navy brig in Norfolk, Virginia, for taking a pipe wrench to an officer. That was the longest stretch, and the last. I only mentioned your being a con so that you understand that I know.'

'Understood. What has Whelan told you about me?'

The captain sniffed, almost a laugh. 'Whelan doesn't know shit except what's written down in front of him. The formal stuff. And I guess that's not much.'

'Which brings us to what I'm doing here.'

'Yeah. I liked the Whelan boy, Bev. But he was a fool, just like his father. I've known the type, all my life. Kid had a suicide wish, and it sounds like he got it.'

'Whelan said you tried to talk Bevan out of leaving the *Monterey*.'

'Of course I did, Aussie. The kid was clever enough, but a romantic. I tried to smarten him up here on the *Monterey*, but he wanted more. He wanted to stare right at … the ugly truth. I thought that might damage, break him a little. I didn't think he'd end up dead.'

Cutler thought about that. 'No chance he's still alive?'

The purse seiner had left the islands behind them. With a firm hand O'Reardon had steered the ship west into the ocean, according to the compass on the instrument panel, and then ever so slightly nor-west, toward the equator.

O'Reardon stared ahead, the midday light making the deep blue sparkle. 'Out here, he might come across a passing ship, if he had something to float on. But where he was last seen? No chance. Nothing out there except … us, and not many at that. He went overboard at night, according to the Taiwanese captain. With the currents, the hypothermia, the sharks that follow us, primed to feed off our scraps? He was gone by daylight. The story rings true.'

'Whelan reckons it's very unusual to lose a man overboard on a ship like this.'

'Whelan is right. Might be the only thing he's right about. I don't know why he's sending you out there. You can look after yourself, I can see that. But you ever been at sea? Long hours, bad drugs, lack of sleep. People begin to grate on one another. Small things turn into big things. You'll be a long way from any help. You're gonna have to sleep with one eye open.'

I can do that, Cutler thought. I've been doing that all my life. 'Why are you helping Whelan? I know he's an investor in your processing plant.'

Cutler had offered the last sentence as a provocation, but the captain's reaction surprised him. Deadpan, he looked straight ahead, not even at their reflection. 'I owe him more than money. I let his son out of my sight. I knew his father, too, worked for him a bit. And besides, it's not too far out of my way. The question is, what's the point? If the captain of the *Shuen* hasn't already dumped his crew, that just means he's got them cowed enough to keep their mouths shut. They're either not paid at all, or indentured and so deep in debt, they're fucked for life. Why would they tell you anything?'

'Fair point,' Cutler agreed. What O'Reardon didn't know was that getting people to tell him things was Cutler's job, tricking them into acting against their own best interests. 'In that case, Whelan just wants me to observe, make a report, do the job that Bevan didn't get to finish. Maybe get the *Shuen*, the company it belongs to kicked out of the PNA waters. Maybe get the captain charged with Bevan's disappearance, the ship impounded.'

Now the captain laughed, but it was laced with bitterness. 'That's what got Bevan Whelan killed, right there. His father's naivete, passed to his son. What does any of that change about anything? I'm a bit insulted, son. You've left out the other part of the equation. What happens if you miraculously *do* find out what occurred, late one night, far out in the Pacific? What're you gonna *do*? I've already told you I know what you are. Not just an ex-con, that's for sure. And not a *report* writer, either.'

They'd arrived at the truth, a bit sooner than Cutler expected, but they'd got there anyway. Cutler turned and looked at O'Reardon's profile, forcing the man to meet his eyes.

'Maybe Whelan's not as naive as you think he is.'

O'Reardon looked long and deeply at Cutler, who didn't look away. Cutler was the first to speak. 'You wanted me to know, that you *knew* I'd done time, because of your daughter. I'd mentioned her twice.'

The captain turned back to his ocean, a hiding place for his thoughts. 'Sure enough. She's a bit like the Whelan boy. A bit of a romantic. You're the kind of fella she takes to. Make sure that doesn't happen.'

Cutler smiled. 'You don't have to worry about that.'

Downstairs, someone was banging a pot lid. The comms on the instrument panel squawked, as a gruff voice spoke a single word – *Chow*. O'Reardon nodded his head to the stairs. 'I get mine brought to me. You go and eat. I'm an old man and I like to eat good food. The cook's been with me for seventeen years. Enjoy. *Wait*, before you go.'

Captain O'Reardon walked toward a steel cupboard beside the stairwell, which he opened, before reaching a hand in and plucking out a book. It was *Travels with Charley*. He passed it to

Cutler before returning to the wheel, speaking over his shoulder, 'That book's got nothing to do with the sea. Where you're going, you'll thank me for it later.'

Cutler slid the paperback into his trouser pocket, ducked his head inside the stairwell and listened to his feet echo on the steps as he descended.

4.

Chow consisted of a steel table laden with Tupperware bowls filled with smoky cabbage, yam, potatoes and kumara, and platters of pulled pork, chicken and beef. The meal was served by the cook, Jonah, a tall man with a shiny scar down one side of his face. He said it was cooked in an earth oven called a *lovo* by his mother. There were steel trays laid over the cooktop that contained more of the meat, which suggested that the meal would stretch to dinner as well. That was alright by Cutler, who took a bit of everything and joined the men outside in the sun. Like them, he forked the food into his mouth and stared at the water, at least until his throat began to tingle. The tingle became a burn, and he felt his throat begin to close.

The man nearest him, who wore a Brisbane Broncos rugby jumper, thumped him on the back and pointed at Cutler's plate, specifically at a stringy green vegetable that looked like silverbeet. Because everything was cooked together, the meat and the vegetables all tasted similar – smoky and meaty. Cutler had barely noticed the green on his fork, so busy had he been staring at the ocean.

'You ate too much *rourou*, too fast. Yam leaf. Don't worry, you won't die.'

41

The other men laughed, and Cutler smiled through his discomfort. 'I'm Paul.'

One by one the men introduced themselves. The young man in the Broncos jumper went by Joseph, or Joe. He watched Cutler take another mouthful of the yam leaf, nodded approvingly.

Some of the other men were looking at the scars on his bare legs. Cutler's tan did nothing to hide the pink weals and glossy dials where pins had been inserted into his legs, and braces set to frame the pins.

Joseph pointed to another raised pink disk on Cutler's thigh, just above the knee. 'That's a bullet wound.'

Cutler swallowed his mouthful, looked down at his leg, nodded and looked into the men's faces. 'Yes, it is.' He lifted his leg and clutched the back of his thigh. 'Came out over here.' He put his fork into a slab of kumara, lifted it to his mouth. He thought that the men were waiting for more, but instead they glanced at each other, smiled shyly. Cutler looked closely at each of them now, saw the machete wound on one leg, a bullet scar on the bicep of the man seated next to him. Joseph put his arm around Cutler's shoulders, pointed to his lower leg, a mess of knifelike scars that circled his shins to where a chunk of his calf was missing.

'Farming, fishing and *fighting*.'

The other men murmured in agreement, as though the mantra was a prayer. 'All of us, eh, the captain only hires veterans. We're all peacekeepers, brothers, at different times. Me in Iraq, Adi there in Lebanon, James in Solomons, old boy David there, was INTERFET in Timor, two years.'

The older man, who Joseph had called David, sat forward. 'We understand esprit de corps. Makes for peaceful times on a fishing boat. We work harder than other bastards, too. More fish is more money for my family.'

'What about chain of command?' Cutler asked, more out of curiosity than anything else. His practice on a job was to worm his way inside, see if there were chinks in the armour, opportunities to play one against the other. It was effective because every gang, group or organisation depended on loyalty, reward or fear for cohesion, sometimes all three. Many down the chain were ambitious, knowing that a way of life that led either to prison or death meant that the only way *out* is up. Up meant replacing those already there.

Cutler's usual MO was to amplify garden-variety resentment, especially where fear ruled. If he was careful, he could turn tinder into flame, break the foundations that way. Sometimes he did nothing with what he learned. Sometimes, shared secrets were a bond sufficient to themselves. Shared secrets inspired trust. Trust was also a weapon he could use, when later called upon.

The men looked at one another and then their plates, resumed their chewing, except for Joseph. 'You want to know about our captain? I want to know about your leg.'

Cutler finished his mouthful. 'You want the true story, or the tall story?'

Joseph roared with laughter, patted Cutler on the neck. 'You must be shot not long ago, if the true and the tall story aren't same thing. My story, I never told it, even to my brothers here, because I want it to stay true. What they see when they look at my leg is the truth. True enough for anyone.'

Cutler smiled. 'You're a wise man, Joseph.'

At this the rest of the men laughed. 'You not so wise then, young man, you think that,' said old David, which made Joseph laugh harder, even as he made himself bigger, thrust out his chest. 'Wise enough to know we got two ears, and only one mouth, for a reason.'

Cutler finished his plate, scraping a slice of yam over the juices. The story of his leg would keep. He took out his cigarettes and tapped off a few, offered them around, then tapped out more. He went around the circle of men and put flame to their smokes.

Joseph took a long inhale, blew the smoke out his nose. He looked at the brand on the side of the cigarette. 'Winfield, eh? You a true Aussie.'

'On special, duty-free. I normally smoke Stuyvesant.'

'Benson & Hedges, me,' said old David. 'Joe, tell Aussie about the first time you saw a cigarette. Tell 'im that story.'

Joseph smiled, blew on the end of his smoke, brought it to a glowing point. 'I'm from a small village, top of Viti Levu, long way from any big roads. Real village then, mostly grass huts like you see in the old photos. I was just a little boy, maybe three or four or five, had never been far from the village, except to fish, work in the garden. My job was to use a cane knife to cut the grass, weeds, jungle back. Hadn't even been to school, didn't know how to speak English, the priest made the service in Fijian. My big brother went away for a while, to work on the sugarcane. I was asleep but got woken by the noise, everybody coming out of the huts, talking. I went to the edge of the hut, saw all the elders, the adults, gathered around the fire. My brother had returned from being away. It was dark, real dark, the kind of dark when there's no electricity, no stars, no moon. There was coals in the fire but no flames. They couldn't see me, standing in the door of the hut, it was so dark. I wanted to go to my brother, but then I saw something in his mouth, little glowing ember, red like fire, get brighter, and then was gone. Then while I watched, he looked over at me, saw my shape in the doorway, looked at me, blew out a big cloud of smoke. I thought he was breathing fire! I started crying! My mother saw me and came and picked me up, took me to the others. My brother showed me the cigarette, held it under my nose. It smelled really bad. The smoke. He put the cigarette to his mouth and there was the fire again, and then the smoke. I started howling. All the adults were laughing. That was the first time I saw a cigarette.'

The men murmured, nodded in agreement, their expressions graver than Cutler might have expected as they emerged from reliving the story. Beside him, Joseph pinched off the end of his cigarette, dropped the butt in a dead can of Fanta, went around the men so that they could do the same.

David looked at Cutler. 'Captain, he talk to you about smoking?'

Cutler shook his head. 'Because of the fire risk?'

'Yes, and he don't want any butts in the ocean, or even ash near the net. That net's worth forty thousand dollars, American. We lost one a few years ago because of a small fire, put the season back two weeks. Make sure you collect your butts. Not good for turtle or fish to eat them either.'

David looked at his watch. 'We've got to work now, Aussie. Always cleaning to do, down below.'

The men stood as one, nodded to Cutler and took their empty plates into the kitchen to make a neat pile beside the sink. Cutler followed them in and did the same. The kitchen was empty and so he busied himself washing the plates, placing them in a drying rack on a shelf above his head. The crew of the *Monterey* seemed pretty tight. He hadn't sensed a moment of tension or disagreement, and he could see why O'Reardon preferred veterans. They were used to the routines that preceded times of chaos and stress, as he imagined occurred during the setting and collecting of the purse-seine net, and the long hours of sorting, butchering and cleaning that followed. The men appeared loyal to the captain, but most of all to one another, and it didn't appear to be a product of fear, so different to most of the outfits he'd worked in over the years.

Jonah entered the kitchen just as Cutler placed the last plate on the rack. Unlike the other men, the cook seemed intense, his eyes a little haunted and his mouth set. He nodded his thanks but there was no warmth in his expression, whether because Cutler had taken a liberty by entering the kitchen in his absence, or because Cutler hadn't done a simple thing the right way, or perhaps because he didn't trust strangers, Cutler didn't know. He got the message, though, and replaced the tea towel slung over his shoulder on the wire above the sink, went back out into the afternoon glare, the breeze passing gently over the undulating swells. A sudden burst of flying fish broke the surface, parallel to the ship, dozens of them gliding through the air before spearing into the water and emerging again, their iridescent flanks and wings beautiful in the sunlight even as they fled from the predators beneath the silvered blue.

5.

The instrument panel cast a pale glow over Casey O'Reardon's hands as she held the ship's wheel. In the thirty minutes they'd been talking, she hadn't turned the wheel except when a large broadside wave hit the starboard side of the *Monterey*, and then without pausing her speech she glanced at the compass and gripped the wheel tighter and held her course. There were no lights on in the wheelhouse, because Casey preferred it that way, and beyond the pall cast by the forward lights mounted on the bow, the ocean rose and fell in a vast black silence until the next wave reared from the east and crashed into the hull, gripping the boat with foaming fingers until the deck drained, and Casey's grip on the wheel tightened, and then relaxed as she checked the instruments. The scene repeated itself every twenty seconds or so, and Cutler looked at her reflection in the bridge window and marvelled at the brute force of the ugly engine that drove the massive steel boat, narrowed down through wheels and pulleys, shafts and rods to a circular terminus linked to the rudder that required little effort beyond Casey's fingers. She moved with the flow and tilt of the ocean, not the boat, and the boat seemed an extension of her hands and arms, her eyes that never left the blackness that passed across the boat even as the starbright sky wheeled and turned.

The flags on the roof above fluttered as the gentle wind entered the open window beside them and passed out the other side. It seemed remarkable to Cutler that the air could be so windless, and yet the waves so large, formed by the trade winds thousands of kilometres away. They were nearing the equator, and Cutler couldn't help himself – every few minutes he leaned across the instrument panel and let his eyes wander the length of the Milky Way, centred in the sky, like a vast glittering tunnel running north to south.

The first time he did this Casey remarked, 'That's why I keep the lights off. Lights on, I have to navigate by the panel, and spend twelve hours looking at my reflection. On a still night, when the stars are reflected off the ocean, it feels like we're drifting through space. The darkness on the water and in the sky, and the bright stars above and around us ... it's magical. You know, like the old saying, *there are no atheists at sea ...*'

Cutler wasn't allowed to smoke in the wheelhouse, or anywhere inside the ship for that matter, but he didn't want to leave Casey and the soft sounds of her voice as she took her twelve-hour shift at the wheel. Out there on the open ocean it wasn't unusual for captains to set the course and leave the ship on autopilot while they bunked for an hour, because there was nothing else out on the water, but Casey preferred to stand or sit in front of the wheel, and when she was alone, listen to audiobooks, averaging one a night over the course of a journey. When they were on the tuna at night, which was often, despite the lack of seabirds or dolphins signalling the presence of the giant pelagics, instead using echo sounder and sonar to home in on large schools, Casey ran the bridge communications to the teams that ran out the net with the launch skiff, keeping the ship steady as the net was cinched and ultimately drawn and emptied into the hold. It was exciting work, she said, she couldn't help the excitement, despite her sadness at the occasional entrapment of turtle, porpoise and dolphin. They used nets that were supposed to enable cetaceans an exit point, but they didn't always work. When this happened, if the dolphins or porpoise were on the surface, they were scooped out and tipped aside the net, although sometimes even this didn't work. The sadness in her voice was genuine.

'I grew up in Guam watching the spinner dolphins playing in the surf on the reefs below our house. I got to know some of them, too, they'd come and greet me when I went out in my kayak. I'd anchor up and dive with them. They seemed to be familiar with me, or humans at least, waiting for me to catch up when I followed them, nudging me when I played dead, laughing when I opened my eyes and surprised them.'

Cutler wanted to change the subject from the dead porpoises in the *Monterey* nets. 'On your mother's side, the native people of Guam—'

'The *Chamorro*. In answer to your question. I don't know. I don't know if Mum's people swam with the porpoises or ate them, for that matter. She grew up in Hawaii, and so did her parents. She only returned to Guam as an adult. She isn't great with family. I know I have second cousins, uncles and aunts, but Mum likes to keep to herself.'

Cutler didn't know much about Guam except its World War II history, and the fact that it housed a large American military presence, focussed on monitoring the Chinese influence in East Asia. He'd often heard it described, unoriginally, as a tropical paradise.

DAVID WHISH-WILSON

He wanted to know more about the Chamorro people, but Casey wasn't finished with the porpoises.

'It isn't just the Pacific fleets. Not just the Asian, US or South Americans. Some of the worst fishing practices are done in the middle of Europe, in the Mediterranean, or off the west coast of Europe. It was Europeans who destroyed the cod fishery off Newfoundland. Wiped out a fishery that could have fed humans for millennia. They're doing the same in the Mediterranean with the bluefin tuna. You know why there were Somali pirates last decade, boarding tankers in the Indian Ocean? Europeans and others overfished their territorial waters, but not only that. According to Dad, European mafia companies working in waste disposal took ships full of toxic waste down through the Suez Canal and dumped it off the Somali coast. You can hardly blame the locals for becoming pirates.'

Cutler agreed. He'd heard about the Somali situation. An old friend of his had left the army and worked security on some of the ships passing through the Red Sea. He'd lived on an offshore base, basically a moored ship housing mercenaries while they waited for their next assignment. The money had been good until the fleets started hiring Russians, anyone prepared to work for less. He'd moved on to working the security detail of some oil and gas CEO, increasingly worried about environmental protestors taking matters into their own hands.

Casey had continued talking, listing the bad practices of a range of different operators – the squid fleets off the Galapagos, the toothfish pirates of the Southern Ocean, the Chinese sardine fishery off West Africa, operating within view of the shore and literally taking food out of people's mouths. As she spoke her voice rose in pitch, carrying a weight of frustration but also of sadness. She was a scientist who worked in an industry where the science was either ignored, or manipulated to encourage further excess, all in the name of politics and greed.

He didn't want to interrupt her, but it was exhausting him. It wasn't that she was idealistic, or naive, or combative or moralistic – it was because she was clearly exhausted by it too.

Cutler had seen this before, in its many variations, although the people he'd spent time with over the past years, Khalil's targets, didn't care about things like animals, or anything as abstract as the environment, or the future of the planet. Mostly, they cared about themselves, and their anxieties applied solely to their own survival, or freedom, and those of their immediate families. For all but the most sociopathic, this took a toll. Cutler's own survival depended on his constant vigilance, and close reading of these people, and of himself when among them. The picture they presented of humanity wasn't pretty, and Cutler had also done things that he wasn't proud of. It was the selfishness, however, across a range of families and criminal organisations that wore him down. What was the point of anything if, across every system, criminal or civilian, people who lacked something that he considered central to any definition of humanness – empathy – were the ones who thrived?

Cutler could see that Casey was trying and, like him, perhaps failing to find ways to live with her own version of despair, in the face of economic systems that cared nothing for her thoughts, or her efforts.

'You're no doubt wondering why I work on a fishing boat,'

she said, 'and not some research vessel. The answer is because, despite everything I just listed, I don't blame fishermen and women themselves. Unless they're Australian, or New Zealanders, or American or German or Northern European. When *they* get greedy, I blame them. That's just greed, and not giving a shit. I'm probably not making much sense ...'

'Go on,' Cutler said, because he genuinely wanted to hear.

'Those countries are different. Those countries are mainly meat-eating countries. Fish has never formed a huge part of their diet, unlike in Asia, or Africa. The price of fish is quite high in those developed countries. As a result, and because of quotas and restricted competition, commercial fishers make a lot of money compared to fishers in most parts of the world. Fishing can make you a millionaire in Australia, or like Bevan's dad, a multimillionaire. It's not like that everywhere else. Fishing is usually a poor person's activity. A lot of fish is caught and sold, because a lot of fish is eaten – it's the main source of protein in the diet. It takes a lot of fishers to do that. There are the big Asian corporations, but by and large fishers do it out of poverty, as a way out of poverty. They can get ruthless because of that – overfishing, pirate fishing, ignoring quotas and rules, selling on the black market, because they're only one mistake away from being broke. It's worth bearing that in mind while you're out here.'

'Thanks, although that doesn't make me very hope—'

'Because you haven't told me *why* you're out here. Except to take over Bevan's position on the Taiwanese boat. You're a good listener, I like that, but you haven't told me anything about yourself.'

Cutler swore inwardly at himself. For a moment, he'd relaxed.

CUTLER

Had his mask slipped, or had Casey's dad schooled her on who he was, and why he was there?

'Happy to tell you about myself, although it's not that interesting. I've spent my life in institutions doing what I'm told. Before I tell you more, you haven't told me your area of research. You said you first-mate the *Monterey* during the season, but study and research the rest of the time …'

Casey glanced at him, and there was mischief in her eyes. Perhaps she understood that he was flustered, caught out or embarrassed. 'Crown-of-thorns starfish mitigation. The prickly guys who kill a reef, eat everything in their path. Good metaphor for extractive industry.'

She was grinning now, and Cutler smiled back, although he wasn't sure why. He'd heard of the starfish, spreading down the east coast of Australia, a major threat to the Barrier Reef and beyond. He hesitated in replying to her. He didn't want to have to continue the lie, unless she already knew the truth.

The door behind them opened and a gust of briny air swept through. Casey's smile only grew larger, as though she'd been expecting her dad, standing there in the doorway with a bottle of rum in his hand. He held it up, a little shakily – he'd already had a few.

'Ratu rum. Good Fijian export. Come and have one with the boys.'

Captain Rick's eyes were fierce or perhaps it was the drunkenness, but he wasn't making a request. He'd taken off his long-sleeve and now wore a singlet and denim shorts. Even in the semi-darkness his arms and legs were a mess of pale cancer-operation scars, and there were other scars besides on his nut-brown skin. In the shadows he looked like a barnacle-encrusted figurehead, a likeness that would probably please him.

Cutler nodded to Casey, then followed O'Reardon down the stairs and into the warm night air.

6.

Captain Rick could drink, although Cutler shouldn't have been surprised. They were two bottles in, out on the deck on the leeward side, the harsh fluorescent lights mounted on the wall beside them dimmed by a draped tee-shirt. O'Reardon filled a tin mug for Cutler and passed it over. He raised his own.

'*Sláinte!*'

'Cheers,' Cutler replied to the men, who watched him take his first sip. The rum was spiced with cloves, allspice and cinnamon, with a sweet coconut flavour in the background. Taken neat, the drink was strong and tasty, and Cutler smiled at Joseph and David, who were waiting for him to speak.

'I like it,' he said, then took another draught.

'*That* is the nectar of the gods, my young friend,' said David, the older Fijian man. 'The essence of the islands – beautiful and a little spicy. Like the islands, it will bring you home to it, wherever in the world you stray.'

'What a bunch of bullshit,' said Captain Rick, to the laughter of the men, including David. 'Most Fijians can't afford it – it's rum for tourists.'

'That is true,' said Joseph, the younger man. 'Kava is a better drink. It makes even a bad man gentle and sleepy.'

'What were you talking to Casey about?' asked O'Reardon.

Cutler took another sip of the rum, which was deceptively strong. He met O'Reardon's eyes. 'Not much. I was asking her about Guam, about the ... Chamorro ... people.'

O'Reardon smirked. 'You interested in that stuff? Native peoples and their ways?'

'I suppose so, although we didn't really—'

'Did she tell you why they're called Chamorro? They were colonised by the Spanish for three hundred years, and then by America. Before that, when the Spanish found them ... what they found. The word "Chamorro" derives from the highest caste there. It wasn't all unicorns and coconuts, Aussie. Underneath the Chamori, the highest caste, were the Manachang caste, who were shorter and darker than the Chamori. They did all the work, mate. They weren't allowed to mingle or marry with the higher caste. It was a form of slavery. You don't look surprised.'

Cutler looked down into his drink. 'I'm not surprised. Though because their society wasn't ... unicorns and coconuts, it doesn't justify it being colonised, does it? You'd understand that – O'Reardon's an Irish name.'

The captain laughed. 'Good man. So we've established that you're not totally naive, like young Bevan was. We had fun with him, didn't we, boys?'

David leaned forward and accepted one of Cutler's cigarettes. 'Yeah, we had fun with him. Told him how the old people used to tenderise a body, before they ate it, by brining it in a reef-pool for a couple of days. He didn't believe me at first.'

The captain raised his mug to David's. 'And that's why Fiji was never colonised. That's why you boys make the best jungle warfare soldiers in the world, except for maybe the Ghurkhas. *Sláinte!*'

O'Reardon topped up their mugs, finishing with Cutler's. 'So, if you're not totally naive, what do you think makes for the perfect society? I'm not having fun with you – I'm genuinely curious.'

'So am I,' interjected Joseph, 'because the one we got sure isn't.'

Cutler thought about his answer. 'That's true. There's no balance. A system that depends on growth isn't going to sustain itself for long. Long enough to make a few bastards wealthy, I suppose, but as for *utopia*, it's not something I've given much thought.'

'But if you *had* to think about it,' said David, who'd finished his rum in a single gulp.

Cutler didn't need to play a role with the three men. He took a mouthful, and then a drag of his cigarette, watched the blue smoke of his exhalation drift away on the breeze. 'Fair enough. I think that the agricultural revolution should never have happened. I think we should have stayed living in small groups, as hunters and gatherers.'

O'Reardon sucked air through his teeth. 'Man, that's a big call. You'd give up hot showers and canned food and all the rest?'

'Let him finish,' said David, scratching at a wound on his elbow. 'Why?'

'Human nature,' Cutler answered, hearing the rum in his voice, its new volume. 'Human *fucking* nature. I'm no historian, but I've spent a lot of time these past years with bad dudes – psychopaths, sociopaths, ordinary criminals and those who enable them. In small bands of people, the kind of arseholes I'm talking about who fuck up every society – the deceivers, the manipulative ones, the ones who lack impulse control, the ones who want power over others, the ones who enjoy others' pain – they're more *visible*. In every other society – tribes, monarchies, democratic and communist nation states – those people not only exist but thrive. In a small group of related people, there are checks and balances that don't allow those character traits to get any leverage, because survival is at stake. Dudes like Adolf Hitler or Donald Trump, or even your average crime boss or corporate manager – people would recognise early on that there's something wrong with them. They'd be—'

'I'll tell you what they'd be,' cut in David, his eyes bright with conviction. 'They'd be taken on a hunting trip and accidentally ... All the hunters would come home and say, *Sorry about old mate, but he got accidentally shot in the back*. Everybody would know, but nobody would say anything.'

Joseph smiled. 'Except maybe for his mama, who'd ask: *If it was an accident, why does he have two arrows in his back?*'

O'Reardon laughed, looking at Cutler. 'I kinda agree, though I like my hot showers. But we can't go back thirty thousand years, so in the meantime, what do we do?'

Cutler smiled. 'Fucked if I know. Do what you've done, I suppose. Find your own way, and your own people.'

'Get the fuck away from people, that's what I've done. Except for the ones I can trust.'

The captain necked his drink and topped them all up again. He raised his mug in a toast. '*Cos the smell of the sea is like victuals to me, and I'd trade in my leg for a new wooden peg, and my head is as bald as a newly laid egg, and the life of a sailor is all of my joy.'*

Cutler raised his mug to the old sailor. 'What's that? An old pirate saying?'

'Aye lad, it is at that,' said O'Reardon, his imitation Cornish accent making David and Joseph shake their heads.

'You ever get pirates out here?'

David's eyes hardened, but O'Reardon laughed it off. 'Not this far out. The odd pirate fisher, or poacher. Plenty of them closer to PNG and Indonesia, but rarely this side of the Solomons.'

'They ever get caught?' Cutler asked.

Now Joseph's eyes hardened as well. Both he and David looked away at the stars.

O'Reardon's voice was still playful, but there was a new edge in it. 'There's no law out here, son. That's what people don't understand, except those of us who live here, away from the land. There's no law in international waters, and hardly any in territorial waters, except our own laws. That's why you've been sent on a fool's errand by Whelan Snr, who should know better.'

'Fair enough,' said Cutler, although O'Reardon wasn't finished. He looked a little stupefied, but his eyes were clear.

'I mean, son, have you ever been on the high seas? Have you ever been at sea?'

Cutler lit another cigarette. He could feel the rum in his limbs, comfortable on the warm steel deck. He thought about what he could tell them, decided he would tell them the truth.

'Once. A couple of years ago, for about a month. I was on a job, inserted as the third man on a smuggling operation.'

Cutler hoped that was enough, but he'd been too scanty with detail. Joseph and David leaned forward with questions on their lips, but O'Reardon got there first.

'What kind of job, and what kind of boat? What do you mean you were put in as the third man?'

Cutler passed his mug over, and O'Reardon filled it. Stories were a currency away from television sets, streaming platforms and podcasts – why Casey O'Reardon listened to audiobooks he supposed, and the captain pressed books on people. On a tight crew over long stints their stories must get recycled, or perhaps stale.

'It was a yacht. Flagged to New Zealand – I think it was a twenty-two-metre boat. Had three crew members in Bali, where it was stuck awaiting repairs. I might have had something to do with the damaged engine—'

'Tell the fucking story, man. How did you sabotage the engine?'

'That I can't say.'

'Arsehole!'

'Yeah, sorry, Captain. If you want to hear the story, there's going to be a bit of that. Do I continue?'

The answer was there in O'Reardon's raised hands, his eager expression.

'One of the men was assaulted in the port, on his way home at night. Before the drugs were received. By then I'd become a friend, hanging around the same bars, the same people. I didn't have anything to do with the assault, but I know who did. Two dudes on a scooter took out the Brazilian fella's legs at high speed with an iron bar, broke one of them clean in half. I was a natural replacement.

They were Kiwis and already trusted me. I'd sold them some stuff, off the black market. They knew I wasn't a sailor, but—'

David had a grave expression, which told Cutler that he wasn't only enjoying the story, but also scrutinising every word for a lie. 'What?' Cutler asked him.

'Why did they break the Brazilian man's legs, and not one of the Kiwi's?'

'Yeah, that's simple. Of the three, he trusted me the least.'

'He was the smartest then,' said David.

'I guess he was.'

Joseph had a question of his own. 'Why didn't the Indonesian government arrest them there, in Bali? Why let the yacht make the journey to Australia?'

'I wondered that myself. The answer is that the guy they really wanted was in Australia. The three guys in Indo were just smugglers. Everything had been paid for by the Australian man, but with bitcoin – hard to trace and pin on him. They kept the Indonesian government in the dark about it. The drugs were put on late one night when I wasn't there – a quarter tonne of coke, hidden in the walls. From then it was go-time. I was invited to help crew the boat the next day. They didn't tell me about the coke, of course – it was pitched to me as an adventure. They'd pay my flight back when we arrived in Perth, they said. The guys weren't killers, and I let myself be talked into it. We left the next day, and they taught me the ropes as we went. Sailed down across the Timor Sea in perfect weather, got there in about a week. They stayed close to the coast, which made me think something was up. They could have docked in Dampier, or Port Hedland, but they kept south. I'd planted a tracker on her and so wasn't too worried—'

'Were you armed? Joseph asked, wiping his forehead of sweat with the sleeve of his Broncos jumper.

'Nah, not armed. I knew they'd search my stuff after I boarded. I did plant a recording device, though – little camera and microphone about the size of a pea, inside the kitchen and sleeping area. They talked stuff through when it was my turn at the wheel. Funnily enough, one night when we were talking – we ate pretty well – talking over chow, I'd had a few drinks, I mentioned the idea of smuggling to them, using the yacht, just to gauge the level of danger, and they'd played along, said they'd thought about it, asked me how I'd go about it. My answer was that I didn't know, but would probably drop the drugs off at sea, using a GPS or the like, or if the boat wasn't too valuable, have it dragged up onto a larger vessel and scrapped at sea, just stuff like that. They clearly weren't on to me – they had their own ideas and agreed that we might give it a go one day. From there it all proceeded pretty much as planned. I was placed with them in case the plan went sideways, and they tried to flee Australian waters, but there was no need. They sailed into Geraldton harbour, Customs checked them over and passed them through, as was the agreement, I suppose. They paid my bus ticket down to Perth, and then I was debriefed by my handler, cut loose, the end of my part in it …'

Cutler had deliberately left it hanging, but he couldn't resist the expressions of frustration, the three men's childlike need to know the end of the story. 'Ok. The two Kiwis are doing a stretch in Perth. The Mr Big, a Sydney mafia dude, got taken when the drugs were offloaded, put into a shipping container, trucked across the country. They'd been swapped out, of course, but he was nabbed at some depot in Sydney. He's doing a stretch as well. Was a long court case, and he nearly got off – claiming innocence of the shipping container's contents, but they had some surveillance on him too. The whole thing was sewn up from beginning to end. I was just a small part of it. Got to sail for a few weeks, saw some beautiful ocean, didn't even get seasick it was so mellow.'

Cutler made no claims about his skills as a storyteller, especially in circumstances where he had to leave so much unsaid, but the three men seemed appeased enough, nodding and thinking about what he'd told them.

It was young Joseph who leaned into the circle, fixed him with a stare. 'When we sign up to put on uniforms, we have the job to do. It's after that when the questions begin to trouble us. What about you? You feel bad about putting those men in jail? Not the gangster, the other two.'

Cutler didn't need to think about his answer. 'Yes, I felt bad. I grew to like them, even before we left port. At one point I thought about warning them, but that would probably have meant that the Indonesian police would have got them. I justified it by thinking they were better off doing time in an Australian prison, than the jail in Bali. They would have got the death sentence there.'

O'Reardon grunted. 'Doesn't make it any better. You've done time yourself. Knowing that, how could you turn the key on another man? I could never do that.'

'That was before I did my stretch. But I agree with you.'

Old David had been listening carefully. There was a silent

judgement in his eyes. 'How do we know you're not here, doing the same thing to us?'

Cutler tried to laugh it off, but it fell flat. David's question required an answer. Better to get things out in the open. 'You're not doing anything illegal that I know of, and these aren't Australian waters. But what would you do if I was?'

The three men laughed, glanced at each other. O'Reardon was an old lag, knew that you never verbalise things ahead of time. Old David had the same wisdom, no doubt learned the hard way.

'You a good swimmer?' asked Joseph, still smiling, although his eyes were wary.

'Not really.'

O'Reardon filled their mugs. Cutler, David and Joseph lit cigarettes. In the awkward silence, the four men looked up at the stars. They were the same stars that Cutler saw at home, the Southern Cross angling toward the invisible horizon. The wind seemed to have dropped, and waves were no longer slamming the hull on the other side. The booze fumes and smoke settled among them, until the engine eased back, knocked a few times, then died off completely.

7.

Captain O'Reardon looked at his watch.

'That time, eh?' asked Joseph.

'Sure is,' replied O'Reardon.

Cutler assumed that they were going to put the net out, but he was wrong. From the wheelhouse the iron steps rang out with footfalls, and then Casey emerged onto the deck, wearing a black one-piece swimsuit, tucking her hair into a ponytail.

'You a good swimmer?' she asked Cutler, which made the men laugh. If she wondered why they were laughing, she made no comment.

He made the same response. 'Not really.'

'We do this every night when it's calm. And besides, we've crossed the equator, which means as a rookie you need to take a dunking.'

'You're going swimming? Here?'

'Yes, and so are you. It's a matter of bad luck if you don't.'

Casey was teasing him, and in her voice was the truth that she wouldn't hold it against him. Still, his head was fuzzy with the rum and smokes, and despite the fact that it was midnight, out in the middle of the ocean, with no land for hundreds of kilometres, at that moment he actually felt like a swim.

Cutler stood and peeled off his tee-shirt. He expected Captain O'Reardon to be watching him, but the captain's eyes were on his daughter, and they were soft and full of love. If the *Monterey* was indeed the job, Cutler knew, the way to the alpha-dog captain would be through his daughter, because the man clearly couldn't say no to her, and would forgive her just about anything.

Cutler followed Joseph, who'd also stripped to his shorts, down toward the stern, beneath the crow's nest and beside the net, past the skiff and to the back of the boat, low in the water. By the time Cutler got there Casey had already dived into the inky blackness and had yet to surface. He waited while Joseph rolled down a ladder and hit the switch on floodlights that shone deeply into the water. Cutler could see Casey down there, floating a metre beneath the surface, waving to him. Already, small silvery fish had joined her, darting around her kicking legs.

'You aren't scared to swim here?' Cutler asked Joseph, who grinned.

'No. My village has protection from the *qio*, from sharks. My ancestors made an agreement with them. I am protected. Do you want to have the light on or off?'

'Off.'

Joseph killed the light and braced himself on a low railing, did a perfect somersault into the ocean, which was calm, although the swell still lifted the ship, raising the ladder in and out of the water. When the ship came down on the filmy surface it slammed hard, and Cutler didn't want to be anywhere near the stern when that happened. He followed Joseph's lead and braced himself on the railing, did a quiet jump as far away from the ship as he could, legs spread and arms out so that he wouldn't go deep.

The water was colder than he expected, the surface warmed by the sun licked away by the earlier wind. He stayed under as Casey had done, equalising by breathing out most of the air in his lungs, opening his eyes to make sure he hadn't drifted anywhere near the stern of the *Monterey*. It was dark underwater, but even from a metre beneath the surface he could see the sky studded with points of light, and the big moon shining down. He waited until he was purged of oxygen before letting himself drift to the surface.

The *Monterey* was a good hundred metres away, the current stronger than he expected, and he felt a twinge of panic that he was so far distant from the voices of Casey and Joseph. He couldn't see them, and struck out with sidestroke toward the safety of the floating steel island, a creature of the land whose instincts played out in dread vulnerability, aware of the heat leaching from his body, the uselessness of his feet and fists and vision, senses and weapons that gave him so much confidence on land. His legs kicked strongly, but he made little headway toward the boat, instead took his bearing and a deep breath, slipped beneath the surface again and swam froglike toward the position of the voices, swimming until his head began to blacken and his chest ache, emerging in a silent breach a dozen metres from the pair, then swimming casually toward them.

'Thought you were going to drift to Japan there, Aussie,' laughed Joseph, who was treading water in the darkness, his teeth and eyes flashing. 'We could have put the net out, scooped you up.'

Casey had been lying prone when he approached, but now she trod water too. She came close to Cutler, put her hand on his arm, measuring him in some way.

'You're too stiff in the water. Try and relax. It's not hard. You know we share most of our DNA with fish.'

'Whatever that means,' Cutler managed to stutter, still gassed. 'We also share eighteen percent of our DNA with yeast.'

'You're not going to get a *rise* out of me. But seriously, our heart, lungs, brain, skeleton, eyes, digestive tract, all come from fish. Humans in the womb often have gills. What I'm saying is that we're not alien to the ocean. We know it, too, deep in our coding, our brain stem. You just have to relax into it. Try and float next to me. I'll hold your hand. Just make sure to keep kicking, gently so to not attract attention. Joseph, you take his other hand.'

'Sounds like a baptism,' said Cutler, although he didn't protest when Casey and Joseph swam to either side of him, and he gave them his hands. As one, they lay on their backs, kicking against the current but remaining otherwise still. Cutler steadied his breath, took their lead, allowed himself to relax, to let the comfort of not caring wash over him, the strange poetry of believing that he belonged in the ocean as much as them, as much as the unseen creatures who lived in the depths beneath.

The water lapped at his ears, the stars and moon bright above him. He could feel the warmth of their fingers against the palm of his hands. He focussed on slowing his breathing, his heart rate, felt his limbs soften, his buoyancy easy now, his back slightly arched where his lungs rose to join the air that he inhaled and exhaled gently. The moon seemed giant and close above them, its cratered surface visible through his smeared eyes, his ears bobbing above the water, the only sound a deep silence, the occasional smack of the *Monterey*'s stern as it hit the water.

'Tell him the story of the moon,' said Joseph to Casey. 'Not our stories, but the science story.'

Casey was silent for a while, as if weighing up whether to tell the story. Finally, she began, Cutler making sure that his ears were above the waterline.

'By our stories, Joe means the stories of our ancestors. But this is a scientific theory about the creation of the moon. Most theories point to the earth being hit by a giant collision of some kind, and a part of it breaking off to create the moon, which is made of the earth, they're sure about that. The moon is made of the earth at a particular point in its history, due to the presence of the same minerals in the earth's surface, at a time when there wasn't a crust. But my preferred theory is slightly different, a bit older, although it still explains why the earth and the moon are made of the same materials, formed at the same time. The earth has gone on to develop and age further, as more magma rose from its molten core, but the moon has stayed the same, fully cooled, no longer molten. The older theory, the one Joseph and I prefer, describes the earth at a time before oceans, before the time of water, when the surface of the earth was itself molten rock, but not static at all; instead, the spin of the earth made the liquid rock move in vast waves across the earth's surface, waves that had nothing to break upon, nothing to slow them down, and so they rolled around the surface of the earth in vast swells like the kind we're floating upon now, faster and faster, whipped by eruptions and cyclonic winds, faster and faster until the molten waves rose higher and higher, the waves catching one another to form a giant wave that still had nothing to break upon, growing larger and faster and higher until at some point the wave broke into the sky without atmosphere, as its crest was thrown free into space, flying until gravity caught it, and it cooled, and curled in on itself, and became the moon, while beneath it the earth also began to cool, creating landforms and continents, and once it had cooled sufficiently, the ocean, because it is all one ocean not many different oceans ...'

Cutler liked the sound of Casey's voice, even the strain of earnestness that was so unlike the voices of the people he'd known. The rhythms of Casey's story also suggested that she'd told it many times. Cutler thought about it for a while before answering, and even then, he didn't have much to say, looking up at the moon and imagining its birth in fire and fury, according to either theory.

'I like that story,' was all he said.

'Tell him what we're floating over,' said Joseph.

'Yes, we are floating above it,' agreed Casey. 'What Joseph means is that the evidence for the wave theory of the formation of the moon is the great depth of some of the trenches in the Pacific, and the presence of the same rocks on the surface of the trench floor that the moon's made out of – unusual geology given the billions of years that followed. If you look at the trench we're basically floating over, not the intercontinental trenches formed by plates crushing beneath one another but this one below us, it almost looks like a long wave has broken off it, back before the oceans were born.'

Cutler smiled and looked at the moon with a new interest,

thinking about the rip line in the earth's surface beneath the kilometres of ocean under him. He looked beyond the moon to the glittering silk of the night sky, the billions of constellations and the impossible depth of time and space and finally he relaxed fully, a speck of dust or a floating minnow in the vastness of the ocean that, like Casey had said, was one ocean, churning and dark in its depths and clear and sunlit on its windswept surfaces. It felt good to be floating there, despite the things he had done and seen, of little significance to the ocean or the sky above him. It was only when he realised that Casey and Joseph were no longer with him, no longer holding his hands, that he dipped his head and righted himself, saw that they'd clambered back aboard the *Monterey*, Joseph's glistening shoulders spotlit by the lights strung above the launch as he walked toward the mound of netting. Cutler felt another moment of panic at being left alone, but he pushed it away, trod water and wiped the hair from his eyes, cleared his nose and paddled back toward the stern of the boat, gripping the ladder and hooking his feet over the lowest rung as the swell lifted him out of the water, then dunked him again, until he began to climb.

Their bottles and mugs had been cleared from the deck. There was no sign of O'Reardon, or Joseph or David, or any of the others. Beneath his feet the engine began the throb, and then turned over as the propellor engaged, and the *Monterey* began to move into the easterly swell. Casey was back in the wheelhouse. Cutler looked at his watch, and it had gone two in the morning. They'd been floating in the ocean for nearly an hour, and only now did he feel the cold, the beginnings of a hyperthermic reaction – goosebumps on his skin and little shivers in his legs.

In Casey's bunkroom Cutler dried himself, brushed his teeth and climbed into some fresh shorts. The ship was quiet except for the regular pulse of the engine. He killed the overhead light and opened the laptop Whelan had given him, plugged through the pages until he reached the AIS graphic that showed the *Shuen*'s position, not far from their own. They would reach the Taiwanese vessel soon, by the look of it. Cutler opened his duffel and took out the plastic bottle of pills, knocked out two valium and swallowed them dry. It was going to be hard to sleep, mainly because swimming in the ocean had opened all of his senses. He sank into the bunk that smelled of Casey and stared at the blinking light of the *Shuen*, clearing his mind of what tomorrow might bring while he waited for the valium to kick in.

8.

Cutler awoke with a dead arm, tucked beneath his torso after he'd rolled in the tight confines of the bunk. His legs were too long for the bed, slanted against the cold steel wall that no longer throbbed with the pulse of the engine.

A golden light shone through the circular window, the sky blue and clear to the horizon. He lifted his dead arm away from his body, tried to clench his fist but failed. He lay it on his chest and waited for the blood to enter it and awaken the nerves.

The *Monterey* wasn't moving, and outside the room he could hear excited shouts from the deck and the tinny sounds of O'Reardon's voice, shouted through the tannoy. Cutler looked around Casey's bedroom and made sure that everything he'd packed was at hand. He slipped on a tee-shirt, plugged in the laptop to charge and put on his sunglasses.

The *Monterey* was on tuna. Cutler's first feeling was annoyance at the fact that O'Reardon had strayed from his promise to escort him first to the *Shuen* before beginning his search for fish. O'Reardon's comment that he owed Whelan a debt wasn't the whole truth – Whelan was also paying for the *Monterey*'s fuel, sufficient at least to get Cutler to the Taiwanese vessel, and then to their regular hunting grounds south of Palau.

Cutler thought of climbing up to the wheelhouse to confront

the captain, but instead he went downstairs to the deck, where old David and some of the others were watching the distant skiff, driven by Joseph, leading the net around a chopping school of silvery missiles, seabirds Cutler couldn't name dive-bombing the shoal and emerging with smaller, pilchard-sized baitfish in their beaks. He couldn't see Casey anywhere, presuming she was still asleep after her night shift, until she emerged from the galley with a pair of fins and a mask-and-snorkel set, which she placed against the port bulwark, staring down into the mess of darting fish. Joseph and the trailing net were still distant, the net pouring off the deck of the *Monterey* as the skiff reached a point directly opposite them, then began to tack to their bow, the floats on the net bobbing behind until all of the net was gone from the deck. The excitement among the fishermen wasn't what he'd expected, given their long experience. He'd expected a workmanlike approach, the product of long routine, but their smiles and seeming fascination at the sight of the large, cigar-shaped tuna bursting to the surface surprised him, their striped flanks giving away their species as skipjack tuna, missiles whose speed and grace was evident even to a spectator like Cutler. He walked to the deck beside the others, the polarising lens on his glasses allowing him to see into the clear blue water. Casey noticed him now, the same excitement evident on her face as well, flushed and open. Both of them returned their gaze to the water, shot through with beams of sunlight reflected off the tuna rising from the depths and corralling, spearing into the baitfish, darting back into the deeper blue.

Beyond the shoal and the screeching birds, Joseph was headed toward the ship, the skiff straining under the weight of the dragged net. The fish were unaware, seemed to share the same excitement as the spectators above them, their glossy black eyes and golden-ribbed flanks visible between spurts of incredible energy, accelerations that churned the water into a vortex of trailing bubbles and surface froth, the baitfish massing and splitting, forming balls that stretched and rolled, split and formed again. Joseph had nearly reached the bow of the *Monterey*, cutting his engine, hooking a lead float with a gaff and passing it up to David, who leaned down to reach it. He turned with the float and drew up a lead line, which he connected effortlessly to a barrel winch that he engaged, drawing in the line that whipped him with sprays of water. Overhead, the power block that held the float line also engaged, beginning to draw in the net to the winch, slowly at first and then more quickly as the two lines were drawn onto the ship.

Joseph drew the skiff away from the ship and circled to the stern, where Cutler presumed it would be winched on board. There was movement all around him, but he had eyes only for Casey, who was peering into the depths, her excitement replaced with a deep concentration, her brow furrowed, her legs braced against the railing as the ship shuddered and the float line and purse lines were drawn aboard. Finally, Cutler could see the heavy rings of the purse line come into view, the mesh of the net that drew itself into a purse beneath the shoal strangely sinister, visible and yet invisible, and he saw the first sign of animals who realised they'd been trapped, larger tuna spearing into the net, turning them back into the maelstrom where they became invisible and indivisible from the mass of glittering, frightened tuna that darted in every direction, never seeming to clash with one another, broaching the surface and tails juddering but only ever driven to the centre, the net closing around them.

'You looking for dolphin?' Cutler asked.

Casey nodded but didn't take her eyes off the shoal. 'Or porpoise, or turtle. There's a Medina panel at the back of the net for the cetaceans, but it sometimes helps to guide them there, before the weight crushes them. Fortunately, it wasn't birds or porpoise who drew us here – it's that.'

Cutler lifted his hand to shield his eyes from the glare. A few hundred metres distant bobbed a red buoy, next to a floating platform that looked wrecked, with bits of wood and rope floating around it.

'It's a GPS marker buoy, placed near a FAD, a fish aggregating device. The marker buoy belongs to the *Shuen*. Got a GPS on it, so they can find it. Where they set their longline.'

Casey spoke while looking down into the net, smaller still now, the mass of fish driven to the surface, Cutler seeing species he didn't recognise. 'Is that a barracuda?' he asked, but Casey laughed.

'Jesus. You're a fisheries scientist aren't you, or at least a monitor? That, my friend, is a wahoo, and very likely on the dinner menu tonight. Their signature blessing as a species is that they're solitary, and therefore hard to wipe out in numbers. Unlike tuna, which like one another's company, just like humans.'

'So you plan to wait for the *Shuen* here?'

'May as well. Despite the wide-open spaces, it's not exactly … cordial, to look like we're chasing them. According to Dad, who radioed them this morning, they've not only gone radio silent, but have turned off their transponder. They could be anywhere, or nowhere. They know that you're coming, right?'

'So far as I know. They were informed by the PNA office that their observer was being replaced. Reminded that it was a condition of their licence that they carry an observer at all times. Were told to stand by.'

'Then I guess we wait. But first, we need to stand back. This next part gets crazy.'

'Ok. But how do you know that the *Shuen* will come back here, if it's trying to hide?'

Casey glanced at him, smiled mischievously. 'Because it won't know we're here. Dad's turned off our transponder too. The *Shuen* isn't far from here, we know that.'

'Won't they be angry that you're fishing on their ... buoy?'

'Yes, they will. Another reason for them not to hide from us. They've turned their transponder off, which is highly illegal. They're using a FAD in these waters, even if it's not theirs, near their GPS buoy, which is also illegal. Dad will claim ignorance of their interests here, which is fair enough. Have you eaten yet? Where you're going, unless you've got an iron stomach, the food could be hard to bear if you're not used to it. If I were you, I'd fill mine now. Last we heard from Bev, he was eating the same food as the crew, which is customary, but he said that it was weevilly rice slathered in fish sauce, and even then, only one meal a day.'

Cutler had seen Bevan's communications, but he couldn't tell Casey that. 'Good idea. Will do. Wait, what's that?'

Cutler had been distracting Casey, and she looked annoyed as she now saw the turtle, helpless on the surface at the far reaches of the net, one of its legs caught in the line between floats, being dragged inexorably toward to the ship.

'Shit,' said Casey. 'You coming in?'

Cutler didn't have time to think, despite looking down into the threshing panic of the boiling ocean beneath them. Casey took up her fins and mask and leapt overboard. He saw that she landed near the hull, where the water was clearer. He shed his tee-shirt, put one foot on the railing and followed her in, landing next to her. She passed him the goggles, and he put them on and looked deep into the net, following her around the perimeter of the float line. He could see the tuna massing now in the middle of the column of water, as though they sensed the net closing in, their movements less explosive, their tails chugging more slowly. A small mako shark, long and sleek, was nosing the net beneath the tuna. Cutler heard a splash behind him and panicked, just about levitated out of the water until he turned and saw Joseph, diving down through the tuna toward the shark, kicking like a dolphin until he reached it. He grabbed the small shark by the tail and dorsal fin, held on as it tried to turn into him, pushing and pulling the twisting shark up toward the surface.

Cutler felt a whack on his arm, remembered Casey, turned to her and kicked along the float line. They reached the turtle together. Its flipper was even more tangled where it had rolled onto itself, and Casey went to work. 'It's a green turtle. Watch its back legs, but hold onto the shell, hold her steady.'

Cutler did as he was told. The turtle was heavy as he grappled with it, preoccupied with keeping his head above water while on the other side of the shell he could feel Casey pulling and jerking. At one point one of his own feet became caught in the net, and he kicked in panic, which only made his toes more tangled. He let go of the turtle, folded himself and manually freed his foot, returning to the surface inches above the turtle's beak. It looked at him calmly, bubbling water in its mouth, the folds of its neck brown and ancient. He swam behind it and grabbed its shell, wasn't sure what to do next, until Casey shouted, 'Push her!'

Cutler pushed, and the turtle kicked over and above the float line that Casey had submerged with her feet, out into the deep blue, shot through with brilliantly lit motes, moving slowly and without looking back at them. Cutler turned just in time to see Joseph guiding the small shark by its tail and dorsal fin toward the rim of net, hoisting it across and into freedom. Together, they crossed the net into the open ocean, swimming quickly toward the back of the ship, and the waiting ladder – Cutler made aware by Joseph of the three large sharks looming on the edge of his vision, oceanic whitetips, moving as imperceptibly as their shadows, attracted by the terror of the corralled fish, watching him back as he kept as close to Joseph as possible.

9.

The deck was awash with fish dead and gasping, David and Joseph moving through with short gaffs that they used to hook the largest skipjack tuna into the yawing mouth of the opening that led below decks, to the brining tanks and processing stations. Smaller fish were nudged through scuppers or tossed overboard by hand, some juvenile sharks among them, squid and smaller baitfish, plenty of fish that Cutler didn't recognise. He'd offered to help, but Captain Rick had insisted that he keep out of the way and let the experienced crew do their work.

Cutler returned to Casey's bunkroom and opened the laptop, checked his email and saw that there was a message from Whelan, with a zip file attached. Cutler opened the folder and then the video clip. The connection to the satellite on his hotspotted satphone was slow, and the file didn't open. Whelan's email message consisted of two words – *Call me.*

While he waited for the file to load Cutler took up the satphone and punched in the preset number. Whelan answered on the third ring.

'Where have you been? Did you see the film?'

'It's still loading. The coverage here's patchy. It's taking its time.' As Cutler spoke, the laptop screen went black as it entered sleep mode. He logged back in and the file was still loading.

'What am I looking at?' Cutler asked.

'Hard to say. I just got it, from a PI we have on the payroll. He's based in Spain, keeps an eye on the toothfish poachers for us, does a little of … your line of work. He's got contacts all around the globe. He was sent the clip a few days ago, from an informant in Thailand. His mate was sent it by another mate; you get the picture. We're trying to trace it back to the person who filmed it – it loaded yet?'

Cutler refreshed the screen, but the hamster wheel kept turning. 'No.'

'Listen. I know you're not squeamish, or … our mutual friend wouldn't have suggested you, but you're going to want to be sitting down when you watch it. It's fucking horrible. I haven't been able to—'

'Alright. Shut up now but stay on the line. It's opened.'

The grainy footage began, then paused, then began again in fits and starts. It was filmed from a ship. Daylight, a bright sun overhead. Men in the water. Six or seven men, clinging to wreckage. Filmed from a phone, it seemed like, the swell lifting the men every few moments, another ship to the right of the men, a bow-shaped shadow on the water to the men's left. The men were screaming, shouting, waving their arms. From the deck where the filming was taking place men were shouting, in what sounded like Chinese, laughing too. From beside the camera holder the unmistakable bark of a shotgun, blasting the water and hitting one of the men, his head disappearing in a red mist, his arm releasing a blue fender, slipping below the surface. More laughter from on deck. The ship to the right of the men came into view, a rust-stained bow and rusted chain, half a name in English and Chinese script, the swell lifting and dropping it with a surge that sent the men underwater, emerging screaming, pleading, the retort of a handgun now, the round lodging in the wrack, more laughing. Whoever was holding the phone began yelling at people around him, the voice elevated with adrenalin, sounding upset, the words rapid and unintelligible. The engines on the ship groaned, and the ship pulled away. The ship to the left was still out of vision, and Cutler could hear it now as the shadow of its bow grew longer, then the blasting of a machine gun, which Cutler knew was an AK-47, an arc of frothing water cutting across the ocean toward the begging men, then homing in, raking across them, instant blood in the water, the shooter going through a whole clip while cheers rose from the two other ships. One man was left clinging to a squarish plastic bottle, barely enough to keep him afloat, and not a man but a boy, no longer begging but praying, his lips moving, then a shout from on deck, so close it might have come from the man filming, an oath of some sort, followed by the coup de grâce from the shotgun, the boy's head and the water around him lifting in a circle of spray, centred with blood, to more cheers, the video ending abruptly.

'Jesus Christ,' said Cutler, then was silent.

Whelan too was silent. Cutler closed the laptop screen. 'You still there?' he asked.

'Yeah, I'm here. The boy, the last one. We think him and the others were from Indo. We've had a lip-reader on it. It's far from certain, but according to the lip-reader, it looks like he was saying what everybody says, when they know – *bunda*, or mama.'

'The man filming the killing. Chinese?'

'Yes, but dialect. The man filming is speaking coastal Min, or Hokkien. One of the men next to him, the one shouting, is speaking Hakka. They could be from mainland China, or from Taiwan. I'm having trouble getting it more specific than that.'

'The man shouting. What was he saying?'

'I think the rough translation is "fucking pirate, die".'

'So it's a revenge killing? They've corralled a pirate ship, sunk it, killed everyone?'

Whelan didn't answer right away. Cutler heard the hiss and click of a butane lighter.

'Thought you didn't smoke, after your wife.'

Whelan coughed, his lungs unused to it. 'I don't. Or didn't. But this … this is too much. My experts, and the lip-reader too, they don't think it's a pirate ship. One of the bits of stuff floating, in the middle, looks like the mast of a *prahu*, an Indonesian fishing boat. Not the kind of vessel used by pirates, who almost universally prefer speedboats. So, pirate fishers probably, but not pirates.'

Cutler longed for a cigarette too but remembered Captain Rick's rules. He tapped one out of a packet and went out on deck, which had nearly been cleared, old David pushing a broom through a slurry of blood, scales and water toward the nearest scupper, the muscles bunching on his glistening shoulders, his grey hair sparkling with beads of sweat.

'It's shocking footage,' said Cutler. 'But why have you sent it to me? And why did your Spanish PI send it to you?'

'This kind of thing surfaces every now and then. It's not as uncommon as you'd think. Go back and look at it again, and then again. The ship to the right, you can see coloured paint on its bow, just above the waterline. It did the ramming, we presume. But the Chinese words above, the characters, you might recognise them. It's impossible to be certain, but it looks like a *Shuen Ching* vessel. At the very least, from the same fleet.'

'How many *Shuen*s are there? Is there only one *Shuen Ching 666*?'

'Yes, only one, although there's two dozen or more in the *Shuen Ching* fleet. But not in that area, at that time. The film, we've had it analysed by some tech boffins. It's time stamped. Two months ago. We've then gone back to look at transponder positioning. Most of the *Shuen*s were out in the Eastern Pacific, too far east to encounter an Indonesian fishing boat like a *prahu*. They're hardy little vessels, you find them in Australian waters sometimes, poaching trochus, but not out near Easter Island, or even further east, by the Galapagos. This likely happened east of Indonesia, or the Philippines, between Palau and PNG.'

'The *Shuen Ching 666* that Bevan was on. You mentioned that it was unusual, fishing on its own. It was in the Western Pacific when Bevan disappeared.'

'Yes, he couldn't have been aboard when the ... massacre happened, but he might have heard something about it, from the crew. But ...'

'But what?'

'Transponders aren't always turned on, as you've learned. The *Monterey*'s is turned off now, according to my AIS data, which is why I asked where you were. It could have been Bevan's ship, which we know had its transponder turned off at the time the footage was taken, or it could equally have been another ship, also gone dark. I just thought you should know. If Bevan saw the video ...'

'Leave it with me,' said Cutler, knowing what witnessing the murder would mean for Bevan Whelan, both in Cutler's world and the world of the fishermen.

Cutler ended the call, the sunshine warm on his face, the smell of fish and saltwater rising from the deck beneath him. He could see dozens of oceanic whitetip sharks cruising just below the seabirds scrapping on the surface, a slick of blood and oil around a circle of dead juvenile tuna and baitfish floating belly up beside the starboard hull. Casey O'Reardon emerged from the shadows behind the winch boom, wearing knee-high gumboots flecked with blood. She mock-saluted him, her teeth white even at a distance, and he returned the gesture, turned back into the coolness of the white steel chamber behind him.

10.

Captain Rick O'Reardon barely glanced at the laptop screen once the video started playing. The *Monterey* was stationary, waiting at the *Shuen*'s GPS buoy site for the Taiwanese vessel to appear, but despite this he was at the wheel, staring at the ocean when Cutler had joined him. The day was now hot and still, the swell moving across the ocean's glassy surface in broad, mounded sets that lifted the ship gently, rolling more than pitching.

When the men in the water started screaming, O'Reardon took a hand off the wheel, waved Cutler away. 'I've already seen it. Don't need to see it again or hear it.'

This was news to Cutler. 'Did Whelan send it to you, too?'

O'Reardon smirked, scratched his ear and kept staring out at the horizon. 'No, he didn't. It was sent to me by another captain. He was shown it by a crew member. That little video, like all the ones before it, will have been seen by people all over the world. It's probably on YouTube already. Fishermen from Patagonia to Hokkaido will have watched it.'

O'Reardon's expression was neutral, his voice unimpressed.

'What will most of them think of it when they see it?'

'Civilians like you, yeah, it's pretty disgusting. Shocking. For fishermen ... and fisherwomen. Plenty would cheer.'

'Really? Wouldn't they put themselves in the position of the men, the boy, in the water?'

'Maybe, some of them. Most, I doubt it. If they're old enough, they'll have seen something similar in their time. Nobody likes pirates.'

This was getting interesting. 'How do you know the men in the water were pirates?'

O'Reardon was clearly tiring of the conversation. He clenched his hands on the wheel. The muscles along his jawline hardened. 'The man who sent it to me, he told me it was pirates. He was probably told the same thing, by his crew, and so on.'

'According to Whelan, the wreckage in the water belonged to a *prahu*, an Indonesian fishing boat. There was part of a broken mast in the water. Painted wooden planks. Not your usual pirate vessel.'

Now O'Reardon looked at Cutler. His eyes were wary. 'I didn't notice that. I was looking at it, not looking at it, if you know what I mean.'

'I know what you mean. If Whelan's right, where do you think it might have happened? He thinks one of the ships involved might have been a *Shuen Ching* vessel, whose transponder was off at the time.'

Cutler had been stared down by some hard men over the years, but the heat in O'Reardon's eyes was intense. 'He thinks Bevan was there?'

'No, because the footage was taken two months ago. But my question. Indonesian boat, not big, made for coastal waters. Where do you think it might have taken place? Whelan reckons between Palau and PNG. Where you regularly fish.'

O'Reardon lifted his gaze to the horizon once more, turned

back to the wheel. 'That, my young friend, is an impossible question. Subsistence fishermen, without modern tech, or even an understanding of marine territories, national borders, they follow the fish. You'll often hear people say, fish don't respect borders, and neither should we. They're fishermen. They follow the fish.'

'My question.'

'If that's a *prahu*, it likely has a small outboard, uses sail-power when necessary, and if it's Chinese crew on the other ships, it could be anywhere from east of the Philippines, east of Indonesia, north of PNG. Even out here.'

'The Indonesians pirate-fish in PNA waters?'

'They follow the fish. Of course they do. Indonesia's not that far, and for the most part it's fished out. Their fishermen have to go further, depending on the season.'

'So it could have been the *Shuen*, one of the ships present that day, that came across the *prahu*?'

'Yes, maybe. Or any other ship in the area.'

'Any other ship in the area? See a lone old-fashioned fishing boat, poachers but not pirates, think they'd ram it, sink it, murder the crew?'

'Watch your tone, Aussie. I've answered your questions. I don't have to. But I mean, where do you think we are? I told you last night – there are no laws out here, except the captain's law. Or when there's a mutiny, the natural justice of desperate men. But no laws beyond that. That's what people don't understand. That's what I tried to explain to young Bevan Whelan, the fucking fool. People eat fish. They don't care where it comes from. It's like *fucking Bismarck* and his sausages. Your average consumer just wants what he wants, and even worse, wants it cheap. Cheap for the consumer means cheap everything … and everyone, in the supply chain. Cheap lives, cheap practices. Cheap laws. Cheap conditions. Cheaply bought politicians, public servants and scientific *experts*. So yes, sometimes, out here, a captain might see someone encroaching on their fish, their quota, their favourite spots, and yes, they might send that someone down into the depths, where there is no evidence to be found, no witnesses to speak to, no consequences to be had. I don't condone it, but I understand it. Thought you'd understand too, as an ex-con.'

'I do understand it. I'm not Bevan Whelan. You make your own laws out here. Try to do the right thing, but there's nobody watching, except other fishers, so sometimes things happen you wouldn't get away with anywhere else.'

O'Reardon looked appeased, as Cutler hoped he would. The man had spoken more in the past five minutes than in the days since Cutler had boarded. There was a new rigidity to him that suggested the conversation was over, but Cutler was wrong.

'Barometric pressure's dropping fast. The waves are getting bigger, riding the swells, even though there's no clouds. There's a storm coming. Might be a big one.'

The skies were still blue, darker at the horizon where it blended with the ocean, paling in the canopy of sky above them, whitening at the sun's wide corona. Blue sky in every direction.

'Yeah, it don't look like it,' said O'Reardon, 'but it's coming. Same as usual, from the east – you'll see it on your laptop.'

'What does that mean for you? Do you leave?'

O'Reardon laughed. 'We don't leave. Where would we go?

If you're worried about your new ride not turning up, don't be. They'll be here.'

'What makes you so sure?'

'I've been at this a long time, son. I know. They'll want to scoop this GPS marker buoy up before the storm hits, for a start. You haven't listened to me much since you got on my boat, but I'll say it again. Go and get yourself some chow, tell Cook I sent you. Eat as much as you can, then get some shut-eye. That ghost ship of yours could turn up any minute.'

'Then what?'

O'Reardon smiled. 'Then the fun begins.'

11.

The sun was headed to the wavering line of the oceanic horizon, the curvature of the earth visible in every direction. A quiet had descended upon the *Monterey* while the crew straightened and piled the line of netting, or else gutted fish below deck. Cutler had done as O'Reardon suggested and spoken to the cook, who'd worked up a plate of leftovers from last night's dinner – mounds of roasted meat and starchy potatoes, yam and kumara. The cook was braising something on the range that smelled like Irish stew when Cutler returned his plate, refusing the offer of seconds. He'd taken instead a mug of steaming coffee with him back to Casey's bunkroom, where he'd tried to read the Steinbeck, but wasn't able to concentrate. He tried then to sleep but wasn't able to close his eyes for long. His heart rate was up, and he could feel the blood in his ears. It was often like this before a job, a kind of listless dread that made everything except strenuous physical exercise seem unappealing.

He was in the process of repacking the gear that he'd laid out in a comforting grid on Casey's bed when she entered without knocking. He didn't notice her at first, too busy checking the magazine in the Glock, thumbing down the first round to test the spring, and when he turned to replace the pistol in its secret compartment, he got a start.

If she'd been smiling when she entered her room, that smile was now gone, staring at the weapon, barrel pointed at the ground. Cutler put it in the case and covered it with the padding.

'Who are you?' she said to his back.

It wasn't the first time that Cutler had been asked that question. He'd never given a straight answer before, but then again, he'd always found it easy to ignore the hurt in the faces of those he'd betrayed.

He hadn't betrayed Casey O'Reardon, or at least he didn't think so.

'I honestly don't know,' he replied, a little wounded at the disappointment in her eyes. He thought of the foster homes he'd lived in, each one better than the last, until his final home with the retired sergeant and his wife in Dubbo, the closest he'd come to having parents. He thought of the different names he'd lived with, the dozens of nicknames, the moves from town to town, city to city, the way his story kept changing, and how the stories he told others had ended up becoming the stories he told himself. If the stories he told himself weren't true, then what of his experiences? They were real enough, but the person living them had been a fiction.

Casey's eyes didn't soften, although her voice did. 'Then I genuinely feel sorry for you.'

Still, she didn't leave. Cutler liked her too much to say anything. He waited for the disappointment to rise again into her fierce eyes, into the lines around her mouth, knowing that he would never see her easy smile again.

'Why do you do it ... whatever it is you do?'

Cutler knew the answer to that question, as pathetic as it was. 'I'm good at it. I don't think I'm built for anything else.'

'I hope you are, *good at it*, I mean,' Casey said, turning away into the corridor.

—

Out on the deck Cutler smoked, watching the strings and bladders of fatty offal get picked off by the diving terns as it was conveyed over the side from a portal below deck. The surface of the ocean was slick with smeared oils and blood, lending extra clarity to the waters beneath. Still the giant sharks circled the descending columns of muck that the birds missed, waiting for their chance as juvenile tuna, striped along their silver sides, darted at the baitfish attracted by the blood. Cutler admired the gracefulness of the sharks but pitied them their eternal watchfulness, until he remembered Casey's words, wondered if he was any different.

The sun was now an ochre line across the water, the blackness of deep space behind it and the foreground of ocean mixing to produce an inky grey, chasing the last blues out of the water and sky. Cutler heard someone pad the steel behind him, but he still got a surprise when Captain O'Reardon grabbed him, tilted him over the bulwark.

'Don't fall in, Aussie. There be monsters. Though you might want to turn around, see what's coming starboard-side.'

On the horizon to the east, where it was darker, a white shape like a giant gull, wings tucked in, small lights for its eyes, nosed quietly toward them.

'You packed?' O'Reardon asked. 'Its transponder's still off, but I caught it on radar. I'll get the skiff launched.'

The *Shuen Ching* didn't appear to be getting any closer. 'Why's it just sitting there?' Cutler asked. 'Doesn't it want to see what you're doing?'

O'Reardon barked out a laugh. 'It knows what we're doing. But it won't risk coming any closer. You'll understand why when you get transferred.'

'I want to know now.'

O'Reardon looked at him thoughtfully, nodded. 'Because the crew will likely dive in, swim across to us, to be rescued.'

O'Reardon wasn't joking. 'Maybe you should approach *it*, then.'

The captain put a hand on Cutler's shoulder. 'Spoken like a man who's quietly shitting himself. I'm not in the business of rescuing sailors, son. On the high seas, they step on my boat, they become my responsibility. And besides, that would compromise your … mission, wouldn't it?'

O'Reardon was right, and he knew it. He passed Cutler his binoculars. Cutler adjusted the focus for the five-hundred-metre range. There was nobody on deck bar a man in a grubby tee-shirt, illuminated by a yellow light, cradling an AK-47, his eyes hidden beneath a New York Yankees cap.

'Come with me,' said O'Reardon.

—

In the wheelhouse Cutler looked through the binoculars while O'Reardon took the short-wave mic from its cradle. The man on the deck of the *Shuen* hadn't moved. The wheelhouse on the other vessel was dark, bar the flaring of a lighter, the red glow of a cigarette. On the climb up to the bridge Cutler had duly noted Joseph and the other men taking cane knives out of a cupboard in the kitchen. They stood on the deck below, lined along the bulwark rails. Old David quietly loaded a pump-action shotgun with red shells.

'*Shuen Ching 666*, this is Captain Rick O'Reardon of the *Monterey*. Do you have copy? Over.'

The comms speaker crackled, but no voice emerged from the static.

'Do you have copy? Over.'

A man cleared his throat. '*Monterey*, what are you doing here? Get away from my GPS position. Over.'

The gruff voice surprised Cutler with its clean, barely accented English. If there was an accent, it was standard English, the kind learned in baccalaureate schools all over the former commonwealth, in places like Hong Kong, Singapore and KL.

'Thank you, Captain,' replied O'Reardon. 'I am not interested in your operations, or your equipment. I am here by request of the PNA, just like last time, to replace the observer you ... to provide you with another mandatory observer. You will have already received communication from PNA headquarters related to this matter, over.'

The speaker crackled. 'I have received no communication. We will take an observer when we restock in Palau, next month, over.'

'Captain, I have brought you an observer. You are familiar with the law. You are not allowed to fish these waters without an observer present. I assume that you intend to fish during the next month? If you didn't receive any formal communication from the PNA office Nauru, then I am happy to read to you the official communication I received when I agreed to bring you your observer, over.'

The speaker was silent for a long while. Finally, the grey noise spiked. 'Why is your transponder turned off, Captain, over?'

O'Reardon shook his head. 'I could ask you the same question, Captain. I could also lie to you and tell you that it's broken. I turned off my transponder because I wanted you to find me, over.'

'Get away from my GPS buoy and leave the area. This is your first and final warning, over.'

'I don't care about your warnings, Captain. My crew are ready to respond to any threat. One of my crew is a trained sniper. You undertake any aggressive action against me, or my crew, or my vessel, I can assure you that your children will be orphans before you can blink. You are well within range, over.'

The speaker began to hum. Cutler took up the binoculars again and saw the man on deck respond to something, begin to depart the deck, crouching. Cutler looked down toward where O'Reardon's men were standing, perfectly still in the darkness, the moon rising on the southern horizon. Tucked into a corner near the killing floor, Joseph sat on a stool, a high-powered rifle leaned upon a coil of rope, the scope at his eye.

Cutler had assumed that O'Reardon's brinkmanship was just a ploy, but in the tension of the men below and the cold precision with which Joseph aimed the rifle, the captain's warnings about the absence of law on the high seas, and therefore of consequences, no longer seemed exaggerated. At that moment anything seemed possible.

Cutler was already going into a potentially dangerous situation, but if the *Shuen* accepted him now, essentially as the product of gunboat diplomacy, then the stakes had been raised higher than he wished.

If O'Reardon was incorrect before, about Cutler quietly shitting himself, he was no longer wrong. O'Reardon glanced at him, caught Cutler's eyes then sighed, tired of the game. 'I have a young scientist observer standing beside me, Captain, who looks very alarmed at your strategy here. He doesn't deserve this, and neither do I. Allow me to bring him to the *Shuen* so we can both get back to catching fish, over.'

'Or?' was the only response.

'Or I will notify the PNA in Nauru that you are now fishing illegally, that you have threatened a fellow captain in their waters. And I will destroy your GPS buoy for the insult you have shown me here, over.'

The radio went silent but not for long. 'I will drop a ladder and hold my position. Bring him, then leave this area. You are lucky there is a storm coming, over.'

The lights on the deck of the *Shuen Ching* were suddenly illuminated, from its bridge to its stern. With the stars burning brightly above it, in the distance it looked like a fallen constellation, come to sit over the dark waters.

O'Reardon lifted the mic a final time. 'Thank you, Captain, over.'

The older man turned to Cutler and nodded toward the door. 'That was easier than I expected. Now get your bags and meet David at the skiff. Joseph will be watching you, if you know what I mean.'

Cutler put out his hand, and O'Reardon looked at it before shaking it quickly. 'Three officers, and only one of *you*. Don't trust the crew either. They're desperate men, and will do anything to survive, as will you, I hope.'

'Yes,' Cutler replied. 'I will.'

O'Reardon turned to his wheel, taking it in both hands, a slight tremor there, his eyes staring out across the silent waters.

12.

David pushed the throttle on the skiff and it surged from the *Monterey* toward the east, where the darkness was thicker, woolly on the horizon, and the *Shuen* lay waiting. The only sign of movement aboard the ship was a boiling at the stern, where water poured from the deck and silvered the ocean.

Cutler lit two cigarettes and passed one to David, who stared at the profile of the Taiwanese vessel as a rope ladder was thrown from its waist. 'You need to change your face,' he said, pulling back on the revs as a large swell came at them. 'You look like you're going to war.'

Cutler didn't reply, knowing that David was right. He was going to have to play the part of the young scientist, resolute and idealistic, eager and friendly despite his fears. He didn't have much time to reflect upon it anyway, as David sliced a broad arc with the powerful outboards before pulling back on the throttle, surfing the flank of a swell and riding the next with perfect timing, bringing the skiff alongside the *Shuen*, whose white steel hull rose like a wave that threatened to break upon them. David's cigarette hung from his lips. He shook his head as the smoke rose into his eyes.

Cutler hooked his duffel across his shoulders and hoisted the heavy suitcase.

'You can climb a ladder with one hand?' David asked.

Cutler took his point, adjusted his grip to put his hand through the handle, so that the weight of the suitcase was transferred across the back of his wrist. The skiff idled alongside the hull, looming above them, the rope ladder whipping in the swell.

Because David wasn't going to say anything by way of farewells, Cutler took the ladder with one hand, the skiff and the hull rising and falling. 'Tell Captain O'Reardon that I accidentally packed his book. The Steinbeck. I'll post it back to him.'

That made David smile. '*Travels with Charley*? He's been trying to get me to read that book for years. Keep it, please. And quickly, now. It's dangerous sitting here.'

Cutler nodded, cinched his duffel tighter on his shoulder, tried to crack an excited smile. 'How's my face now?'

'You look like a crocodile trying to smile.'

Cutler laughed, turned to the wall of steel. The ladder was made of hemp, with plastic slats, poorly tied. Some had slipped. He put his foot on the first rung and left the safety of the skiff. The hemp strained under his weight, and the slat bowed. Cutler reached as high as he could, and hoisted himself up three slats, panicked when his feet couldn't find the rope, which was whipping beneath him. He hooked his leg inside one of the slats and it took his weight while he hoisted himself higher, and then again, until his left hand gained the steel bulwark, his right hand weighted with the briefcase feeling like it might break at the wrist. With an effort he swung the briefcase over the rail, hoping that nobody was there, letting it go onto the deck where he heard it crash. Lighter now, he scampered up the last three feet of ladder and hurled his chest over the bulwark, sliding the duffel off his shoulder to join the briefcase on the deck. He looked back a final time at David, who hadn't left the *Shuen*, but was idling away from the hull in case Cutler fell.

David put his hand to his mouth and shouted, 'When I get back, wave your hat from the deck if everything's ok, and Joseph will stand down.'

Cutler gave him the thumbs up. He was a bit scratched and scraped where his elbows had hit the hull, and his breaths came in shallow, painful sips where his chest had been constrained by the heavy duffel, but he waved goodbye to David, and swung himself over the rail and onto the deck of the *Shuen Ching*.

The first thing he noticed was the smaller deck area of the vessel, despite it being larger than the *Monterey*. In the semi-dark he made out winch drums and racks of hooks and floats, and baskets filled with gaffs and gumboots, everything strapped down. Cutler looked up to the wheelhouse, which unlike the *Monterey* occupied the midship area of the vessel rather than the bow, where a dim light shone through a bank of small, salt-stained windows. There was no welcoming party, and no sign of life elsewhere on the ship. He dragged his gear away from the bulwark toward the stowed equipment near the bridge, which smelled of dried fish. The paint-blistered walls of the ship glittered with a mosaic of fish scales, strangely beautiful in the dim light. Large roaches scuttled out of sight at the sound of his boots on the steel. He walked beneath the bridge, which spread right across the deck, with only a narrow passage either side allowing access to the rear decks, passing a padlocked iron cover inset into the floor, which presumably led below to the fish processing and storage areas. He tried the door to the bridge, which was built over three levels. It was locked. He shook his head at the stupidity of the captain, until he remembered the suspicion in the man's voice over the comms.

Cutler was reminded of David's request and turned to the *Monterey*, barely visible except for the bridge lights casting a filmy, reflected light over the ocean. He took off his cap and waved it, put it back on and looked behind him to the bridge. From across the ocean he heard the *Monterey*'s engine grumble into life, and then the whine and throaty roar as it began to leave the area. Beneath his feet the *Shuen*'s engines likewise came alive, juddering the old steel as the ship began to fight the swell, making the hull groan as the heavy propellor shifted water and the driveshaft whistled. The *Shuen* picked up speed quickly and ploughed the swell, slowing only when the ship reached the GPS buoy, blinking red in the night. The engine began to idle, chuckling the steel wall of the bridge as the vibrations decreased, then ceased altogether. A light came on in the wheelhouse, and a searchlight mounted on the bridge roof swung an arc across the waters, fixing on the buoy.

Cutler heard feet inside the bridge, descending a staircase toward him. He stood back from the heavy door as the lock disengaged. He remembered David's advice, and put on his face. The door creaked open, no light behind it. A small, thickset man with a doughy face, the man he'd seen earlier in O'Reardon's binoculars, pushed past him, waddling toward the bow, his flip-flops squeaking. He knelt and with the rope of keys at his belt took up the padlock on the floor, and clicked it open. He straightened his back and hefted the heavy steel door, which he walked until it was vertical, and then laid down on the deck, hinges squealing. He never once glanced at Cutler, even as he wiped sweat off his face, kicked at the mouth of the entrance, barked an order that Cutler didn't understand, although it had an immediate effect. From below deck came the sound of whispered voices, and presently a man's head emerged from the hold, thin and brown-skinned, with large, liquid eyes. He held up his hands, and it was then that Cutler saw he was chained at the wrists, with a longer and thinner chain passing through the steel cuffs. From the string of keys at his belt the Taiwanese officer unlocked the cuffs and slipped the man's wrists free. The chain fell behind him, clanging as it was stripped, as more men arose from the darkness of the hold to have their cuffs unlocked.

Unlike the officer, each of the men glanced at Cutler, although none of them returned his smile, or his nodding to them. They each gave him a single glance, then looked at their feet, or massaged their wrists, or looked away across the waves. Cutler knew that look, the same as he'd seen on incarcerated men the world over – the men were ashamed of their chains. Their refusing to meet his eyes gave him a chance to look them over, however, even as the officer pulled the chain from the hold, wrapping its links around his hand and elbow. There were five men, although the youngest looked not much older than a boy. He looked Filipino, and his crewcut made him look even younger. He was short, like each of the men, except for the man who'd exited the hold first, who was tall and lanky, with curling black hair, his skin much darker than the others, apart from patches on his arms that were mottled pink, and resembled birthmarks. He looked Indian, and like the others wore board shorts and a singlet, his feet bare on the steel deck. They were each of them thin, their muscles bunched and lean with hard work. One by one they glanced up at him again, but none of them met his eyes. The officer pointed at the bow and without a word the taller man and the boy went to the baskets of rope and gaffs. The taller man took out a long coil of rope that he hitched onto his shoulder. While Cutler had been watching, the officer had waved the other men back below deck, and by the time Cutler noticed, the final head was bobbing out of sight, only the sound of feet ringing on a steel ladder to say that they'd been there. The officer went to the two men at the bow, observing as the rope was made into a loop. The three men leaned on the railing and began the process of retrieving the GPS buoy.

Cutler turned to the door behind him, which was slightly ajar. Leaving his bags on deck, he slipped inside the fetid darkness of the bridge. This floor appeared to house sleeping quarters, and a small mess that smelled like instant noodles. There was a toilet that smelled of piss but looked clean. Cutler climbed up the narrow stairs to the next floor, which again housed sleeping quarters and a storage room, where cleaning products and boxes of food were stacked in a corner. Cutler climbed up the stairs to the wheelhouse, glancing inside before he knocked. A small thin man was at the control panel to the left of the wheel and was clearly startled when Cutler opened the steel door. The man closed the ledger he'd been reading, tossed it onto the tabletop beside him, took off his steel-rimmed glasses and began to clean them on his shirt.

Cutler approached him, remembering his educated British accent, put out his hand to be shaken. The man looked at it like Cutler's hand was a dirty tissue. Cutler let his smile drop. The standard approach in a situation like this was to forge ahead, let an artificial enthusiasm overwhelm the stranger, to use charm to demonstrate likability and inoffensiveness. The man continued to regard Cutler very closely, without showing anything himself, and so Cutler reverted to plan B, and put on his most defeated expression.

'Have I done something wrong?' he asked, genuine regret in his voice.

The man grunted. 'You not come in here. Not in here, you understand?'

Cutler nodded apologetically. His PNA observer guidelines meant that he was supposed to have access to all of the *Shuen*'s records, especially catch numbers, to marry them with the tonnage of species in the hold, but he let it go. The other thing was that this man, dressed in khaki shorts and an old Manchester United shirt, wasn't the man who'd addressed O'Reardon over the short-wave.

'Ok,' Cutler agreed. 'Not in here. My name is Paul … Cutler. It's nice to meet you. I'm sorry to have arrived in these circumstances. I apologise for the captain of the *Monterey*. He was very rude. I don't know why he did that. *American*.'

The man's focus on Cutler sharpened. 'My name is Captain Yang. You not come in here, understand?'

The repetition was deliberate, the man's dark eyes hidden in the shadows of the bridge, the blinking lights of the instrument panel and the harsh lights outside silhouetting his face as the last traces of orange glow sank beneath the watery horizon.

Captain Yang wasn't what he'd expected, wasn't what he'd been led to believe the captain of a distant-water vessel might look like – more like the oafish junior officer directing things out on the deck. Apart from the steeliness in Yang's eyes, and his clear perceptiveness when it came to reading men, his lack of physical stature was a surprise. This wasn't a matter of his height, but of the softness of his hands, and the fact that his slender arms were also soft, unused to physical work of any kind. Cutler had been led to believe that most captains worked their way to the position, with the emphasis on work. Perhaps Yang was a 'lucky' captain – knew where the fish were and how to get them, or perhaps he was in the position because he was a good leader, however that might be defined.

Cutler had to play the long game on the *Shuen*, but the signs weren't promising.

'Can you show me where my quarters are?' he asked, his voice soft and tentative. He remembered his cigarettes, and tapped one out, offered it to Yang, who shook his head, wasn't inclined to answer his question either. The man was so pale that he must rarely see the sun. With his glasses returned to his face, his eyes were slightly magnified, his focus on Cutler even sharper.

'Why you come here?' he asked, suspicion in his voice.

Cutler had been hoping for a question of this sort, and he answered eagerly, as per the role he was playing. 'I've always wanted to work at sea. I took the first …'

His voice trailed off when it became clear that Yang didn't understand. Perhaps he'd been talking too fast. He opened his mobile and tapped a word into the translator that'd been recommended to him. He pressed play and held it up to Yang's face, trying to make his own match the excitement and stupidity explicit in the word – *màoxiăn* – spoken clearly in a woman's voice.

'*Màoxiăn*!?' he repeated incredulously. '*Màoxiăn*?'

'Yes, *màoxiăn*. Adventure. Adventure.'

Captain Yang muttered to himself, his eyes shot through with hatred, likely fuelled by the frustration of being saddled with another naive foreigner. 'Passport. Passport! Show me.'

Cutler had come prepared, and he made a show of exposing his money and cards in the traveller's wallet that hung from his neck. He took out the PNG passport and opened it to show his photo.

Yang snatched it, looked it over and compared the photograph with Cutler's face. When he was satisfied, he closed the passport, but didn't give it back.

'You're not PNG. You're *gwailou*, white man. Not PNG.'

Cutler smiled, his answer rehearsed. He began to speak, but opened his phone again, tapped out 'father makes coffee in PNG.'

Once more the young woman's voice recited the words. Once more Yang was incredulous. '*Kāfēi*! Father makes *kāfēi*?'

Cutler played along, laughing, as though a great breakthrough had been made. 'Yes, father makes *kāfēi*. You like *kāfēi*?'

The question wasn't worthy of an answer. Yang flipped the passport onto the desk beside the ledger. Cutler looked at it mournfully but didn't say anything.

'Where your bag? Show me your bag.'

Cutler smiled, put on his most helpful voice. 'My bags are downstairs, on deck. Downstairs.' He mimicked with his fingers the walking necessary to retrieve or inspect his bags, but Captain Yang was already pushing past him.

Out on deck the darkness felt weighted, pushing between the

dim lights to form pockets of solid shadow. The temperature had dropped with the barometric pressure as he led Captain Yang toward his duffel and suitcase. The stocky man supervising the retrieving of the GPS buoy turned and saw them, muttered something to the gangly worker pulling in a rope with long, exaggerated motions, face turned from the spatters of water that leapt from his hands. The stocky man clicked on his headtorch, which bleached his broad face and yet made his dark eyes glisten.

Cutler watched him come and so put out his hand, introduced himself again, but for the same result. The man proceeded directly to Cutler's bags, and he realised he had to intervene. He cut off the stocky man and knelt between him and the bags, his back turned. He ripped down the zipper of the duffel and felt around, until he located what he was looking for, cool and solid in his fingers.

Cutler turned and offered the bottle of Johnny to Captain Yang. 'Take it,' Cutler said. 'A present.'

Yang looked coolly down at the bottle but didn't move. It was the other man, who now that he was close smelled like bait left in the sun, oily and desiccated, reached out his calloused hand and took the bottle. He held it up to the spotlight above them.

Cutler stood and again put out his hand. 'Paul ... Cutler. Captain Yang didn't give me your name. What is it, your name?'

Cutler looked to them both, exchanging glances. He put out his hand again, and this time it was accepted, but not out of friendship. Cutler felt the hard squeeze that he let crumple his fingers, put unbearable pressure on every one of the twenty-seven bones in his hand. He winced, the pain genuine, allowing the man to see his discomfort, to enjoy it even, before he let go of his hand.

Cutler had to step sideways, out of the interrogatory glare of the headtorch, to capture the man's expression.

'My name is Li,' he said, the cruel smile still edging his sunburned lips. Without the torch in his face, Cutler could make out the deep pocks on the man's cheeks, his chin, whiskered black and grey. His skin was dark with sun and salt, the colour of old leather, his breathing deep and regular. Cutler held out his cigarettes and Li took one, waited for it to be lit, enjoying the silver service.

Cutler had never met these men before, but their meeting reminded him of so many others – the cool, observant leader, hands clean, and his muscle: crude and potent, happiest when his hands were dirty.

'Are you the first mate? An officer?' Cutler asked, because he wanted to hear the man speak more.

Li smiled, his teeth blunt and white, the glare from the headtorch deepening the dark well of his mouth, his throat. He sucked greedily on the cigarette, held it up to the light as he'd done with the whisky, nodded when he saw the brand.

'I'm Chief Officer, Deck Department. First Mate.'

Cutler nodded respectfully. 'What do I call you, sir? First Officer Li?'

Li glanced again at Yang and laughed. 'Yes, sir. Yes, sir. Or boss!'

'Is there another officer, engineering department?'

There was something off about his question, judging by their reaction. The men glared at him, the headtorch bright in his eyes, making them water. Cutler held up a shielding hand. 'Shall we drink? I could murder a whisky.'

Li's English was pretty good, although it wasn't as good as the man who'd addressed O'Reardon on the short-wave, the reason Cutler had asked about an engineering officer. Similarly, Cutler's statement about his thirst was deliberate. Through the glare he saw Li register the idiom, even as the captain beside him froze, his eyes sharpening.

'Murder a drink. Thirsty.'

Cutler mimed the action, pointed to the whisky in Li's paw. 'Whisky. Shall we drink?'

Li smiled in response to Cutler's invitation, although his eyes were cold. 'Yes, we drink. But first, your bag. Take everything out, put it on deck, so we can see.'

Cutler had to play along. He looked reproachfully at the two men, as though he resented the command, until he shrugged, bent to his duffel and began to pull out clothes, toiletries and supplies. Li sifted through the gear with the toe of his thonged foot, barely interested. Both men were focussed on the impact-proof suitcase, which Cutler unclipped, opened, carefully extracting his empty shoulder bag, laptop, satphone, the maps in their waterproof sheaves, holding up each item and laying it neatly on the deck, which still carried heat from the day's sun.

'What is that? Show me.'

Captain Yang pointed at the EPIRB, red and glossy in the harsh light of Li's torch, the size of an apple.

'Floating transponder. EPIRB. New rule from PNA. All this stuff is from PNA.'

The men looked at each other, and neither seemed satisfied.

'GPS,' Cutler said again. 'Like … that!'

He pointed toward the bow, where the two men who'd retrieved the buoy were now waiting, watching them, their faces hidden in shadow. Beside them, and out of the water, the buoy looked heavy and expensive, like a floating streetlamp, still blinking from its red eye and dripping onto the deck.

It can't have been easy hoisting it out of the ocean, and yet the men had worked silently and steadily in the background.

Li had clearly forgotten them, because now he barked an order that Cutler didn't understand, until he repeated it, each word sliding into the next. 'Packit, Packit. Fucking packit.'

The two men slid into practised movement, the taller man placing his arms under the heavy end of the buoy while the other hooked his arm through a rope. Together, they braced their knees and lifted the device, from hip to shoulder in a single fluid lift, then began staggering toward the open storage deck beneath the bridge.

Captain Yang's eyes hadn't left Cutler's open suitcase. Cutler didn't want the man to look too closely, and so he knelt and began stowing his gear back into the duffel. He half expected the captain to kneel beside him, but the man didn't move until Li did, together with the two crew, who followed the first mate to the hatch in the forward deck, which they climbed down, all without speaking, even as Li closed the hatch, kicking a bolt to lock it from outside.

Locking the men in the hold, in front of Cutler, was the first challenge. The first of many, he assumed. A PNA observer might be expected to enquire as to the crew's welfare, but Cutler didn't want to question the men's rules aloud, not yet. He let his eyes wander from the hatch to the two officers, and put on his shyest expression, catching the challenge in their stares. He looked away at the ocean and knelt again to the suitcase, which he clamped shut.

Cutler's primary objective on this first night was to get a listening device into the wheelhouse. The voice-activated bugs behind the suitcase lining, together with the Glock, linked to a receiver on his laptop, had a range of fifty metres in good conditions. Captain Yang had been too suspicious, too combative when Cutler had entered the wheelhouse, to the point that Cutler had been reluctant to even look for a suitable location for the bug – somewhere out of sight but easy to access – easy to plant and retrieve, should that become necessary.

He stood and hefted the duffel and the suitcase, looked at them expectantly, ready to be shown his quarters, but Yang had other ideas. He reached out a slender hand toward the suitcase.

'Give me this case. I will lock it in safe, with passport.'

Cutler shook his head. It was a pity, but this was a challenge that he had to meet. 'No, I need my laptop. I need to take notes.'

Li sucked air through his teeth, his thick neck puffing as he lifted his head and squared his shoulders, which in the semi-darkness made him resemble a toad. 'Many thief here. No computer outside wheelhouse.'

Cutler tried to smile, as though it was all a misunderstanding. 'Captain Yang said I can't go into the wheelhouse. I need my laptop to work. I'm sorry, but I need it.'

Cutler despised the plaintive notes in his voice, but he persisted. 'Listen, I'm very tired. Sleep. I want to sleep.'

He put his free hand under his chin, tilted his head, the universal symbol. 'Sleep.'

The two officers exchanged a glance. Captain Yang nodded to Li, who stepped aside, indicated for Cutler to follow him. Cutler half expected him to grab the suitcase from his hand while he was laden with the duffel, but the man merely stared at him as he passed, a distant look of victory in his eyes, a small and cruel light there amid the dark expression of hatred that flushed his face and stiffened his posture.

Cutler entered the darkness of the ground floor and shuffled aside as Li made for the stairs. Captain Yang swung the heavy steel door, bolting it from the inside.

13.

The sleeping quarters that he was to share with Yang and Li was a low-ceilinged box with two sets of steel bunkbeds opposing one another. The space between the beds was barely wide enough to stand in, and at the end of the beds were two steel cupboards whose doors were open, shelves laden with clothes and boxes of snacks. Captain Yang stood outside in the doorway and pointed with his chin to Cutler's bunk. 'You sleep there. Bag on bottom bed.'

Cutler was tall enough that he could reach across the top bunk easily, and so hoisted the duffel off his shoulder onto the top bunk, placed the briefcase beside it.

'No, bag on bottom bed. Bottom bed.'

There was no way that Cutler was going to give Yang and Li easy access to his bags during the night, and so he nodded to the captain and then pointed to his genital area, made a walking figure with his fingers, back and forth to the toilets.

'Toilet. I don't want to wake you, getting out of bed.'

Cutler did the walking finger puppetry, pointing to his genitals, until the ridiculousness of it made the captain grunt and turn on his heels toward the wheelhouse stairs. Now Cutler was alone in the bunkroom that was to be his home. He sat on his bed and looked at the bunk opposite. At the foot of the bed was a small television with a DVD player, gaffer-taped to a milk crate. In a cardboard box beside the television were dozens of knock-off DVDs, splayed open and covers slid out. Finally alone, he looked under the beds and sifted quickly through the cupboards, looking for anything that might belong to Bevan Whelan, whose bag and laptop must be on the ship somewhere, waiting for the next time the *Shuen* was in port when, according to Whelan Snr, it was supposed to be freighted home. There was nothing in the room that looked like it might belong to the young Australian, all of the shirts in the shelves were size small, and smelling musty like they hadn't been worn often. There were a few stick mags underneath a pile of manga that looked like they'd been at sea for decades, old Euro porn from the seventies with pasty men and women, and eyes that looked heroin dull, but apart from that the room seemed just like he'd imagined crew quarters at sea – cramped and messy, badly aired and functional – used for sleeping and not much else.

Cutler stepped into the hall and scouted the storage rooms beside the bunkhouse. He wasn't sure of Li's location, and didn't want the first mate catching him unawares. He returned to the bunkroom and, before opening the briefcase, remembered to do a survey of the room. It was surprising that he was bedded down with the two officers, even more surprising that there didn't appear to be any engineering officer on board, essential if there were repairs to be made. It was unlikely that the captain would be watching him from the bridge, but it was better to be careful. Cutler looked into the corners of the room and up in the light fitting for any hidden cameras. Just in case, he draped a tee-shirt across the television screen before opening the briefcase, ears pricked for any sounds from outside. Very quickly, he scooped out the first bug, a silver pellet the size of a bean, with a removable sticky-taped surface, and slipped it into his shorts pocket. He held on to the second device, a micro-camera the size and colour of a long grain of rice, then replaced the padding in the suitcase. After removing the laptop he closed the suitcase, twirling and setting the combination lock.

Cutler stood in the doorway and looked back into the room. If he placed the camera on the ceiling, inside the light fitting, whatever happened on the bottom bunks would be invisible. He stood inside the doorway and crouched. On the left-hand side wall was a raised edge of steel where a painted-over speaker, the combs of its face still visible, gave a view over the length of the room. Cutler took out the superglue he'd brought for this purpose, a small generic tube kept in his toiletry bag, and dabbed a spot of glue onto the side and top of the camera. He wedged it beneath the speaker, where it was largely concealed from view, being roughly the same colour as the industrial white walls. He knelt and blew over it, then gave it thirty seconds, and tapped it with his finger. The camera remained in place.

Next he opened the laptop, logged in and opened the software that would be triggered to record when the camera detected movement. He switched the feed to live, waved his hand at the camera and caught his image clearly on the screen. He closed the software and opened the similarly branded software for the listening device he hoped to place in the bridge. He ran the start of the program and coughed into his pocket, saw the sine wave rise as the sound was recorded.

The placing of observation tech on the site of a new workplace was routine – Cutler did it on every job, after all, and was familiar with the strengths and weaknesses of the devices, usually monitored by third parties in law enforcement. A laptop was a commonplace item, and even the most suspicious target usually overlooked a closed laptop as a site of continual, 24/7 monitoring and recording. Unless he was physically forced to open the locked software in front of a hostile agent, the surveillance tech remained hidden within the standard Microsoft video-player software application, recording visual or aural data in real time to be reviewed later.

There were no sheets or blanket provided for the bed, and so Cutler got out the silk inner-lining for his light sleeping bag and laid it across the mattress. There wasn't a pillow and so he placed the sleeping bag at the head of the bed. Despite what he'd told Yang and Li, he was nowhere near ready to sleep. He wanted to get a bug up there in the bridge as quickly as possible, at a time when they were likely digesting what his arrival meant for their fishing operations, whatever their culpability in Bevan Whelan's disappearance.

Cutler closed the door to the bunkroom and went outside on deck, lit a cigarette and stood at the bow, watching the clouds gather above him in the turbulent darkness like spooling fairy floss crystalline and grey, rolling and rising in time with the swell that had lost its broad shape and was becoming choppy, discordant, the wind-driven waves crashing over the deeper, current-driven swells. The air smelled of ozone, of stratospheric gases pulsed down to the surface, freshening the denser smells of salt and diesel. The wind chewed at his shirt collar and the back of his shirt, eating up his cigarette in fierce glowing draws. It was getting colder, but he waited at the bow, deliberately presenting as a slightly romantic figure, staring out over the darkened ocean, buffeted by the wind and swell, wanting them to think of him as precisely that – another naive young westerner in thrall to the idea of service to the ocean, and all the creatures it contained.

Cutler pinched off his cigarette and put the butt in his pocket, just like a young marine scientist would do. He walked past the locked hatch where the crew were imprisoned without looking at it, couldn't hear anything from below deck except the tinny sounds of K-pop, played through a mono speaker. The negative pressure inside the bridge structure made it hard to pull the door open, but he managed and made his way to the bunkroom, snatching up the second bottle of whisky before climbing the stairs to the wheelhouse, the bug in his short's pocket easy to hand, just as the engine of the *Shuen* stroked into life, sending a judder through the steel hull that settled as the engine found its rhythm.

14.

The door to the wheelhouse was locked. Cutler peered through the glass into the room lit by the panel of lights and a sideboard lamp beneath which Yang and Li were busy with a game of chess, an open thermos and two plastic mugs beside them. They looked up when Cutler knocked, glancing at each other.

Cutler had expected the two officers to be openly hostile, based on Yang's earlier attitude and Cutler's stated desire to sleep, but the captain and first mate both rose, the first mate smoothing his tee-shirt over his belly as he approached the door. Behind him, Yang reached into a recessed cupboard and drew out a third plastic mug.

The door wasn't only cracked for Cutler's benefit but opened widely. Li stood aside and ushered Cutler in, his eyes not meeting Cutler's but his mouth open in an attempt at a smile.

Cutler held up the bottle of whisky. 'I couldn't sleep. Do you want to have a drink with me?'

He'd addressed the captain, who he'd assumed would say no, but the captain waved Cutler to the little bench-table. Yang tipped out the tea from the mugs back into the thermos, which he capped, placed back into the cupboard.

They were clearly going to play it differently than Cutler expected. They weren't all-in on the change in direction, however, their smiles a little forced, their bodies tense and their eyes cold, but either way, Cutler regretted not having the bug in place earlier. He would have loved to have recorded the men's discussion, as they described the strategy behind deciding to befriend Cutler rather than excluding him entirely.

It could be that the men had bought Cutler's acting the part of the harmless adventurer, or it could be that their strategy was all about making a good impression, in light of the ongoing investigations into Bevan Whelan's disappearance at sea. They had been ordered to return to the nearest port, in their case to Palau, to allow a PNA official and a police investigator to board the vessel and ask the appropriate questions, but the captain had refused, stating that his orders from the company who owned the vessel were to fish out his current day quotas before returning to port. It could be that Captain Yang had spoken to his company while Cutler was downstairs, and been ordered to play nice with the new PNA observer, or it could be a stratagem developed between the two men, but either way the change in their attitude toward him was clumsy and disingenuous, and either way Cutler welcomed it – it would make his work easier.

Now all three of them would be acting a part. Cutler knew from experience that while everyone was deceptive, and while everyone was accustomed to wearing masks, few except those pathologically inclined were able to maintain a high-stakes role, minimising the distance between the real and the fake to the point that the psyche was stable over the longer journey. Where the distance was too great, or where, like with Yang and Li, the acting was forced or strategic, it was easy for someone like Cutler to manipulate the other party into a position where the mask might slip, at a time of his choosing.

At this point, their reverting to hostility was the opposite of what Cutler wanted. Right now, the two Taiwanese men welcoming him to their table and pouring him a whisky, Li even clapping him on the shoulder, was useful to him. Cutler glanced around the room with an expression of rapt gratitude, looking for a place to secure the bug, his eyes fixing on a small ledge on which were secured maps and documents in plastic folders, only two metres from the intercom and short-wave microphone, and a satellite phone velcro-strapped to its holder.

Cutler raised his glass and toasted the men in Chinese, his poor pronunciation making them laugh appreciatively. An alarm went off on Li's wristwatch, and he stood, went to the wheel. The engines were now warmed up, and he put the vessel in gear, turning the *Shuen* toward the west and away from the coming storm.

Cutler looked to Yang, catching him a little off guard, the captain having to pull his smile up quickly.

'The storm,' said Cutler. 'You go away from it?'

Yang understood him, nodded, finished his whisky. 'Yes, go away. To the deep. Very deep. Here, too shallow. Waves bigger.'

What he said made sense, and Cutler smiled into his cup. He was accustomed to speaking pidgin-English, the universal creole shorn of pronoun and often subject, and in some ways preferred it to standard English. 'When do you start fishing?' he asked, mainly so that he could keep Yang's attention, the eye contact a form of reinforcing his innocence, his naivete, his eyes as soft as his voice.

'When storm finished. Soon, too big waves. Bad for lines.'

'Fish go deeper?' Cutler asked, mirroring Yang's English in a way he hoped didn't sound condescending.

Yang made the universal fish shape with his hand, then angled it down. 'Fish go deeper.'

There was an element of suspicion in Yang's eyes when he regained Cutler's own, as though the behaviour of pelagic species in storms was something that a young fisheries scientist should know.

Cutler conceded his mistake, topped up their mugs again. He smiled, opened his phone and the translation app, spoke into the microphone. 'I learned many things at university, but this is my first time at sea. My father says that life is different to books.'

Cutler felt that Yang understood him, but pressed play on the app, the sound of the young Chinese woman taking Yang by surprise. He nodded toward Cutler's phone, who passed it over. The Captain pressed play again, and said something to Li that made him laugh, his shoulders trembling as his hands gripped the wheel. Yang spoke into the phone and passed it back to Cutler, who pressed play. The transatlantic tones of a male voice, the absurd Kermit-the-Frog American accent modulated by Irish warmth, speaking the words clearly and succinctly. 'Your father is a wise man, although he must be worried that you have chosen to run away to sea.'

Cutler smiled with relief. He held up his hand and waggled it a little. 'Yes, a bit worried. What about you, Captain Yang? Was your father a fisherman?'

Yang looked down into his cup, then back at Cutler. 'Yes, a fisherman.'

'Is he still a fisherman?'

'No, father is … dead.'

'At sea?'

'Yes, at sea. Big storm. Many ships …'

Yang did the falling through water motion again, his eyes never leaving Cutler's, a trace of resentment there at being asked the question, clearly not something he was expecting. He let Cutler soak in his glare a little while, showing something of the steely captain that Cutler had first met, before remembering himself, reaching for the bottle and refilling their cups.

'Where?' Cutler asked.

Captain Yang shook his head, stared into his cup. It was Li who spoke, his voice choked, but not by emotion. Disuse perhaps. He waved his right arm around. 'Here. Pacific Ocean. Tuna longline fleet. Ten ships sunk. Here.'

Cutler knew better than to make eye contact any longer. He kept his eyes on his hands. 'I'm sorry, Captain Yang.'

There was no reply from Yang, but his first mate laughed angrily. '*Sorry.* Scientist say he sorry! Pacific say she don't care. Pacific say the truth.'

There followed a long silence, and Cutler let it settle around them, pondering on the hurt that sat alongside the disdain in Yang's words, and what that meant for his next moves. The swell had picked up, and even in the darkness it was clear that the sky had lowered upon them, dark shapes coalescing and breaking apart through the bridge window as the ship pitched and slammed and aimed her bow at the night before inevitably falling again. The wind too had got up, carrying whips of spray from the bulwarks that expanded as they flew, hitting the window in heavy lashes that bubbled on the glass, tossed away as the ship dived into the next trough.

'Pacific always say the truth,' Li added, his voice quieter now, his stance at the wheel a little crouched, his knees bent and ready for the next slamming wave or gravity drop into nothingness.

The silence allowed Cutler to fully survey the room. He let himself be spooked by the conditions, allowed his eyes to betray the fear that was genuine and getting worse. Even deep in an operation, and a long way from help, he always felt in control, always felt like with a decisive act he could turn the tables, flip the script, shatter the illusion that had bonded him to the men and women who were his targets. Even at the mouth of the grave dug for him by the bikies, even with his hands bound, he'd felt capable of action, waiting for the opportunity that eventually came. But fear was infectious, and even though Yang and Li were calm and inured to the sounds of the ship's hull slamming and groaning, the roiling water testing every seam and weld, he understood that this was because they too were afraid, no less than him perhaps, but more because they were *ready*, had perhaps been ready their whole lives, for the time when the hull breached, and the water came flooding in.

Cutler, too, tried to be ready, despite the sounds of metal under duress, and of a wind that didn't blow so much as shriek, raining a foaming spittle across the bridge window. He took the bottle of whisky from the table lest it topple, filled his cup and passed it to the captain, who filled his own.

Cutler nodded to the chessboard. 'Do you want to play?'

Yang muttered something that once again made Li guffaw. Yang leaned closer. His eyes were a little unfocussed, his contempt clear despite the smile. 'You play?'

'Sure. Not very well, but I like the game. It's getting pretty rough. Big waves! I don't think I can sleep.'

Yang understood him perfectly, shrugged and finished his whisky, held out his cup to be refilled. Cutler filled it, and wedged the bottle between his thighs. He bent over the table and reset the board, giving Yang the white pieces and first move of the game.

Cutler was getting a little drunk himself and decided to ease off. Yang advanced a pawn and Cutler rushed to move, just as a big wave hit the *Shuen*'s stern, making everything on board quake, the men included. Cutler didn't want to think of the men below deck or mention them just yet. It was playing to a racial stereotype, but he looked at Yang and wondered, then asked the question. 'Make a bet? I bet you?'

Yang looked perplexed, and Cutler dug out his phone, used the translator. Yang listened to the voice, nodded and for the first time gave Cutler a genuine smile, his teeth crooked and uneven, much like Cutler's own.

'Yes, I bet. How much?'

'Five dollars?'

Yang laughed cruelly. 'Five dollars? Why such a little?'

Cutler shrugged. 'In PNG, five dollars is a lot of money.'

Yang read him closely, ascertaining the truth of the statement. He nodded toward the board, indicating Cutler's move. Cutler advanced the pawn nearest his hand two spaces, kept his eyes on the board. He didn't lift them for the next ten minutes as he and

Yang traded moves. On two occasions the bridge tipped as the
Shuen was caught in a swell, the magnetic pieces holding fast
even as the board slipped. Yang's moves were interesting. He
wasn't trying to win, but rather using the moves to test Cutler's
chops, and more particularly his temperament. Between each
move Cutler weighed up the role he was playing against what
his next move might say about him. He wanted to present as a
little impulsive, and so rushed at a couple of opportunities that
were in fact traps, feigning both surprise and then annoyance
at himself. Move by move, he projected that same rashness of
temperament by aiming for high-risk, low-reward manoeuvres.
Yang allowed him to take his queen, feigning displeasure himself,
when in fact he had Cutler boxed in a corner, both horses a
move from checkmating him, albeit from a clever distance. Yang
made the final move, acting surprised at his own good fortune,
holding out his moist, soft hand for Cutler to shake. Cutler
shook, but that wasn't what the gesture intended. Yang kept his
hand outstretched, rubbing his thumb and fingers together in
the universal gesture.

'Oh, I gotcha. My wallet's in my room. But I don't have a five
dollar note. Play again?'

'Double.'

'Play for double? Ten dollars?'

'Yes, ten dollars.'

Cutler kept the bottle pressed between his thighs while he
reset the board. Yang again played white and advanced the same
pawn. There was a faint glimmer in his eyes, and the hint of a
smile as he watched Cutler's pawn hesitate over two squares.

Perhaps it was the whisky, or perhaps it was Yang's desire to put Cutler in his place, but the older man proceeded to play out the King's Gambit opening, confident that Cutler would accept the bait, and take the central, sacrificial pawn, which he did. Yang maintained his poker face as the gambit exposed Cutler at the back. Cutler had learned the movement from the old sergeant, his stepfather, and then again in prison. He had a role to play, either way, and he submitted to the strategy that told him a lot about Yang, both his knowledge of the game, and also his belief that he could take the younger man in open play. Cutler saw the moves coming, but he allowed Yang to dominate him, indicating his youthful enthusiasm and stubbornness in response, but also the fact that he was out of his depth with Yang, who concluded the game in fifteen moves. There was no satisfaction on the older man's face as he held out his hand for the winnings.

Cutler projected a little disappointment, but also a lack of awareness of what had just happened to him, looking at the board appreciatively for clues before reaching into his shorts pocket and extracting a twenty-dollar note. It was new currency, supplied to him by Whelan, and Yang held it up to the light and rubbed his thumb over its linen textures.

'You think it's fake?' Cutler laughed. 'Straight from forex in Suva. That's a lot of money for me, but fair play to you. Let me try again tomorrow.'

Yang shrugged, topped up his own whisky as Cutler put away the pieces inside the board, clipped it shut. Yang was a little drunk in his movements, his eyes slippery, his breathing heavy as the whisky did its work. He made ready to stand, bracing himself on the table, and while Cutler wanted him to stand, so that he might plant the bug, he also needed to seize the moment.

He touched Yang on the forearm, who flinched. Cutler nodded then spoke into his translator app. 'People like me. PNA observers. How do you find us? I think we've got off to a good start.'

The Chinese voice repeated his words, and Cutler watched Yang's face closely as he digested them. Yang grunted, which made Li laugh at the wheel, muttering something under his voice. Yang made to stand again, having decided to ignore the question, and once again Cutler touched his arm, nodded toward the phone in his hand. He held the translator close to his mouth, his eyes on Yang, who stood and moved away from him, turning his back.

'What happened to the man I'm replacing? Why did he quit your ship? I don't want to repeat any mistakes. I want us to work together.'

Both Yang and Li clearly understood the questions, because they went very still, even before the translation filled the silence. Cutler's own gambit was risky, but it needed to be done. Both men turned and stared him down. Cutler kept his best, earnest expression, looking from man to man. He pressed repeat on his phone, until Yang raised a hand. Cutler killed the quiet Chinese voice.

'You didn't know?' Yang asked. 'Nobody tell you?'

This was the moment where everything could fall apart. Yang's voice was shot through with disbelief.

'Tell me what? I don't understand.'

Yang was angry now, and Li's body language suggested the same, raising himself taller. Cutler didn't know how they would play it. Would they lie?

Yang went to speak but thought better of it. He glanced at Li, whose face said nothing. 'The PNA. The America captain. Nobody tell you?'

Cutler kept his voice even. 'They told me I was replacing a man. A man from Palau. He quit ... quit ... *finished*.'

'No!' Yang shouted. 'Not man from Palau. Australian man. He didn't quit. He ... die. He go ...' Yang did the swimming hand gesture again, going deeper. 'He die. He go over. Disappear. You replace him, not man from Palau.'

'The Pacific takes him,' Li added, reading Cutler closely. Cutler made his face darken, registering shock. He put the phone down, looked at the men. 'Why didn't they tell me?'

Li grunted again. 'Because you are again ... stupid boy. You don't belong here. PNA don't care. You keep out of our way. We catch fish. You keep away. Ocean is dangerous place. Easy to go ... into water. Never seen again.'

It felt like Li's words were more warning than threat, but behind him Yang smirked, until a big wave hit crested the bow, cleaving the water that clattered onto the window, blinding the ship as it dived into a trough. Li turned and faced the next wave, his feet wide and knees bent.

Yang waved dismissively toward the door. Cutler stood, and Yang staggered to the instruments, bent to the task of reading the depth sonar, glowing green as another dark wave broke over the bow.

Cutler reached into his pocket and peeled off the sticky plaster from the bug. He stood and braced himself on the table, planted it deep against the wall, staggered toward the door, which tilted and rose above him as the ship dived once more into the darkness of ocean and sky.

15.

Cutler stared at the bunk above his head, tried to centre his vision on a particular rusted spring that was broken and bent under the others. The room pitched and yawed, and the ship groaned with the duress of forging through the giant waves that smashed it from the rear and portside, the sounds of the propeller churning in his imagination like the blades of a drowning helicopter, underlaid by the sound of grinding teeth. He tried to centre his vision on the busted spring, but his mind wandered inevitably toward the catastrophic, his senses and imagination coupling in visions of ruptured steel and exploding glass. He wondered at the men below decks, and how many storms they'd endured, knowing that they were imprisoned behind iron doors, should the ship begin to sink. He tried instead to imagine the creatures beneath him, uncaring of the storm in the peaceful depths, but he knew that this too was an illusion, and that every creature beneath him bar the largest predators and the mighty whales were always hunting, and being hunted in turn.

His laptop was closed on the bunk above, but even so, it would be recording the conversations of Yang and Li. He had expected one of them to return to the bunkroom to sleep, but an hour had passed and still he was alone. He hoped that the men were talking, conferring and even better confessing, so that he could do his work and leave the *Shuen*. The idea was to hotspot his satellite phone with the laptop and its Iridium software and email the recorded files to Whelan back in Australia, who would have a translator at hand. He hoped that the two men had fallen for his act, and that their guards were sufficiently down, at least enough to speak candidly about him, and his question about Bevan Whelan. Then he could proceed with his plan of disabling the vessel, at least so that it required returning to the nearest port, where the PNA and local police could do their work. He'd been surprised to have confirmed, up in the wheelhouse, that there wasn't an engineer on the *Shuen*, someone whose job was to make sure the vessel performed at its best, and who would be the first person to identify sabotage. This was unusual for a working vessel, and he had to assume that either Yang, or more likely Li, had the skills to perform this role. The fact that the crew were chained during his arrival confirmed his worst fears about their general treatment, and more specifically O'Reardon's belief that they might try to swim to his vessel to be rescued. That kind of desperation told him that the engine room would be hard to access, so that the crew couldn't sabotage the inner workings of the ship, for the same reason of forcing a return to port.

Cutler went over his memory of the two officers. There was nothing that changed his first impressions of a solid bond between the two. He hadn't sensed displeasure, or envy, or resentment – something that he could work with. Whelan had told him that the two officers had worked together on previous, smaller vessels. That kind of history might make for a strong bond, but not necessarily. Perhaps in the coming days, either from the recorded data, or his own observations, there might be something to get a lever under, to prise apart something more significant, and useful. He wasn't getting his hopes up in that regard. The history they had, the work that they did, the pressures they were under and the secrets they kept required a lot of trust. There was a chain of command, but Cutler hadn't witnessed Yang abusing that. Each seemed perfectly formed, physically and psychologically, for their roles of leader and muscle, and he doubted that Li had ambitions beyond his current station. In previous situations he had been able to sow doubt and mistrust among leaders, but that was among people where there was time and space to work, which wasn't the case on the *Shuen*. The crew was a more likely option for him to garner information sufficient to his task, should he have the opportunity.

Cutler had met plenty of men like Yang and Li before, but Yang was the more interesting one. The man was clearly intelligent, and quietly capable. He displayed a violent calmness, even in moments when anger had risen to his eyes. Unlike Captain O'Reardon, who was a proud maverick, prone to volatility, a fixer of his own problems, Cutler got the sense that Yang was always in command of himself, but that he also drew power from a broader system of control, backed up by the corporation he worked for, perhaps. His father had been a fisherman, and Cutler wondered if he had other family in the company that not only controlled the fleet of *Shuen Ching* distant-water vessels, but also the manufacturing and distribution of its finished product – canned tuna for the general market. If anything, Yang seemed too intelligent and capable for the role of captain. Normally, that might be something Cutler could work with – a little opening, the sense of grievance from a career stalled, the potential for disloyalty to those above him – but Cutler wasn't getting that feeling at all.

Yang reminded Cutler more of the law-enforcement officers he'd worked for rather than the criminals he'd sought to undermine, and ultimately entrap. Whatever misdeeds Yang had committed, it seemed likely that he was doing them from within, rather than from outside a larger framework of law. Captain O'Reardon, and even Whelan, had reinforced time and again that the captain of a distant-water vessel was a law unto themselves and – especially when in international waters – subject to no laws or consequences at all. This was problematic, but the alternative was even more troubling: the idea that the companies and governments such vessels worked for provided the blessing for these men to operate as they wished, for as long as they were productive, out-competing the vessels of other companies, other nations.

Was the favour of such companies and institutions, never mind the rewards, worth killing for, especially when there were no consequences? The answer was yes. Men killed, and routinely killed, for less. But what had Bevan Whelan seen, or done, that made his demise not only possible, but necessary?

Cutler was getting ahead of himself. He needed to try to sleep.

He stopped staring at the bunk above him and closed his eyes. With the movement of the *Shuen* it felt like he was riding a raft down a turbulent river, white-water surging across him, canyon walls on either side. The only way out of the canyon was forward, and Cutler leaned into his paddle and kept his eyes on the bright light in the distance.

16.

Cutler awoke to the tidal susurrations of Li's snoring from the bed beside. He groaned and untangled himself from the silk liner that had become a blanket sometime during the night. His ankles were sore from his feet hanging over the end of the bed, and his head a little foggy from the whisky, but the sun was out, and despite the small porthole between the bunks, the room was flooded with light.

The storm had passed, or rather they'd eluded the storm, because while the swell was making the ship rise and fall, there were no waves breaking on the hull.

Cutler didn't know what time Li had entered the room, but a glance at his watch told him that he'd slept late. Trying not to wake the first mate, who slept with a black Singapore Airlines mask over his eyes, Cutler stood and edged between the beds and out the door. He went into the head and drained himself, then splashed water over his face, cleared his eyes of sleep.

There was no need to change his clothes, and he wasn't hungry. From the bunkroom he took his cigarettes, laptop and satellite phone, and a large notebook and pen. He climbed down the stairs and unlocked the bridge door. Outside on deck the light was fierce, and the air strangely humid. A breeze caught the flag above him but left no trace on the surface of the ocean, blue to the horizon.

Standing at the bow smoking his cigarette, he saw that there was detritus in the water, with plastic bottles bumping against the hull, and a chunk of polystyrene tangled in monofilament that nudged its way around the bottles. Cutler didn't know if the garbage had drifted on the ocean currents, or had been turfed overboard from the ship, although he got his answer when he saw a splash from the stern of the vessel, watched a lidless plastic bottle of Coke take on water, begin to sink. This was followed by a fluttering of noodle packets, and a polystyrene noodle cup, that drifted to the surface and floated away. He couldn't see who was emptying a bin, even as a bucket of slops was tipped over the edge, which hit the water in dark gouts.

Cutler pinched off his cigarette and pocketed the butt. It hadn't occurred to him to wonder why the ship was stationary, but now that he noticed he felt a moment of panic. Out there to the horizon was a world without trees, or birds, or hills or roads. For all its beauty, the skim of the ocean's surface seemed like a desert, the real life happening below. The image congealed, and for a second the idea that they were sitting on the surface of the ocean, with the ocean life beneath them, became inverted, and it felt as though the sky were beneath him, like a pale blue ocean floor, and the ocean above, teeming with life that looked down on him.

He closed his eyes and shook his head clear. He had work to do, and he needed to engage. Up in the wheelhouse, Yang's face was hidden behind the dark, salt-stained glass, but Cutler knew that he'd be watching. He picked up his materials, already heated with the midmorning sun, and walked confidently toward the open hatch near the bridge, from where he could hear the sound of men at work, dragging barrels and pulling chain. He was halfway down the stairs before he began to look around. He'd assumed that the crew were quartered there, but the space was filled with fishing equipment – huge bales of monofilament, wrapped in clear plastic, and steel tubs laden with poles, gaffs and oily machinery. The room stank of fish and diesel, and he couldn't see where the noise was coming from. He stepped through a bulkhead doorway into a larger area, where cleaning stations and a small conveyor led to an opened door in the hull. The room smelled even more strongly of fish, with remnant blood and scales visible on the cleaning tables and conveyor rollers, and on the heaped pile of plastic aprons thrown on the wet floor. Behind the stations was a bank of what he assumed were blast freezers. He went and opened the first one, which was eerily empty, the ceiling lined with heavy-gauge steel hooks, the floor a mess of ice and frozen blood. The next freezer was half-full of hanging fish, the size of the tuna a little shocking, hooked through the mouths and their pale fat bellies wide and long, their eyes misted with frost. The species was bigeye, and he opened his notebook and cursorily wrote the number of fish contained within, the smaller ones hooked toward the back, the dozen or so larger fish clustered at the front. Each of them looked like they weighed a couple of hundred kilos, which he also noted.

He'd assumed that a fishing boat would be a busy place, and yet he still couldn't see any crew. The next freezer was chock full of skipjack tuna, what he'd been told was the primary catch, the world's most popular canned tuna. The fish were small, their heads and tails docked. There were too many to count, but he nudged at a few inside the door, and then he saw them – the layer of shark fins and tails, both large and small, that the tuna rested upon.

Cutler shut the freezer door. He didn't look in the remaining freezers, instead glanced above to the chute where the fish were relayed downstairs. Based upon O'Reardon's characterisation of the *Shuen* fleet, he realised that he expected the fishing operation to be a lot messier, a lot less hygienic, a medieval operation of sorts. There was congealed blood in every crevice along the stations and conveyor, but every other stainless-steel surface was clean and shining in the dim light. The racks of knives, the chainsaw and axes, were clean and fixed in their brackets along the wall.

He exited the killing floor through another heavy bulkhead doorway just as the engine kicked into life. This room was toward the stern, and the noise of the engine as it turned over was tremendous, even as the drive shaft engaged with the propellor, and the ship began to shift in the water, making him grab for the doorway to brace himself. The steel walls of this wide room were painted an industrial green. This room too was used for storage, containing barrels of oil and maintenance tools that were stowed in crates. Crates of detergents and lubricants and rolls of synthetic rope. Boxes of food and supermarket shopping bags full of cleaning materials. There was no place for someone to hide, or to be stowed, only the sign indicating the engine room opposite him.

Cutler scanned the walls around him, and the ceiling, but he couldn't see any cameras, confirming what he'd observed in the wheelhouse last night. The captain of the vessel was connected to the workings of his ship through the instrument panels before him, but there wasn't any sign of surveillance beyond the range of the human eye. Considering how vulnerable a ship in the middle of the ocean was to a disabled engine, especially one that carried a reluctant crew, this surprised him. He tried the door, but it was locked. He glanced back at the bulkhead door he'd entered from and knelt, peered inside the heavy locking mechanism with its standard keyhole portal, saw that it could be picked. He also smelled exhaust fumes, so strong that they made him wince. The ship was chugging along at a gentle pace, and despite the regular oscillations of the pistons, and the heavy steel doors and walls, the sound in the room was increasingly deafening.

Cutler opened the final bulkhead door to the stern. Even though he understood that there was nowhere else left on the ship for the men to be quartered, he was still shocked to see the crowded hammocks and the mess on the few available horizontal surfaces, in the smallest room he'd encountered so far. The noise in the bunkroom was even louder than next door. The welded steel plates that protected the drive shaft trembled and were hot to touch. The plate above the shaft was covered with a thin mattress. Even worse was the smell. Sweat, farts, stale clothes and the exhalations of men through the night, but also something else. He climbed amid the mattresses and mosquito nets, the empty water bottles and strewn sheets and a pair of steel buckets. He remembered the bucket tipped into the ocean while on deck, and saw that they were shit-buckets. The door behind him could only be locked from the outside. During the storm last night, the men had been locked in the small space, loud with the sounds of the engine and the buckets of their waste, but even worse was the obvious smell of exhaust in the room. Expanding foam had been sprayed into gaps in the steel coping that covered the drive shaft, but the air in the room was heavy with exhaust fumes. Cutler had assumed that the engine exhaust would exit via a smokestack of some sort, and perhaps it did, but not only was the muffling of the exhaust damaged, so too was the delivery system. He'd been in the room a matter of minutes, but already he felt light-headed. There weren't any ashtrays in the room, and he could guess why – not only was it already hard to breathe, but it felt as though a spark might ignite the air around him.

Because of the noises he'd heard below deck, he expected to find crew in the bunkroom, or at least at work somewhere, but the room looked like it'd been abandoned at short notice.

Cutler went back the way he came, shutting each of the doors as he passed through them. He would return to the engine room another time, but so far hadn't seen any trace of Bevan Whelan's belongings, or any sign that he ever worked on the *Shuen*. There would be a safe in the wheelhouse, and likely stowed weapons too – he'd already seen evidence of an AK-47 – but everything Cutler had seen so far told him that Yang and Li were cautious to the extreme, and that their secret places would be hard to access. Now was the time to push his luck, however, while they were still pretending to be friends.

17.

Cutler counted his steps as he approached the hatch. A shadow crossed the box of light that was the chute on the killing floor, and only then did he hear the activity on deck. This was important, because even with the doors open down in the hold, from the back of the ship where the crew were quartered, he hadn't been able to hear anything from up on deck, despite the obvious activity. Depending on how Bevan Whelan's going overboard went down, and when, it would've been impossible for the confined men to have heard anything from up on deck – not an argument, not a push, certainly not a splash. He had assumed that the crewmen would be key to unlocking what happened to Bevan Whelan, but he saw now that that his intended enquiries with them could be pointless, if they weren't actively engaged in fishing, and so on deck to observe.

Actively fishing was what they were engaged in now. Climbing up the stairs to the deck, Cutler could hear the drum line unspooling, hear the shouts of the men as they worked. He emerged from the hatch a little blinded, and stunned by the blanket of heat that fell upon his shoulders. Away in the distance the GPS buoy winked in the glare off the ocean. Cutler skirted the deck, keeping out of the men's way.

The taller man with the mottled skin was adding hooks to the snoods that whirred toward him before baiting them with a rapidity that was startling, hooking a small fish that looked like a mullet through the eye as the line peeled away. He was shirtless in the bright sun, for the simple reason, Cutler supposed, that if he were accidentally snagged, he would be dragged overboard. The young man who'd accompanied him on deck the previous evening was controlling the pace of the unspooling line. The three other men, who Cutler didn't get a good look at earlier, were occupied replenishing the buckets of baitfish and baskets of line that were carried to the tall man who was adding a hook that he baited every few seconds before the line went into the ocean. There were no seabirds scrapping for the bait, which Cutler was glad of. Casey had told him that one of the main bycatches of the longlining system was seabirds, hooked on the bait and dragged under, to be drowned at depth. She'd described how half a million seabirds and an estimated hundred thousand albatross were killed each year this way. The line kept unspooling off the drum and the man kept hooking the baitfish and the line kept drifting out into the ocean.

Cutler took a seat on an upturned bucket and tried to keep out of the way. None of the crew were talking, each of them too busy to meet his eye. The three men bringing and passing the bait looked Indonesian or Malay to Cutler. The eldest had a hennaed beard beneath the peaked cap he wore, indicating perhaps that he was a Muslim, while a man around Cutler's age wore a hastily assembled *udeng*, or Balinese headscarf, to keep off the fierce sun.

The third man wore a checked sarong, folded above his knees. He was the first man to glance at Cutler, taking notes against the wall, but there was nothing in his eyes to indicate friendliness, or interest of any kind. This didn't matter in the short term, but either way Cutler hoped that he was correct in identifying the men's ethnicity. At some point in the coming days, Cutler hoped to show them the destruction of the Indonesian *prahu*, and the murder of the fishermen. Unlike everyone he'd shown the video clip to thus far, he hoped that the men would be sympathetic to the murdered fishermen, and thus forthcoming.

Cutler put down his notebook and opened the laptop. He tilted the screen so that it wasn't visible to anyone, then turned on his satellite phone, opening the settings so that he could turn on the hotspot facility. He glanced around a final time before uploading and emailing the file he'd automatically saved when he'd ended the night's recording. He watched the blue line slowly creep across the page to indicate that the file was transferring, then closed the program and opened Excel, where he listed the date and time, and the rough GPS location recorded on his phone. He pretended to input data while the file transferred. He didn't want to smoke while the men worked, the sweat soaking into their shirts, with the exception of the tall man who Cutler estimated had already baited hundreds of hooks, his hands working automatically but his eyes fixed on his work. The GPS buoy with its radio transmitter looked to be nearly a kilometre in the distance, and yet the spool of line on the drum was still a metre deep. There was another drum laden with line behind it, ready to be rolled into position, and another behind that. The work of setting the line was clearly going to take many hours.

Cutler's role was to observe the men's work, but it didn't sit easily with him. The boy on the drum line and the bare-chested man baiting the hooks were focussed solely on their work, practised and concentrated despite the heat, but the other man carrying buckets of bait and baskets of line and retrieving the empties could do with a hand. While the man with the hennaed beard passed the fish to the tall man, and while the man in the sarong scooped baitfish into the buckets from the freezer alongside the wheelhouse, the man in the Balinese headwear ran the buckets there and back. The buckets each weighed a good twenty kilos, and Cutler tightened his cap and slipped off his thongs. While the Balinese man was placing a bucket at the feet of the hennaed man, Cutler placed himself midway behind him en route to the freezer. The man saw what he intended and didn't miss a beat. He was breathing hard, and he flipped the empty bucket to Cutler, who scuttled three steps to the freezer, in time to take the new bucket full of fish. He needed only to turn, take two long steps, and pass the bucket to the Balinese man.

It didn't take long for the six of them to find their rhythm. Occasionally Cutler spilled a couple of the baitfish, which were a type of small mackerel, and which slowed the chain as he retrieved them, but by and large the routine was fast and effective. There wasn't much chance for Cutler to interact with the men, except for a glance every now and then to the two men nearest. After an hour or so the glances became smiles, as Cutler began to tire. He was sweating hard, and his fingers were damp and slippery, but none of the men could take a break while the hooks were going out. Not once did the tall man baiting the hooks break from his work, or miss baiting a hook. He worked like a machine, and yet his movements were graceful, confident and unbothered by the heat, or the fact that his paler mottles were reddening in the sun.

When the first drum line was emptied, there was a minute's break while the drum was swung away, and the next connected to the line that had gone out. Each of the men except the kid raced to the shade where some yellow plastic jerry cans that looked like they'd been fished out of the ocean, were passed around.

Cutler drank deeply. He was well beyond wanting a cigarette, his chest rising and falling like the other men's. He took the opportunity to hold out his hand while he introduced himself. The tall man glanced at the bridge before accepting the handshake.

'Fazal,' he said, 'and this is Wayan,' indicating the Balinese man. 'The man you stopped to help out is Budi,' indicating the bearded man. 'Aadam is working the freezer, and Fernando is working the drum.'

Cutler met eyes with the tall man. It was his perfectly accented English that he'd heard over the comms, when he was back on the *Monterey*. The brown eyes were quietly watchful, and shy.

'Are you from India or Bangladesh?' Cutler asked.

The man smiled, shook his head. 'I'm from Myanmar. Burma. From a small village in Maungdaw township. When there *was* a village.'

'You're Rohingya?'

146

'My government likes me to call myself "Bengali", but yes, I'm Rohingya.'

The Filipino boy, Fernando, shouted something and the men around Cutler melted into action. Cutler held eyes with Fazal, the Rohingya man, nodding his thanks for engaging with him, as the tall man returned to his task, linking the two lines with a sturdy carabiner, painted orange, before taking up his first hook and mackerel as the line began to leave the ship.

The red GPS buoy was no longer in sight, as the *Shuen* continued to move slowly toward the west. It was clear to the horizon, meaning that the first drum carried somewhere near twenty kilometres of line. There were two more drums to go. It was hard to imagine a boat putting out a sixty-kilometre fishing line, baited with thousands of hooks, but that was what he was witnessing.

There was no time to check the computer to see whether the email had been sent. Cutler returned to the line, where the first bucket was waiting for him. He watched Fazal's left hand sliding along the snood line to add the hooks while the other flipped the proffered mackerel and hooked it and let it go, only seconds before the next snood arrived. Unlike the other men, who'd been mute with fear when he'd introduced himself, Cutler already knew, from their briefest of interactions, that Fazal held the answer to his questions about what had happened to Bevan Whelan. He needed to earn the man's trust, but more than that, offer him something for the information. Fazal was trusted enough by the Taiwanese officers to lead the deck operations unsupervised, and to speak on their behalf when communicating in English with other vessels, but at the same time he was chained upon Cutler's arrival, then locked below deck overnight in atrocious conditions. Offering him something better didn't seem too hard, but getting access to him for an extended period was another matter.

Cutler bent to the task of carrying the new bucket, began to watch the other men just as closely. The bridge door creaked open, and Li strode out into the light, wearing nothing but his underpants. He saw Cutler working and laughed, lit a cigarette and walked to the bulwark where he began to urinate. Cutler watched the men even more closely. None of them would meet his eyes now, as he took the buckets and passed them on. The mood on the deck had turned. The men worked even harder, if that was possible, but their bodies were laden with an extra weight, glancing in the direction of the first mate's naked back and pale, hairless legs.

18.

The three lines that were one line had soaked for six hours. The sun had set, and the crew, who'd been busy sharpening knives and cleaning, finally chowed on boiled rice and fish sauce cooked on the deck over a camp stove linked to a propane bottle. Cutler watched Aadam, the cook, while he stirred in the pungent sauce with a spatula before serving. Aadam and the other men ate with their hands, hungrily, finishing the pot in minutes, while Cutler ate more slowly with a plastic spoon.

It was expected that Cutler would eat with the crew, and not the officers. Cutler had gone into the wheelhouse to charge his phone and seen Yang cooking up a pot of stew and rice in the small galley, two plates and chopsticks on the bench beside him.

The fish sauce stung Cutler's cracked lips. His fingers were a mess of blisters and cuts. When he finished eating he offered his cigarettes around the huddled circle.

'Why don't you eat fish with your meal?' Cutler asked, genuinely curious, but also probing for the resentment that the men must feel. He himself keenly felt the need for protein after the hard day's work in the sun. Fazal shook his head at the proffered cigarette, leaned forward and spoke under his breath.

'Only if we catch it in our spare time. This is normal.'

'But there must be plenty of fish offcuts. Wings. Docked tails.'

'They think that if we're allowed to eat those things, that we will carve off extra for ourselves. That we will not clean the fish with the same ... economy.'

'What about species other than tuna? Caught accidentally?'

'Bycatch must be returned to the sea or filleted for sale. For the same reason.'

'They think that you might deliberately try and catch other species on the longline, despite using the same bait for each hook?'

'They think that, yes. This is normal.'

Cutler caught the anger in Budi, the oldest among them, wiping his red-and-grey whiskers before accepting Cutler's cigarette. The same sullen anger was on the face of Wayan, the Balinese man. Cutler was a little shocked and, like the two men, he looked to Fazal for an explanation.

'Every time a new observer comes aboard, we get the same questions. Many of them want to help us with our work, like you did today. But nothing ever changes for us, and you will only be here for a short time, before you return to your life.'

Aadam muttered something in what Cutler assumed was Malay, which made the men smile, except for the kid, Fernando, who, like Cutler, hadn't understood.

'What did he say?' Cutler asked.

'He said, "If you want to help us work, you need to work harder. You make us look bad."'

The same bitterness in Aadam's eyes now, reading Cutler's own, pleased that the comment had been translated. There was a real hardness to the man, despite his small frame. Cutler nodded. He had a point – they all did.

'How did you get to speak such perfect English? And how do you know Malay?'

If he thought that Fazal might be flattered by his observations, he was wrong.

'I don't have to explain anything to you. But to be polite. I learned English at school. My teacher was Burmese Australian, returned for marriage. I learned Indonesian when I was a refugee in Jakarta, for three years. I learned Malay when I worked in construction, in KL. I already know your next question, but I can promise you that I'm not going to answer it. How I came to be here, with these men.'

Yang's voice came over the tannoy, the words indecipherable, although the men rose as one.

Wayan, the Balinese man, was the last to rise. 'If you want to help, you wash dishes. Pot, plates. Pack away in our quarters.'

'Ok, sure. Where do I wash the pot, and the plates?'

'In ocean. Longline coming in now, so wash fast.'

A thin rope had been attached to the pot when it'd emerged on deck. He got to work retying it, so that he could drop it overboard, bring up enough water to wash it, and the plates. The men were moving easily through the darkness. The floodlights came on, at the same time as the lights were illuminated below.

Wayan returned to him, because of something he'd forgotten. It was hard to hear him because of the engine noise, with the ship pulling alongside the GPS buoy. 'Tie rope to pot right way. We don't get new pot if you lose it. Don't help us bring line in, or cleaning fish. Too dangerous for you.'

Cutler nodded, the shadows beneath Wayan's eyes stark, the sweat on his forehead glistening in the harsh light.

19.

Cutler didn't feel like watching the operations from the wheel-house alongside Captain Yang. After the blunt honesty of the crew, the idea of the performed bullshit that he and Yang would both have to endure made him feel ill.

He rehydrated by drinking two litres of warm water, took a seat on an upturned bucket in a corner near the equipment crates, where he could see the fish come aboard, as he supposed his role demanded. He had no desire to witness the death of thousands of marine animals, but he understood at that moment, with the line connected to the drum, the importance of the Pacific Islanders who usually acted as observers. The surface of the ocean away from the *Shuen* was inky black, not even any windblown waves to disturb the glassy surface tension, and it made it easy to imagine that the ocean contained an unlimited number of fish to catch, for those with the will and means.

He'd been assured by Casey O'Reardon that this was not the case, however, and that what he was about to witness was a kind of race to the bottom – smaller catches, smaller fish, the end of the process being the harvesting of fish solely for boiling into paste, reconstituted in a number of ways. Kind of like Soylent Green, she'd quipped. Protein harvesting, she'd also called it, adding, however, that it was more like open-cut mining than farming, which the word 'harvesting' suggested, leaving in its wake a depleted environment. There were an estimated three million, seven hundred thousand commercial fishing vessels at work on the oceans at any given moment. The *Shuen* just one of them, about to haul in sixty kilometres of baited line. Other vessels still using illegal drift nets, and deep-sea bottom trawling, scouring an estimated four billion acres of ocean floor annually.

The numbers defied logic, as did the practices, and all because, as Captain O'Reardon had pointed out so many times aboard the *Monterey* – it happened out of sight and out of mind of supermarket shoppers.

The drum began to shudder, and the line began to wind aboard. This time, Aadam waited near the stern bulwark with a long gaff, while Fernando worked the drum. Budi had gone downstairs to work alongside Wayan, processing the catch and junking anything not considered valuable. Fazal waited, his knees bent in readiness for the first hook to emerge. It came over the gated edge, a small skipjack tuna, around twenty kilos, even its characteristic metallic stripes bleached out by the industrial light. Fernando paused the drum line, and Fazal expertly unhooked the fish, passing it like a rugby ball down the chute, removing the hook from the snood and fixing it to a narrow rail, indicating with his hand that the drum resume its groaning, the silvered line taut into the floodlit ocean, laced with thousands of bouncing droplets. For the first time that day the *Shuen* was stationary, both officers in the bridge observing but taking no part.

The sight of the skipjack tuna thrown down the chute reminded Cutler of something else Casey O'Reardon had described, when she said that it was the pitiful lot of fish to be thought of as a commodity, due to their expressionless faces, the fact that, unlike mammals, their faces were unable to smile. As a result fishes were thought of like grain, measured and sold in tonnes, each individual indistinguishable from the rest, the clue that nailed this observation evident in the lack of plural when referring to them – one fish, ten fish, a hundred fish, a million fish – fish, not fishes, not sentient creatures sensitive to pain and bonded to one another. Reef fish better than chimpanzees at solving intelligence puzzles, able to learn and remember, to form inter-species relationships, to communicate and teach. Humans more like fish than they cared to imagine – the same vasculature, spinal system, nervous system – humans merely fish that evolved to live on land. The list went on, Casey's voice clear in his memory, and not strident or didactic or angry, more … frustrated and sad, at the brutality of the economic systems that demanded cheaper product, and more of it, an algorithm that played out before him now – the work-weary men sweating in the evening not even allowed to eat what they caught, due to the fear of margins, of expense, the economic logic taken to an extreme that malnourished them, living on starch and salt. Allowed to catch fish in their own time, except that they weren't allowed any time, so far as Cutler could see.

Cutler and Casey O'Reardon had lived different lives, but they had things in common. Casey was a student of marine life, a world of perceived simplicity that masked a deep complexity, deeply linked to our own, whereas Cutler saw himself as a student of human behaviour, where the perceived complexity rather masked a deep simplicity. He lived among men and women as an impostor, almost an observer, like a scientist in a laboratory, except that he wasn't objective in his engagements, because that was impossible – dangerous even. The game might be different, the faces and names different, but underneath the surface there was a staggering simplicity, repeated time and again, that explained how those criminal worlds operated. Some among the groups, usually the most successful, felt nothing when they used other people as means to an end. They could order the others about, betray them, manipulate or even murder them, and feel nothing. Such people were human, like every other human, except for that one thing, which was both itself human and less-than-human. They made of their world a game, or they made of it a war, and everyone else became pieces of the game, or casualties of a war. Such people rarely won the game, or won the war, but at the very least they stayed ahead of it, or above it, before moving on and starting again.

The problem for Cutler was what to do with this knowledge? So far as he could see, there was no way around this problem, there was no fixing it – the genie was out of the bottle.

Where he differed from Casey was the way that he struggled with hope. Hope, and the perverse fact that the only other people who understood what he'd learned from his hard lessons among them were such people themselves. Was he himself projecting? After all, *he* deceived, manipulated, performed and wore masks – he played the game and fought the war.

The difference was that he suffered a little for his understanding, and was haunted by his experiences, much like Casey O'Reardon, for whom the more she learned and the more she understood, the more she suffered, and the more she despaired.

And yet she remained hopeful, unlike Cutler. How did she maintain her optimism, caring for it like a fragile garden? There were likely philosophies of hope that he wasn't aware of, and yet would seek out. He needed to do that, at least, even while in the future he worked among those who were convinced of their simple truths, which gave them a kind of power. It was his job to deceive them, to destabilise their vision of the truth, and to take away some of their power.

Early on, his handler, Malik Khalil, had told him that he knew Cutler had a secret. They were debriefing in a café near the AFP building in Canberra, a crisp winter morning, frost on the ground. Cutler had successfully completed his first task among a group of families who'd been rorting the NDIS, stealing money that belonged to disabled people and their carers.

Cutler couldn't help asking, 'What?'

'What is your *secret*? A secret that you've been withholding, even from me? It's that you're smart. More than smart. Highly intelligent.'

Cutler didn't know what to say.

'Because of your upbringing you've had to hide it, be a small target, but do you know what a gift it is in a job like ours, to be intelligent but able to hide it so completely? Emotionally intelligent, too, able to blend in. To be smart enough to know when to shut up and listen, and observe, to be patient and wait for your moment? To say the right thing, or the wrong thing that is actually the right thing, at that moment?'

Cutler had been flattered more than he wanted, but also felt some shame at being caught out. They had been discussing the difference between crime and the law, exploring Cutler's emotional confusion at where the distinction blurred, following Khalil's admission that very few of the people involved in the NDIS rorting ring would be brought to justice, despite the hard work of Khalil's crew and the danger Cutler had been placed in.

Cutler was on board the *Shuen* to identify the perpetrators involved in the disappearance of a rich man's son. That was the crime that was paying his wage. And yet, the crimes before him were manifold and related. Aadam, the Malaysian man, was right. Cutler might learn who killed Bevan Whelan, but the lives of the crew would stay the same. And not just this crew, but the crew on literally tens of thousands of similar fishing vessels around the world.

Cutler had been taking notes automatically. He glanced down at the page in his lap – he had counted off, so far, one hundred and twenty-seven skipjack tuna and seventeen bigeye tuna. As his eyes returned to Fazal's sweating back, whose mottled arms were straining to tighten the monofilament and single strand connected to the hook, the hook was connected to a ten-foot blue shark, gaffed through the tail by Aadam, who removed the giant steel claw and reached to his belt for a club. He proceeded to beat the shark senseless, and its eyes glazed over while Fazal tore the hook from its mouth, before Aadam took the shark's tail and sent it down the chute.

It was only a moment, but he caught Fazal's eye. It wasn't shame that Cutler saw there, but defiance, daring Cutler to judge him.

Cutler thought about beginning a new ledger to count the sharks they caught but thought better of it. The drum was turning again, and they would be at this for another five or six hours at least. He turned back to the page he'd begun, poised his pencil as the next skipjack tuna flapped through the gate, drumming hard on the resonant steel. Cutler heard a large splash from beneath the open port, where the conveyor belt carried waste to be tipped into the ocean. He didn't need to get up from his seat to know that the shark had been finned and its tail docked, before being returned to the ocean alive, to sink and slowly die of asphyxiation and starvation on the ocean floor, two kilometres beneath them.

20.

The ocean was quiet, the time approaching four a.m. Finally, the sounds from the cleaning stations below deck had ceased. The men were congregated at the opposite end of the ship to Cutler – on deck beneath the wheelhouse, at the bow, where a shanty-town arrangement of gaffs and poles had been strapped to the bulwark, over which were spread a torn plastic tarp and sarongs. The men were quiet, speaking in whispers, although with the ship's engines turned off Cutler could hear the angry roar of a propane stove carried on the wind.

The bringing in of the line and the cleaning of the fish had taken longer than he imagined, as fast as the men had worked. He had caught the surprise on Fazal's face when Li had barked that the next line wouldn't go out until after sunrise. The PNA quota system went by fishing days, rather than fish caught, and it made economic sense for the *Shuen* to fish for twenty-four hours straight within the period of a day, to maximise their catch.

Cutler had been watching the software on his laptop throughout the tedium and guilt he felt watching the men work, without a break, through the long night. Whether because Cutler was aboard, or for another reason, the ship's transponder was turned on. PNA officials on shore would be able to establish that they were fishing, based upon their movements on the screen.

Neither Yang nor Li had bothered him as he sat away from the men. He assumed that the game from this point was for the officers to pretend that he was invisible among them, which suited him fine. He had gone into the software that linked to the camera in their shared bunkroom, which was triggered by movement. He rewound the footage that pictured Li sleeping during the night, but earlier, he scrolled back to watch the first mate rifling through his duffel. Cutler felt a pang of fear as he watched the big man shaking the locked suitcase, knew that if he broke open the secret compartment behind the suitcase lining that the jig would be up. Li had shaken the suitcase and listened to it, but ultimately replaced it back on the bunk, beside the duffel.

Cutler refreshed his email, saw that there were no new messages. He had transferred the audio file recorded the previous night, was waiting on the translated transcript, should anything be important. Just minutes earlier he'd transferred the second audio file, which covered all of yesterday and all of last night's discussions on the bridge. The email was routed through a server in Port Moresby, and he was communicating with Whelan Snr as 'Dad'. This must be hurtful to Whelan, he realised, although the tall Australian would put it aside in the interests of furthering his investigation. Cutler had asked 'Dad' if he could send him any readings or links to websites that discussed the philosophy of hope, to give him something to digest during his downtime. Whelan hadn't responded to that, either. He could imagine the man's doubtful expression – there wasn't supposed to be any downtime, and certainly not within the first few days of his placement on the *Shuen*. He wondered if this email, like the others, had been forwarded on to Cutler's handler, as per their agreement.

Cutler looked at the charge on the satellite phone. It was down to one bar. He closed the laptop and turned off the satphone, lit another cigarette and looked to the horizon. The sun wouldn't rise for another couple of hours, and so he decided to hit the bunk, and charge his laptop and phone.

He stood and moved toward the wheelhouse door but paused at the sound of gumboots on the deck. Around the narrow walkway between wheelhouse and bulwark came Fernando, the Filipino boy, who cocked his head for Cutler to follow. As Cutler walked into a breeze stronger on the bow side of the ship, he smelled cooking, unmistakably a curry of some sort. The men were gathered around the stove, still wet from having washed themselves from a plastic bucket tied to a rope. The wind rustled in the tarp, and Fernando nodded Cutler toward his seat among them.

Aadam was again stirring the pot, this time with a filleting knife. He didn't look at Cutler, dipping a finger into the curry, liking what he tasted.

'Thank you for the food,' said Fazal. 'And for the medicine.'

While the men had worked, Cutler had gone to his bunk and retrieved all of the supplies he'd brought, suggested to him by Whelan, and placed them in a plastic bag in the crew's quarters downstairs. Most of the food had been stashed in the bottom of his duffel. Jars of peanut butter, cans of coconut cream, beef jerky and dried jackfruit, dried mango and pineapple, a tube of harissa, small cans of tomato paste and bags of brown sugar – foods dense in protein and calories, but also flavour. Aadam had mixed proportions of the lot in the curry, which smelled like a rich satay, the remnants stored in a small cardboard box with a hat covering it from view.

Meanwhile, Fazal worked with the antiseptic cream that Cutler had also given the men, along with jars of multivitamins, B vitamins, vitamin C and zinc, and several packets of strong, broad-spectrum antibiotics. Fazal applied the antiseptic cream to an open sore on Budi's heel, which looked inflamed and infected. Cutler watched him work – he was gentle but firm. He had the men stand before him while they lifted their shirts and showed him their wounds. It didn't take long before the cream was nearly gone. He finished by rubbing some cream into a nasty gash on his own ankle, which was yellow with pus.

'You and Budi should take a course of those antibiotics. Take one, twice a day, for five days. Don't miss a day or they won't work.'

Fazal didn't raise his eyes from his work. His ankle had begun to leak a thin yolk of infection. He squeezed it to drain it further. 'I know how antibiotics work.'

'Fair enough. But that ankle. It's ulcerated. You should clean it out with the peroxide.'

Now Fazal looked at him. 'How do I apply it?'

'Tip a capful of it directly onto the wound. It won't be pretty. It won't smell good.'

Fazal took up the bottle of peroxide and walked to the end of the bow. He sat and filled the cap of the bottle with the clear fluid. Cutler knew what came next, and instead turned to the food. He realised that he hadn't eaten for more than twenty-four hours, when he'd snacked on two muesli bars. Aadam was straining rice, tipping the starchy water directly into the curry. He spooned the rice into the six plastic plates, then sloshed some of the curry on top. He passed a plate to Cutler, who passed the plate to Fernando, who passed it to Budi. Fazal returned to the circle, the wound on his ankle a deep hole, ragged at its edges but cleaned of infection. He opened the packet of antibiotics and passed a tablet to Budi, and took one himself.

The men were silent while they ate. Fazal ate with his hand, mixing the rice with the curry, while the others ate with an assortment of plastic takeaway forks and steel spoons.

The food was good. Delicious. Fiery hot. Sweat beaded Cutler's forehead, and he felt his ears burning.

The men ate one bowl each before licking them clean. Cutler did the same. There was plenty of food left, which he assumed was for later that day, to be eaten cold perhaps.

From his pocket he took out a double Snickers bar that he'd been saving. He passed it to Budi to divide with the knife, but the older man bit off a section, passed it to Wayan, who did the same. The bar was returned to Cutler with exactly a sixth remaining. He chewed and swallowed it down, savouring the sweetness. He hadn't been on the *Shuen* for long, but already he was losing weight. Now that he'd given all of his supplies to the crew, he would be eating what they ate, no matter what.

'You will have to sleep here,' Fazal said. 'The bridge and the hatch will be locked now. We'll stay here too. Only way down into the hold is through the chute.'

Cutler looked at his watch. It was nearly five a.m. The sun would be rising soon.

'Are you going to sleep?' he asked them all.

Budi shook his head. The skin beneath his eyes was grey, his eyes red-rimmed and inflamed, matching the colour of his beard.

'When will you sleep?'

'When the line is soaking, next time,' said Wayan.

Cutler liked the Balinese man's English, the vowels rounded and stretched for emphasis.

'I won't sleep either then. Fazal. There is a bag of ground PNG coffee in the plastic bag. Shall I make a pot of coffee?'

The men broke into smiles, even Aadam and the usually grave Budi. But it was Wayan who spoke first. 'We don't have espresso machine.'

He was joking, his smile sly and barely noticeable, but his eyes were bright with the irony of his statement.

'I'll make it Norwegian ... Norway style. Just boil it for a while. We have sugar.'

'Sugar. Oh yes,' Budi replied.

'I dream of sugarcane juice, more than anything else,' said Fazal. 'Tea I dream of, too.'

The men cooked with two pots, one large and one medium. The medium pot, which had been used to cook the rice, was missing a handle, but Cutler poured in some water, and a quarter of the bag of coffee. He put the pot on the stove and ignited it with his lighter. The flame was large and blue, and the noise made speech difficult. Instead, he marshalled the stirring of the coffee, thick and muddy as he'd been taught, and when it'd boiled for five minutes he added brown sugar from the packet, stirring that in too. He killed the stove and turned off the propane. The men around him offered their bowls, placing them in a semicircle at his knees. Cutler filled each of them equally, remembering which was his own.

When each of the men had taken their bowls, he offered around his cigarettes. Fazal was the only man to decline, waggling his head but smiling.

The men sat cross-legged, none of them drinking the brew, each of them inhaling the smell, taking deep lungfuls of coffee-scented air.

Cutler had questions he wanted to ask, but that would have to wait. He didn't want to ruin this moment, their enjoyment, each of them sipping the strong liquid, which even with the sugar tasted bitter, smoking between sips, not talking but just enjoying the drink, the interlude before the next round of noisy, dirty, exhausting labour.

As tired as he was, Cutler felt his nerves sharpen as the caffeine did its work, the stars above him cartwheeling toward the northern horizon, which was hidden beneath the bulwark opposite. He glanced at each of them, their eyes illuminated with pleasure but also something else.

'What does the coffee make you think of?' he asked them all. 'It makes me think of my adopted father. His mother was from Norway. He used to make coffee like this while it was still dark, when we had to drive a long way, early in the morning, so that I could play football.'

Cutler's question was genuine, but an uneasiness returned to the circle. Perhaps it was the distance between his memory and their own, the associations stretched beyond what might be shared, or perhaps their memories were too painful to recall – of simpler times, before they were slaves.

'What did your father do?' asked Fernando, an edge of resentment in his voice.

Tell the truth, or the lie, or both?

'He was a soldier. His father had met his mother in Norway, during the war. The Second World War. He was Scottish, and he stayed in the army after the war, moved to Australia later, joined the Australian army, died in the Korean War. My adopted father wanted to serve his country like his father did, I suppose.'

'Not your real father?' asked Aadam.

'No.'

Cutler waited for the questions as to the identity of his real father and mother, or why he was there as a PNA observer if he grew up in Australia, but none of them asked. If word got back to Yang or Li, he would cover the lie by saying his real father was the fictional plantation owner in PNG.

'Did you write in your book about catching the sharks?' asked Budi, his voice neutral.

Cutler looked at the scars on his legs. He had a lie ready for that question, too, but didn't feel like using it. 'No, I didn't.'

'But it's there?' said Fernando, tapping his head.

Cutler nodded, wanting to get away from specifics around his purported role. These men had seen observers come and go – they would be attuned to his deceptions.

'How many sharks?' Fernando asked.

'I counted one hundred and forty-seven. Eighty-two whitetips, seventeen mako, twenty-one silky sharks and … twenty-seven tiger sharks.'

Fazal glanced at him, and there was respect there.

'Good,' added Fernando.

'My father was a shipbreaker, in Chittagong, Bangladesh,' said Fazal, saving Cutler from any further scrutiny. 'My mother worked in the fields while he was away. It was a ship graveyard. They would drive the old ships up onto the shore and, with mainly old tools, the ship would be broken up and sold for scrap.'

'Hard work,' said Cutler.

'Yes, and very bad. It made him sick, the dirty fuel or some other pollution. It ruined the bay as well, killed all the fish. But one day he found something while working. I don't know what it was – a watch probably, or something else valuable. He was able to sell it, and retire, return home to work beside my mother. He is still alive, but only just. Heavy metal poisoning made his blood very sick.'

Fazal didn't want to say any more about where his parents were now, following the destruction of their village. He stared into his empty bowl.

Aadam spoke quietly. 'You are the eldest. You went away to look for work, to help them.'

'Yes, but I was tricked. More than once. People smugglers stole the last of my father's money. I survived on my own. I gave up waiting to be taken as a refugee, because I don't have any papers.'

Now was the time to insert himself. Cutler leaned forward, spoke as quietly as Aadam had. 'Did you try to go to Australia, from Jakarta?'

'Australia,' spat Fazal. 'My cousin Ibrahim, he is in jail there. For being a refugee. For having no papers. Seven years now. They want to return him to Myanmar, but the government there won't let them. So, he stays in prison.'

'I'm sorry,' said Cutler.

'Why are you sorry? You didn't put him in jail.'

Fazal was still angry, his hands wrung together. His anger made the other men circumspect, each of them looking away, at the deck, the stars, their empty bowls.

Cutler knew that Fazal wouldn't thank him for the next question, but in his anger there was also a useful honesty.

'How long have you been at sea, Fazal? How long have each of you been at sea?'

Fazal glared at him. 'You don't have the right to ask that question.'

'Because I'm not going to do anything about it?'

'Yes, that's correct. You will feel sorry for me, and maybe you will remember me one day when you are making coffee, but you won't do anything about it.'

Cutler was silent. He took a deep breath, exhaled slowly.

'Three years.'

It was Wayan who'd spoken. The Balinese man removed the scarf from his head. His hair was pasted to his scalp with sweat. He was already greying, his scalp receding. He placed the scarf back on his head, began to wrap it, folding the edge inside the topmost coil.

'Three years I don't see my children, my wife.'

The other men nodded. 'One year,' said Fernando. 'Three years,' added Aadam. 'Two years,' said Budi.

They all looked at Fazal, who looked back at them all. 'Five years,' he said quietly. 'I tried to go home, after Jakarta. When the killing started. I saw about it in a newspaper. I was told that I needed people smugglers – to go to my own home! I gave them my savings, at the border in Thailand. They put us on a bus, all men like me. We drove through the night. When I woke up, we were in a port. We were put on a boat. We asked questions, but the Thai men just laughed. The boat took us to a big ship, far out at sea. The ship was at anchor. We were put onto the ship. It was full of Rohingya people, like me. Maybe a thousand people. It was like a prison. Small boats came and took people. We never saw them again. We lived on scraps. The small boats were the only way off the ship. Some men tried to take over the ship, to drive her back to Myanmar, but they were shot. The captain laughed, because he wasn't a captain. He was a people smuggler. A slave trader. The ship's engines didn't work. The ship was a wreck-ship, like the kind my father used to scrap. It was a floating prison, out in international waters, full of Rohingya people, so nobody cared. A place to keep men and women until an order was put in, for workers. Some people threw themselves overboard. Some opened their veins. I put myself forward, made myself look strong, although I was sick and weak. A boat took me, along with seven other men. We were sold to fishing captains. The others were sold to Thai boats. I was sold to a Taiwanese boat. The *Shuen Ching 454*. Then this boat, *666*. Before I was captured, I had never been on a boat. Now, I haven't walked on land for five years.'

Nobody spoke. Fazal's anger had broken away, word by word, his voice almost a whisper. Cutler took out his smokes, passed them around again. The men smoked and stared at their cigarettes, the wafts of blue smoke rising into their faces.

'Have you seen any money in that time? Have you been paid?' Cutler asked.

Fazal laughed, but it was strangled with bitterness. 'We do not know if we have been paid. We do not know anything, except that we survive. If we obey, we survive. If we disobey, we are sold again. Maybe worse.'

Cutler's instincts warned him against it, that it was too soon, but he asked anyway. 'The Australian man I replaced, Bevan, did you tell him these things?'

Fazal met Cutler's eyes, and the look held. There was no anger there, instead a question, a reading of Cutler that peeled away some of his disguise. If that was true, Fazal was astute enough to not say anything except, 'Yes.'

Cutler looked to Budi, and Aadam. Fernando was still looking at his cigarette. Wayan had tears in his eyes, perhaps thinking of his children.

'Captain Yang and Chief Officer Li. Do they hurt you? This ship is flagged to Taiwan. Taiwan has labour laws.'

Fazal put his hand on Cutler's arms, shook his head, glancing at the others. 'They don't understand what flagged means, or labour laws. Yang and Li are no better or worse than others. Li is dangerous when he has too much *shabu*. You should be careful.'

Cutler nodded, but Fazal wasn't finished. 'I'm sorry I was angry with you. It has been better since you came aboard. Li has been sleeping, I can tell. Do your job, but don't do it too well. That is my advice.'

Cutler was about to ask the question, the one that he'd been wanting to ask. Was that what happened to Bevan Whelan? Had he done his job too well?

There were bootsteps on the steel, approaching from beside the bridge. Each of the men began to stand, passing their bowls to Aadam, who stashed them next to the stove. It was time to get back to work.

21.

The sight of Li surprised them all. Instead of his regular tee-shirt, shorts and thongs, the first mate was in full uniform, wearing trousers with piping, and a clean shirt with epaulettes, an officer's hat with gold trim pressed down on his great head. He strode toward them, his fists clenched.

None of the crew knew what was going on, that much was clear, their faces betraying confusion and fear. Cutler stayed seated, noticed that Li was ignoring him.

Had the men said too much to him? Had Li been listening?

Li crooked his finger and bade the men follow him back to amidships. They did so. Aadam glanced at Cutler, who nodded toward the cooking implements – he would clean up.

As Cutler stood he saw the ship, half a kilometre in the distance. It was large, and fat in the middle, sitting deep in the water. From his shoulder bag Cutler took out his binoculars, dialled in the focus. The ship was flagged to Taiwan. Cutler knelt and opened his laptop, hotspotted his satphone. He flipped through the pages, the web taking ages to load, until he opened the AIS page. There was the transponder signal for the *Shuen Ching 666*, but there was nothing else on the screen. On the home screen, he saw that there was an email from Whelan, from 'Dad', but he didn't have time to read it now. He closed the laptop and put everything back in the shoulder bag.

He heard a rallying cry from behind the wheelhouse, from the operations deck. Very quickly, he threw the plastic bucket tied to a rope overboard, pulled it up slopping and full. He dipped each of the plates in the saltwater, and the pot used to make rice, and then coffee. He used his hands to remove the rice scum, turned the pot over onto the deck to drain. He took off his tee-shirt and used it as a tea towel, drying the pot and the plates, the spoons and forks. He put the lid on the pot full of curry and rice and put it back into the plastic crate where he stowed everything else, including the propane bottle. He picked up the heavy crate carefully, not wanting to spill the curry, and began to approach amidships.

A small launch had left the larger ship while he'd been cleaning, approaching the *Shuen* rapidly. There was muffled shouting ahead, and Cutler turned the corner to see Fernando kneeling, Li's hand around the back of his neck, the other men already gone below, the hatch open. Cutler remembered what O'Reardon had said about the men swimming to be rescued, and guessed that because the other vessel was also from the same company, they didn't need to be locked away.

Li glanced at Cutler, and his eyes were cold, daring Cutler to speak. Cutler put down the crate of cooking gear and stood nearby, watching the launch approach the *Shuen*, from where the ladder had been dropped. The launch disappeared beneath, and then the ladder took on weight.

Fernando began to whimper, then struggle. Li made Fernando stand, then changed his grip to a chokehold. Cutler could see the veins in Li's neck as he tightened his elbow around Fernando's throat.

'Fernando, are you ok? Officer Li, what's happening? Can I do something to help?'

Li swore at Cutler in Chinese, the curse muffled as the head of a fellow officer rose above the open bulwark gate. The new man was young, barely in his twenties, looked nervously around the ship, just as Cutler had done. He wore a small backpack, which he unslung and laid on the floor. He stood straight, then bowed deeply from the waist, waited a few beats then stood at attention, saluting Li.

Li grunted, gave him an indecipherable order, the young man picking up his pack and scurrying to the bridge door. When he'd opened and closed it behind him, Li began to shuffle Fernando toward the edge. The boy was crying now, wriggling to get free of the larger man's grasp. Li stood him on the edge, and only now did he release the chokehold, returning his right hand to the back of Fernando's neck, pushing him forward so that his face craned above the water below.

Li's intention was to throw Fernando overboard, rather than have him cling to the ladder. Clearly, Fernando was being moved on, perhaps to work on the larger ship, or perhaps to be sold to another vessel.

Fernando's head turned toward Cutler. His eyes were full of tears, but he didn't speak. Cutler wasn't sure of the play. He wanted to intervene, to throw Li overboard instead, who was now following Fernando's pleading eyes back toward him, daring him to do so. Li slipped his right foot behind Fernando's, the classic judo move, in preparation for tipping the boy off balance, sending him over.

Fernando began to speak, very quietly. Li cocked his head to listen, put his ear next to Fernando's mouth, an oddly intimate gesture. Fernando continued to whisper, even as Li removed his hand from the boy's neck. Fernando turned around, his back to the ocean. He brought his hand up, and placed it on Li's breast, held it there, his head bowed.

Li muttered something to himself, waved the launch away. Fernando dipped at the knees, twisted behind Li and ran to the hatch, almost dived down it in his eagerness to leave.

Cutler stared hard at Li, who wouldn't meet his eye. The first mate instead watched the launch return to the larger vessel, before turning to the bridge, giving a thumbs-up signal to Yang. Seconds later, the tannoy began to crackle with static, and Yang's voice ordered the crew back to deck.

Li stood with his back to Cutler, watching the larger ship lift the launch from the water, turning its blunt nose toward the *Shuen*.

22.

It didn't take Cutler long to work out that the *Shuen Ching 121* was a transhipment vessel, a floating warehouse containing the frozen catch of the larger *Shuen* fleet. The practice was illegal, part of the reason distant-water ships like the *Shuen* could stay at sea for years at a time without returning to port, but they were out in the middle of the ocean, and nobody was watching. When Cutler opened his laptop again and logged on, he saw that the transhipment vessel's transponder remained turned off. Anyone observing the AIS data would see the *Shuen* stationary for a few hours, but there was nothing unusual about that.

The two ships were roped together in the gentle swell, huge fenders hung from both gunwales to protect them from accidental harm, while the transhipment vessel craned over mesh-steel crates full of frozen baitfish, emptied by the crew, before returning the crate filled with the blast-frozen tuna and, without even bothering to disguise them, the dismembered pieces of thousands of sharks. When the freezers of the *Shuen* were emptied, and a crate of food had been craned over, while Wayan, Fernando and Aadam were busy packing away the baitfish in the freezer and cleaning the deck of bloody slush, the new engineer supervised the pumping of diesel from the larger vessel into the tanks of the *Shuen*, watching while Fazal and Budi carried over the giant rubber hose that they held at the mouth of the tank, their faces tilted away from the fumes that visibly wavered over them until the tank was full.

Cutler watched the new engineer closely. His job was to maintain the ship's mechanical and electrical features, a difficult and dirty job in the heat of the engine room, although he looked unsuited to the task, sweating heavily in the naked sunshine, his clean officer's shirt stuck to the skin of his back, his pale arms burning, his freshly barbered neck reddening in the hot glare coming off the steel deck and walls. He looked like a kid freshly graduated from the academy, and Cutler hoped that he was. He would be eager to please Yang and Li, his superior officers, but depending on his temperament, and his personal moral code, he might present Cutler his only opportunity to insert a wedge between the officers, creating disharmony or a reduced level of trust. Cutler doubted it, somehow. Yang and Li were thick as thieves, as the saying went, and the young officer had so far deferred to them excessively at every opportunity, bowing and saluting and responding to Li's grunted commands with an almost military response of his own, which Cutler didn't need to be told meant 'yes, sir'.

The email from Whelan was disappointing. Whelan's translator had transcribed every conversation and utterance between Yang and Li and come up with nothing incriminating. Most of the conversations were operational. Cutler was referred to as the *gwailou*, but not necessarily in a disparaging manner. The crew were referred to as *hak gui*, meaning black ghost; again, nothing necessarily disparaging there to indicate a political opinion to reinforce their obvious servitude, except for one use of the word *nú lì*, meaning slave, when Li had reported to Yang that the men were working like slaves, which was a compliment to himself as their slavedriver.

The men's lack of conversation about the new man among them, Cutler, was unusual, although it could be a factor of many things – especially their weariness of PNA observers – Cutler just one more in a long line of men and women who did their tour and then moved on. Cutler had hoped that provoking them to bring up Bevan Whelan that first night might induce some conversation, but he had failed to do so. Perhaps a more direct approach was needed, although that came with risks.

It was always possible that the chief officers feared that they were being monitored, by their company perhaps, but it was more likely that they were men of a kind that Cutler had dealt with many times over recent years. Whatever the crime, serious or otherwise, once it was done, it was never spoken of again – the silence itself a form of conversation, a kind of glue between the guilty parties.

Cutler had saved and sent the next night's recording, right up until the moment the transhipment vessel had departed amid a single blowing of a horn, but without waves, salutes or other formalities. The ropes were released, the fenders stowed, and the *Shuen* engaged her engines before peeling away to the north-west, fully stocked to fish for another month.

Cutler couldn't help himself nodding off as the fatigue came over him, the ship moving easily through the swells, his internal gyroscope finally accustomed to the movement of water, in all its moods.

—

When he awoke, slumped against the bulwark near the bow, the shade that had protected him from the sunlight was gone, the full sun beating down on his bare head. He glanced at his watch – he'd been asleep for nearly an hour, so tired that he hadn't even lain down to sleep. His legs were numb and his back was sore, but he needed to move, and to drink water.

The tannoy buzzed as the ship slowed. The ocean here seemed different, a paler blue, the waves crosshatched with different swells. In the sky above him Cutler saw a large bird, white with a dark beak, a tern of some kind.

Yang's quiet voice on the tannoy roused the men from their shadows on the deck, where they too had been resting. Li appeared from the bridge door, indicating Fazal and Fernando toward the red GPS buoy, laid on a plastic tarp. The cycle was repeating again. Wayan attached a wire to the buoy as Fazal muscled it toward the stern gate, Fernando opening it for him under Li's supervision. The buoy was dropped into the ocean, the wire whipping afterward. Fernando moved toward the drum winch, not meeting Cutler's eye. Cutler didn't know why Fernando had been threatened with being sent off the ship, and he didn't know why the first mate had relented. Cutler was so tired that it seemed like it'd happened days ago, instead of that morning, the sun barely above the horizon.

Fazal took his position near the gate, the ocean sloshing a little beneath the hull. More birds were visible now, circling overhead. Wayan opened the door to the bait freezer, while Budi ferried over plastic buckets. Aadam took a position on the line behind Fazal, stretched the hinges of his jaw and wiped his eyes of sweat. Wayan passed Budi the first bucket of bait, the frosted fish steaming in the heat. Cutler put down his bag and joined the line. The drum began to unspool, Fernando on the brake. Fazal whipped a hook off the rack and fixed it to a snood affixed to the main line, then baited the hook. He attached a float to the line, then the drum unspooled as the men began to find their rhythm, Cutler ferrying a bucket, passing it to Budi, who passed a baitfish to Fazal, the line jerking out into the ocean, the birds beginning to shriek and caw now, diving on the water, frustrated as the baits were pulled underneath the surface. Cutler looked to Fazal, who was glancing from his hands to the water. A beautiful white bird with black edges on its wings hovered above the water, a petrel perhaps, until the next baitfish arrived. It swooped and bit the bait, was dragged underwater, its place taken by an even larger seagull. Cutler looked to Fazal, who winced, but kept baiting the hooks, the birds raucous as they swooped the baits, another one dragged under now, none of the men saying anything.

Li stood beside them smoking, his uniform replaced with his regular tee-shirt and cap. He cursed the birds for wasting the bait, flicking his cigarette after them as he turned back to the bridge.

23.

The line had been soaking for the six hours it took the *Shuen* to motor back to the first GPS buoy. Cutler was sure there was a good reason for doing it, but it seemed to him like a waste of fuel, when they might've stayed stationary while the line soaked, and the fish took the baits. Cutler had been told by Whelan Snr that the triumph of industrial fishing was due to economies of scale, but also the fact that fishing was the most energy-intensive extractive industry on earth – for every two tonnes of fish caught internationally, one tonne of either bunker or diesel fuel was required. Only the largest players could afford this over the longer term – companies either ruthlessly efficient or those whose distant-water fleets were subsidised by their governments.

While the crew rested and the *Shuen* ploughed the swells, Cutler went below deck to introduce himself to the new engineer. The door to the engine room was open, the noise thunderous in the confined space. He peered inside and watched the engineer, wearing a new pair of overalls, gloves, toolbelt and workboots, and a new pair of red earmuffs. He was kneeling beside the engine, working a lube gun into some seals near the drive shaft. Cutler waited for him to finish, giving the young man a fright when he turned and saw the doorway blocked. The Taiwanese man put down the lube gun and indicated for Cutler to retreat into the hold. The man took off his gloves and folded them neatly into his toolbelt, wiped his hands on a new tea towel beside the door.

The engineer shut the engine room door behind him, dampening the roar. He took off his earmuffs and placed them around his neck. He bowed to Cutler, who did the same, then put out his hand.

The handshake was hot and sweaty, the man embarrassed.

'Do you speak English? My name is Paul.'

The engineer smiled awkwardly, composing himself. He was wheezing a little, perhaps from asthma.

'My name is Wen-Hsiung,' he said. 'Perhaps call me William, or Wen. Yes, I speak English. Not so well, but I studied at high school, then at college.'

His English was excellent, the accent American. There was a clear curiosity in his eyes, too, behind the shyness. There was none of the sullenness or jadedness that he saw in Yang and Li, men who'd seen too much, and perhaps done worse.

'How is the engine looking?'

Wen smiled, wrung his hands a little. There was a fastidiousness to his movements, checking that his fingers were clean.

'The engine is good, considering that it hasn't been maintained. The old engines are strong. Not much can go wrong if they're looked after. That, of course, is my job.'

It was better to get this over with. 'Why wasn't there an engineer for so long? What happened to the last engineer?'

Cutler's question seemed to catch Wen by surprise, as if he sincerely didn't know. He was visibly conflicted, his eyes darting from his hands to the bulkhead wall over Cutler's shoulder. Cutler didn't move, or speak, letting the silence work on the polite young man.

'It is very sad,' Wen finally replied. 'He is missing at sea. I was told that he went missing one night. Perhaps ... suicide. Yes, suicide. Or an accident.'

It was Cutler's turn to be surprised, and conflicted. He didn't want to push too hard – he didn't want Wen to distrust him.

'That is very odd,' he replied, deciding that he mightn't get another chance to plant a seed of doubt. 'The man I replaced, as PNA official observer. He is missing too. It also happened at night, apparently. Just two weeks ago.'

Cutler's voice was neutral, while he watched Wen closely. The engineer wouldn't meet his eye, drawing his own conclusions. 'We must be very careful,' Wen said, the meaning of his statement ambiguous, his head bowed a little.

'Yes,' Cutler agreed. 'We must.'

The seed was planted, and he didn't want to pursue it any more. 'When you are finished with the engine, can I make a suggestion? Have you looked at the crew's bunkroom, at the stern? It is very noisy, but there are also fumes. Exhaust fumes. I think the exhaust system is leaking. Can you look at that?'

Wen nodded eagerly, glad for the change of subject. 'Yes, however, the first mate, he told me that the men sleep on deck?'

'I don't know,' Cutler replied. 'Perhaps the fumes are why the men sleep on deck. It's hard to breathe in there. I think it's dangerous.'

'Yes, I will look at the men's bunkroom. For you.'

Cutler didn't hear Li until he was right behind him. He saw Wen blanch, his eyes widening, taking the gloves from his belt.

Li came in at their side, glaring at Cutler while Wen shrank away. Li barked something and the engineer stalled his return to the engine room.

Li's pupils were dilated – he was on the *shabu*. He was sweating more than usual, his movements a little erratic, his hand fluttering, twitching at his side. It looked to Cutler like he badly wanted to make a fist, and then throw the punch.

'Why do you talk with engineer? You don't talk to engineer, you understand!'

Li repeated something in Chinese that sent Wen rushing back to the engine room. Cutler was about to speak when the noise washed over them. The door closed while he tried to make an apologetic face, his eyes on Li's right hand.

'Yes, I understand. I am sorry. I was just being polite.'

Li grunted, bumped Cutler with his shoulder as he pushed past.

—

There was a narrow space under the bulwark in the shade, between Fazal and Fernando. The men's eyes were closed, but Cutler could tell that Fazal at least wasn't sleeping, his chest barely rising and falling, unlike Fernando, who was grinding his teeth, laid on his side, a finger in one of his ears to block out sound.

Cutler placed his shoulder bag against the hot steel, to use as a pillow. He laid himself down on his back, closed his eyes, which were burning with fatigue, little red coronas dancing and spreading until all he could see was red.

He opened his eyes. 'Fazal. The new engineer. He just told me something. It's made me worried.'

Cutler's worry was artificial, but he hoped to draw upon the older man's paternal instincts, so clearly demonstrated in his dealings with the others. He wanted to place himself under Fazal's care, as a shortcut to gaining his trust.

Fazal didn't move, his eyes still closed. 'Why are you worried? *You* have nothing to worry about.'

Despite Fazal and the others' understandable resentment toward Cutler, and all that he represented, there was none of that resentment in Fazal's voice.

'I'm worried because of what he told me. He told me that last month the previous engineer went missing at sea, at night. Just like the last PNA observer did.'

Fazal was silent for a long time. 'Does he know what happened to the man he replaced?'

'No, he just knows that he went missing one night. He thinks perhaps suicide, or an accident.'

'He is probably right.'

It was Cutler's turn to reflect on what Fazal was saying, or in this case, not saying. Both of them knew the next question.

'You know what happened to him. Can you tell me?'

Now Fazal opened his eyes. He sat back on his elbows, glanced up and down the deck. 'What would you do with this knowledge?'

Cutler told the truth. 'I don't know. But I would never mention it to the officers. Never while I'm aboard the *Shuen*, to anyone else.'

'Lie back down and close your eyes. Pretend to be sleeping.'

Cutler did as he was told.

'I don't know why they did it, or what the engineer did wrong. Li eats too much *shabu*. The engineer was a young man, like the new one. We had just put the line in, and the final marker buoy. The engines had started, just as we heard yelling. Li and the engineer were fighting. They came out of the bridge door. The engineer had a swelling eye. He was pleading, in Chinese. I only understood the word *no*, which he was saying again and again. Li had a wooden club, like we use to make the sharks go quiet. He was threatening to beat the engineer, pushing him closer and closer to the open gate where the line goes out. Li was kicking him toward the gate, and the engineer was very afraid. I can still see the look in his eyes. He looked to us for help, but we didn't help him, because we didn't think that Li would do it. But he did it. He kicked the engineer right to the edge, then pointed to the marker buoy, kept shouting at him in Chinese. The man was begging now, but that only made Li angrier. He kicked the man in the stomach, sending him backwards into the ocean. We heard the splash. We were too afraid to say anything, when Li turned to us. His eyes were black, no white in his eyes, just black eyes, like a shark. The engines became louder, and Li went back inside the bridge. We went to the edge. Aadam tried to throw the engineer a rope, but he missed. The ship started to pull away. The engineer swam toward the marker buoy, to get away from the propeller. He clung on to it, then climbed onto it, wrapping his arms around it. He was out of the water, but the buoy was unstable. The ship left the area. We drove to the first marker buoy, six hours away. We drew in the line, taking off the tuna, and the sharks, and the turtle, and the birds. When we were near the end of the line, Li came out on deck. He seemed to be in a good mood, like he is at the beginning, when he's just taken *shabu*. He even offered Fernando a cigarette, which Fernando refused, because none of us could look him in the eye. It had taken six hours to drive to the first marker buoy, and five hours to bring in the line. It was eleven hours later, and nearly dark. Li waited to the side as we pulled in the last tuna. The red marker buoy came in sight. The engineer wasn't there. I was looking at Li's face. He was surprised. A little shocked. He made us hurry to bring in the marker buoy. We drove back over the direction the line had come from, all of us at the bow, with torches, it took us all night, but we never saw the engineer again.'

Cutler didn't say anything. It was worse than he'd imagined. Only Li knew whether he had meant for the man to die, terrified and alone in the middle of the Pacific, or whether, speeding off his head, it seemed like a good idea at the time. His surprise that the engineer had drowned suggested the latter. It sounded like a cruel punishment for some infringement, or betrayal, but either way, if he could do that to one of his own countrymen, a fellow officer, then he was capable of anything.

'What had the engineer done to deserve such a punishment?' Cutler asked. He was so tired with his eyes closed that his horror at the engineer's fate blended with the images of the crew bludgeoning sharks. He could feel himself sinking into himself, like he was collapsing. When he spoke, Fazal's voice sounded very distant.

'We don't know what the engineer did. Maybe something, maybe nothing. It happened before the last observer, the young Australian, came aboard – four weeks before.'

'His name was Bevan Whelan. Is that what happened to him, too?'

Cutler's voice was slurred. He tried to rouse himself, to open his eyes, but it was no use. With this level of fatigue, anything seemed possible, nothing seemed out of the question, right or wrong, or beyond the pale.

'No, I would tell you. You have nothing to worry about. Go to sleep. We have only a few hours. It will be a long night.'

Cutler tried to fight it, to reimagine Fazal's words, to picture the young engineer clinging for his life to a wobbling buoy, jerking in the water each time the drum line was drawn aboard, but the pictures wouldn't come and soon he was sinking, deep into the infinite redness behind his eyes.

24.

Cutler leapt awake, scrambling. The noise was impossibly loud, a smash and then a long animal-growl from the hull. The boat shook, and then the noise was gone.

He looked up at Fazal, preparing his hooks, the other men moving silently in the darkness.

'Don't worry, Mister Paul. The captain ran over a FAD. He does it often.'

'Why did he do that?'

Cutler was still half asleep. He rubbed his eyes, which stung from the sweat on his knuckles. The night was hot and still, the air barely circulating on deck despite the *Shuen's* forward momentum, rocking into the swell and lifting, before falling again.

'The FADs are placed there by purse seiners, or hook and liners. Not good for us, with a longline. That was a big one, with GPS. Somebody's not going to be happy.'

'Thought we'd hit a reef. Scared the shit out of me.'

The men laughed. 'No reef out here, Mister Paul,' said Fernando, who was using a grease gun to lubricate the drum winch cylinder, empty of line. 'Now a long way from land.'

His white singlet was bright in the semi-dark, until with a clank and crackle the overhead industrial lighting came on, which covered everything in a harsh glare that made Cutler's eyes sting even more, and he raised a hand to shield them. He dabbed at his eyes with his tee-shirt, until the sting lessened.

The *Shuen* slowed. Cutler stood and followed Fazal and Fernando to the bow, where they waited with a gaff to hook the GPS buoy and so secure the fishing line. The bow-lights illuminated the waters ahead with twin cones of yellowish light. Cutler looked beneath him and saw a dozen dolphins riding the bow wave.

Go away, he thought to himself. *Go away*. And then, 'Fazal, can we make them go away? Before the line comes in?'

Fazal shook his head, his dark eyes scanning the water. 'Don't say anything about them. Officer Li will come with his automatic weapon, or his shotgun.'

'To be merciful is God's, while to act is man's,' said Fernando quietly, causing both of the men to look at him. 'My *lola*, grandmother, she say this a lot.'

The buoy came into view, the red column dipping in the wash as the *Shuen* slowed, then came to rest. Fazal threw the gaff tied to the rope toward the buoy, drew it in quickly. When the gaff engaged the line, he pulled faster and passed the line to Fernando, who walked it back to the stern, where the gate had been opened.

Cutler helped Fazal drag the heavy buoy out of the water, careful not to smash it on the hull or gunwale as it came over.

'Are you ever tempted to damage the machinery, or break the buoy?' Cutler asked. 'Give yourself a bit of a rest?'

Fazal gave him a look, wiped sweat off his brow. 'That is stupid. It is what Li suspects us of doing, every time something breaks. We have learned to fear his anger. You should learn to fear him too.'

Cutler nodded. He'd been half joking. He turned from Fazal and watched the young engineer weave between the crew, each of them preparing the killing floor. The Taiwanese man looked exhausted. He nodded to Cutler sheepishly, put his hand beside his cheek – the universal sleep symbol.

Cutler wondered as he walked back with Fazal. He would take no part in the drawing of the longline, nor the early excitement of the men as the fish started to arrive, some dead, most alive. The excitement would soon be replaced by a dead-eyed matter-of-factness, as the mechanical practice of killing took over. The crew did the work that machines couldn't do, such as Fazal's job of removing floats, fish and hooks from the line before it was winched, but they were forced to work like machines themselves. Cutler would observe and write down the catch, but first he had another idea.

Cutler went down the hatch, carrying the empty five-litre drinking bottle as a decoy, hoping that neither Li nor Yang would be suspicious. He placed the empty bottle next to the tap near the cleaning stations, where Budi and Wayan were putting on gloves and sharpening their knives. Neither commented as Cutler continued deeper into the hold, toward the engine room. The bulkhead that contained stores was now crammed with the goods that the mother ship had transported to them – twenty-kilo bags of rice and pallets of tinned meat and fruit and, strangely, canned tuna.

On the other side of the bulkhead door was the crew's quarters. It must be frustrating for them to have to live next to the room storing food for the officers, while they subsisted on rice and fish sauce, and the occasional bonus of dried noodles if the catch warranted it.

Cutler tried the engine room door, assuming that it was locked, and yet the handle turned, and the room behind him filled with noise. The *Shuen* wasn't moving, but the engine idled, and then it died and the room became eerily still as Yang turned everything bar the electrics off.

Cutler turned on the light. The room was small and cramped, taken up mostly with the engine itself, an ancient, green-painted, cast-iron, four-stroke Mitsubishi engine, its bedplate newly cleaned of oil. The cooling water inlets and the fuel valve and exhaust valves had also been newly shined, as had the air system and alternator. Thanks to Wen's efforts, the engine looked showroom quality. Against the wall, the generators and various pumps had also been cleaned and the floor washed.

Cutler left the door open a crack in case the engineer returned to lock it. He was largely unfamiliar with the engine but had done a little research. He was looking for a way to disable the engine, should sabotage become necessary. He went first to the air compressor, found against the far wall. The discharge valve was noted in Japanese script, and that was one option. If he turned it off and the engine and the air compressor started, the compressor would blow. Like with any internal combustion engine, damaging the fuel lines was a possibility, but while it would disable the engine, it was also repairable. The final and most dangerous option, but also the most destructive, was to use an oxy torch to set a flame on the crank case while the engine was running, and leave it for a good while. This would cause the crank case to explode, permanently disabling the engine but also potentially killing anyone nearby. There was an oxy torch outside in the hold, presumably for use with cutting and welding, and he stored that away as an option.

What Cutler was mostly looking for was a hiding place. Both Bevan Whelan and the previous engineer had disappeared overboard. Bevan Whelan's personal items, including his laptop and satphone, were locked away somewhere in the wheelhouse, most likely in a safe. Either Yang or Li were always in there, and breaking into the safe without being noticed seemed an impossible task. If Bevan was worried about his safety, and assuming that his laptop and phone had been confiscated, the engine room was the only place that Cutler could think of where a message might be secreted, to be found by another.

Cutler knelt and looked beneath the engine, searching for gaps where something might be placed in a hurry. He followed the baffling that accompanied the exhaust pipe from the engine but couldn't see anything there. There were no cupboards or storage lockers for tools or parts – all of that was out in the hold. Cutler wiped his knees and hands, slung his shoulder bag and went back out into the hold.

There were too many places to look in the darkened space. The room was open to the officers and crew, and he doubted anything would be hidden there.

Cutler estimated he had another four or five hours before the line was completely drawn in again. The ship maximised the daily catch quota by working the crew for upwards of eighteen hours per day.

The light was on in the cramped bunkroom. Wen rested in a pair of boxers with an arm slung over his eyes. The small fan fixed to the wall at the feet of the beds pushed the humid air around.

Cutler tried to be as quiet as he could, unpacking his shoulder bag and placing the laptop and satphone on the lumpy mattress. Except for his first night on board, he hadn't slept in the bed, preferring to rest on deck in the fresh air, which gave him access to the crew, but he'd try to grab an hour now.

Cutler could tell by his breathing that Wen wasn't asleep. As though reading his mind, Wen took his shielding arm away from the light. His eyes were red and bleary, after he'd worked with strong chemicals in the confined space of the engine room.

'Can't sleep?' Cutler asked.

'No. Can't sleep. I have been practising, but it hasn't helped.'

'Practising for lack of sleep?'

The young man smiled. 'Yes, it sounds funny. I have been practising sleeping in three-hour times, forcing myself to wake up and exercise, but the ship is noisier than my apartment at home, if that is possible. I live in a big city and have many neighbours. Have you been to Taiwan?'

Cutler shook his head, sat down across from Wen, reaching into his shoulder bag and pulling out an orange vial. 'You want one of these? Valium. Will help you sleep.'

Cutler could see the indecision in Wen's eyes.

'Take one. Keep it for later if you want. They're not strong.'

Cutler passed across the little white pill and, to his surprise, Wen swallowed it dry, nodding his thanks.

'No, I've never been to Taiwan,' he said, circling back. 'I'd love to go one day.'

'It's a beautiful country. Very good people.'

'Not all like Li, then?'

That made Wen smile. 'No. Not like him, at all.'

'How long is your contract on the *Shuen*?'

'I don't know. I think until I ... you know.'

Now it was Cutler's turn to smile. 'I understand.'

Wen's eyes grazed Cutler's legs, snagging on the scars. 'Do you mind if I ask what happened to your legs? You have many ... accidents there.'

Cutler looked down at the pulpy scars and shiny scales that marked his shins, knees and thighs. He made the universal signal for revving a motorbike, turning up his right wrist, grinning to make light of it but also diverting Wen's gaze, which froze. His whole body tensed. Cutler looked into the doorway to find Li, framing himself there with both arms arched into the corners. His face was red, presumably from climbing the stairs, although he'd been stealthy about it.

His eyes were on Wen, before he hissed out a sentence.

Cutler looked to Wen, who sat up in the bunk, his face blank.

'What did he say?' asked Cutler.

Wen kept his gaze on Cutler's legs. When he spoke, his voice was small, like a child. 'He said, "Why doesn't the white man understand?"'

Li had demanded that Cutler not speak to Wen, something that Cutler had forgotten in his weariness. 'Tell Li that it's a bit hard when we're sharing the same room. Tell him I don't want to be rude.'

Wen translated at length, which made Li grunt a reply. Cutler kept his eyes on Wen, who looked a little shocked. Clearly, his translation would be softened.

'Officer Li says that white men are always rude. That you are lying.'

Cutler decided to play along. He'd like nothing more than to sink a fist into Li's paunch, take the wind out of him, but that wouldn't help anything. He didn't look at the officer, and instead nodded, kept his eyes to himself.

Li hissed out another sentence, clearly a question.

'Officer Li wants to see your ... books. Fishing log.'

Cutler automatically reached into the shoulder bag and took out the ledger. He passed it to Li, who nodded toward Wen. Cutler gave it to him while Li asked a series of questions and Wen responded, running his finger down the tally sheets. Li asked a final question, which led Wen to look through the pages again, before answering.

Wen's answer led Li to enter the room. He stood over Cutler, who now met his eyes, boiling with suspicion, and anger. His breathing was ragged, his hand on the bed trembling with suppressed violence.

Wen leaned forward, a small gesture, coming between them. 'Officer Li asks why there are no sharks in your fishing log.'

'Tell Li that shark-finning is illegal.'

Li grabbed the ledger, flung it into the air, its spine cracking on the ceiling before landing on the top bunk. 'Why you don't write sharks? Why?!'

Cutler tried to keep his voice even, not wanting to give the officer the satisfaction of seeing that he too was angry. 'Tell him …'

Instead, Cutler leaned back, pointed dismissively toward the scars on his legs. 'Tell him that I don't care about sharks. A shark did this.'

Wen translated. When he was finished, Li ran his eyes over Cutler's legs before reading his face, searching out the lie. Cutler looked to Wen, who'd been told another story, but there was only curiosity there. He didn't speak or give Cutler away.

'You don't speak to engineer!' Li shouted. 'Last time!'

Li withdrew his frame from the bed. As he left the room the first mate cursed loudly, heading back to the stairs, his flip-flops squelching.

Cutler went to speak, but Wen put a finger over his lips, pointed out the window. There would be time later to continue their conversation. Wen sank back into the bed, slung an arm over his eyes again.

25.

Wen's breathing had settled, telling Cutler the valium had done its work. Cutler turned out the main light in the bunkroom, and outside the porthole window, the stars were bright despite the salt stains on the thick glass and the jaundiced light filtering from the wheelhouse above them.

Cutler turned on the satphone and hotspotted the laptop, whose charging cable was warm against his legs. He fired up the software linked to his recordings of conversation in the wheelhouse and bunkroom. He made a file of each and opened up his email. There were two new emails from Whelan. Cutler left them for the moment and began a new email, attaching the two sound recordings in a zip file, hoping that it would send. The hamster wheel turned as the data was uploaded and sent, taking several minutes. Cutler rested his eyes, which burned so much that when he opened them to glance at the upload, even the laptop screen made him wince. Finally, the file was sent.

Cutler decrypted the first email from 'Dad'. As Cutler expected, the second round of recordings hadn't contained anything from either Yang or Li indicating culpability in Bevan Whelan's disappearance. The two men had barely conversed, and when they had, their discussions were again largely operational. The only thing of minor importance was Yang's discussion with the captain of the mother ship, part of the same company. This conversation demonstrated the *Shuen* engaged in the illegal practice of transhipment while at sea, but that was hardly going to get them in serious trouble.

The only odd note was Whelan's question again about the recording of the murder of the Indonesian fishermen. He had asked the question in each of the previous emails. This time he was more emphatic. Would Cutler please show the recording to both the crew and the officers, to gauge their response, and find out whether they had recordings themselves?

It was an odd question, and an even stranger request, especially the request to show it to the three officers. There was merit in the idea that showing them the file might provoke some discussion between them, but Cutler couldn't see how that might relate to Bevan Whelan, not when the video, according to Whelan, was now visible on YouTube.

Cutler had considered showing the video to the crew, especially Fazal, but had decided against it. Three of the crew members were from Indonesia and Malaysia. The footage was likely to traumatise already damaged men.

Cutler replied that the time hadn't been right, but that he would proceed as asked. He closed and re-encrypted the email and opened the second, also sent by 'Dad', although the clipped diction betrayed the fact that this email had been sent by his handler, Khalil. Cutler had requested some reading on the philosophy of hope, the email said, and here was a little something to put him to sleep at night.

Cutler opened the attached file, and while he watched the

hamster wheel turn he wondered which university professor Khalil had on the hook for some misdemeanour or other. The file opened to a badly scanned copy of three volumes of a book entitled *The Principle of Hope*, by Ernst Bloch. Cutler saved it to his desktop, re-encrypted and closed the email. Cutler opened the PDF of the book and scrolled through the preface and index pages, before giving up.

He was too tired, and so closed the laptop. His thoughts drifted to the crew, and the perversity of thinking that something written by a German Marxist philosopher seventy years ago might illuminate how they imagined their futures – in light of something abstract called hope. They were workers by any understanding of the word, caught up in a capitalistic endeavour that sought to scour the ocean of living creatures for the lowest possible price. The company they worked for, although it was moot whether they were even being paid, was vertically integrated, controlling the catching, processing and distribution of their product across a globalised food chain. They were not even a big company although, according to Whelan, big enough to collude in bribing ministers in developing countries to gain access to fisheries. At home in Taiwan, the company successfully lobbied politicians for subsidies, and bureaucrats abroad in regional fisheries organisations and UN bodies to achieve their specific ends of making the most fish available for capture, regardless of sustainability or of human rights. They and the countless other companies like them were everything that was wrong with the world, and thinking of them made Cutler feel hopeless, and powerless. He could march upstairs and kill both Yang and Li, and others would immediately take their place.

He could sink the *Shuen* but another would arrive to take the quota. There were even bigger and equally nefarious fishing companies in countries like Norway, Japan, the USA, Iceland, Russia, China, Spain, Tunisia, New Zealand, Türkiye, Italy, South Korea and Australia – all over the globe, competing for the same declining resource. Even worse was the cruel paradox, according to Casey O'Reardon, whereby the scarcer fish like tuna became, the more money they were worth, and so fishing had become sufficiently lucrative that the industry was attractive now to venture capital investors looking for quick returns, banking on stock depletion and higher prices per unit sold.

Cutler closed his eyes to ease the burn, but only for a moment. He rolled out of the bunk, landing quietly on the floor. Wen's breathing snickered as his chest rose and fell. He seemed a good kid, but eventually he too would be corrupted, or burned out by the harsh realities of life on board the *Shuen*. Wen was too green to be of any use in Cutler's regular game. He clearly didn't have the respect of his superiors. He might be useful as an honest witness, depending on what went down, but even that couldn't be relied on.

Cutler filled his shoulder bag with everything he needed. He doubted that he would return to sleep in the bunkroom among the officers. His legs ached as he walked out of the stuffiness of the locked bridge, yearning for the fresh air on deck.

—

Fazal was filling his rack with the hooks taken from the line, while fish skidded and were kicked toward the chute that took them below deck. The ship rolled through the broad swells from the east, where a distant glow signalled the end of another long night. Wayan and Budi were most likely below deck, working the cleaning stations and the blast freezers to take in the new catch. Aadam was positioning the three drums behind Fazal, where the line drawn in had been wound and stored until the next round of fishing. This was usually Fernando's job, given the automated nature of the technology, and his small stature. Aadam didn't look up as he drew line onto the drum winch.

Cutler watched Fazal unhook a flapping skipjack tuna, barely large enough to be legal, then kick it down the chute.

'Fazal.'

Cutler gave the big man a start, which surprised him too. Fazal quickly hid his alarm, the tenseness leaving his shoulders, and arms, unclenching his fists as he returned to his station on the line.

'Sorry, mate. Didn't mean to sneak up on you. You read, right? I thought you might like this.'

Cutler lifted the copy of Steinbeck's *Travels with Charley*. It was a vintage edition, a Bantam paperback from 1963 and Fazal looked at the cover, where a man and a dog sat on a hill looking over the surrounding plains, a romantic image made a little absurd by the presence of Steinbeck's giant poodle.

Fazal looked a little sceptical. 'Why would I want to join him and his dog, in search of America?'

Cutler smiled. There was no malice in the question. 'Something tells me that you'll like it.'

'Thank you,' Fazal said, holding up a hand for Aadam to wait before drawing in the winch. 'I have read *Of Mice and Men*, and

Grapes of Wrath. You are right – I will probably like this one too.'

'Were the others recommended by your Australian English teacher?'

'Yes, and from Jakarta. I befriended a local man, who worked in a backpackers hotel. He gave me many books. He even offered me a job there, but I was too stupid to take it.'

Cutler could imagine. Fazal the refugee, watching the wealthy young travellers come and go.

'I thought I'd make you all a coffee,' said Cutler. 'Is there any left?'

'Of course. We wouldn't drink it without you. Now, I'd better get back to work.'

Fazal turned to the line, standing beside the racks that carried thousands of hooks. Across the moonlit ocean came the red blinks of the final GPS buoy.

Budi and Wayan smiled at Cutler as he passed through the cleaning stations, the cold from the freezers a welcome relief, visibly steaming as it slumped from the rooms where larger tuna were hung on hooks and smaller ones piled in the corners.

For the first time, Cutler was beginning to have doubts about whether he'd learn Bevan Whelan's fate. He'd taken the slow way, earning the men's trust, but that might not pay off if they genuinely didn't know what happened. What Cutler wrestled with was the fact that whatever he learned about Bevan's disappearance, he doubted that he'd be able to leave the *Shuen* in good conscience, knowing the situation of the crew. His mind was turning to ways that he might unite the two objectives.

An obvious way was to offer a financial inducement for information, or some other benefit that might be shared among them,
assuming that information existed.

Another was to manufacture information himself, in order
to help the crew, even if that meant framing Li and Yang. They
were guilty of other crimes, although without Bevan's body or an
eyewitness account, it'd be hard to prove guilt in Bevan's alleged
murder.

A third option was to give up on the investigation, and focus on
sabotaging the *Shuen*, so that it needed to return to port. In that
event, there was every chance, however, that the crew would be
either kept in chains below deck for the duration, or taken aboard
the company mother ship, and parcelled out to other ships. They
were clearly regarded as little more than company property. Apart
from Fazal, who'd been purchased at what was essentially a floating
slave market, the others had been acquired through fishing agents,
responsible for paying them and ensuring their silence. Cutler
assumed that payments were being made to the fishing agents for
the men's wages, in full or part he didn't know. He doubted that
the men would be paid if they abandoned ship and made for home
on their own.

Cutler could live with the last two alternatives. At least they
might lead to the men being taken ashore, and set free, even if
they lost the money owed to them.

Either way, it was time to force the issue, with frank questions,
and possible inducements to the crew. It was also time to draw
some fire himself, by making the two officers suspicious of him, or

at least perceiving him as a developing threat, assuming there was nothing to be learned from the crew.

The light was out in the storage room, the bales of food and non-fishing equipment so tightly packed that it forced a passageway around a pallet of rice, toward the engine room, before he could gain the stern bunkroom, where the men's cooking supplies were kept. As Cutler passed the engine room his eye snagged on movement behind the thick glass panel in the door.

The door was closed. Knowing that the engineer was asleep in his bunk, Cutler pressed his eye to the glass, looked deeper into this room. In the furthest corner he could make out Li's back. He was standing still, his hands clasped behind his head, earmuffs on.

Cutler quietly opened the door, widening his line of sight. Li didn't notice, the earmuffs doing their work. At his feet was Fernando, whose upper body was mostly hidden behind Li's hips and legs. Fernando bobbed there, Li arching his back like a cat.

Cutler took out his phone, and with a stab of his thumb took the picture. He put the phone in his pocket. His blood pressure was rising – he could feel the blood in his ears, despite the deafening noise. All it would take was three steps, and then Li's neck would be available to him. He stepped away, closed the door behind him, counted to ten and then opened and slammed the heavy steel door. The noise was tremendous. He went into the stern bunkroom and sat on one of the hammocks, put his head in his hands. He heard the noise increase as the engine room door was opened, and then closed. The slapping of Li's flip-flops as he negotiated the crammed room, headed back to the deck.

26.

Cutler boiled the coffee on the stove, knowing that Fernando would have to return directly to work.

Now the little scene on deck yesterday made sense – Fernando pleading with Li to not be transferred to another ship, his hand briefly on Li's chest – a gesture of defeat, of submission.

Cutler clenched and unclenched his fists. He had seen the same thing play out in prison, and outside of prison. You could call it coercion, or blackmail, but either way it was rape. Sex in return for favours, or for protection, or to avoid more extreme forms of sexual violence.

The pot boiled and the coffee stewed. Cutler tipped in three tablespoons of the precious brown sugar, stirred it around. He poured the pot into the smaller water jug, then took up the string of plastic and tin mugs – like everything below deck, tied together in case of a storm.

Most of all, he prepared his face. Li would know that someone had slammed the door, someone who must have witnessed him in the engine room. Before he had a chance to terrorise the rest of the crew, Cutler had to let him know.

A cool breeze washed over the deck, matching the faint dawn that barely coloured the steel and the ocean. At the stern, Fazal and Fernando were occupied with hooking and retrieving the

GPS buoy. Cutler poured the coffees and passed them to Aadam, Wayan and Budi, who were still dressed in aprons and bloodstained gumboots, ready to finish the processing. They nodded their thanks, even more when Cutler offered them cigarettes.

Cutler didn't want to look Fernando in the eye, not yet. He poured a mug for Fazal and Fernando, for when they were finished with the buoy.

Cutler was looking for Li, to let him know. To make it harder for him to isolate Fernando again. He drank coffee from the jug and smoked a cigarette, down to the butt. None of the men made conversation with him, perhaps sensing his anger. They passed him their cups and nodded their thanks and quickly returned to their stations.

Cutler had slept no more than a few hours in the last three days. He was accustomed to this, trained for it, and yet it was never easy to examine his intentions in the light of his fatigue, and the likely consequences.

He would have to avoid violence, as much as he felt like dishing it out, unless he was attacked himself. The crew were in no position to support him, without risking everything themselves. Yang and Li could manufacture any story they wished and serve it as the truth.

On Cutler's side were the recording devices in the wheelhouse and the bunkroom, but if anything happened outside of those areas, it would be impossible to prove.

Wen was no longer asleep in his bunk. Cutler ducked into the low room and took out his laptop from the shoulder bag, placed it in its proper padded sheath. He replaced it in his shoulder bag, did the same for his satphone. He cracked open the suitcase and took out the red EPIRB. It was heavy, and he wrapped it in a hat. He threw in a bottle of water taken from a slab beneath Wen's bunk.

He looked at the Glock pistol for a long time. He might need it for self-defence, but drawing it would put him in the firing line later, leaving him open to any number of charges, assuming that they were still in Palauan waters, and not the high seas.

There was no law on the high seas. The thought was now a strange comfort to him, where previously he'd been troubled by it.

Cutler put on the shoulder bag like a backpack, tightened the straps. Even in a tussle, it would be hard to remove, or even open.

He rose through the bridge staircase, taking three steps at a time.

Li was at the wheel, while Captain Yang pored over the instruments. Engineer Wen was cleaning the room, picking up cup-noodle and biscuit packets, and dirty mugs and plates, placing them in a cardboard box.

Only Wen turned to look at Cutler when he entered. Li stared out to sea, but his knuckles were white on the wheel, as though sensing what was about to happen.

Cutler didn't want Wen to have to be part of this. He didn't want to put him in a difficult position. 'Engineer Wen, could you please leave us for a moment. I need to speak with the captain.'

Captain Yang turned to look at them. He spoke quietly to Wen, who didn't put down the box, didn't leave the room.

'Get out of bridge!' Yang shouted at Cutler. 'You go!'

Cutler stood his ground. For the first time, Yang was visibly angry. His eyes were red with sleeplessness, wide and unblinking, but at least his pupils weren't dilated with amphetamines.

Li continued to stand at the wheel, staring across the bow.

Cutler took out his phone, held up the image of Li and Fernando in the engine room. He walked it to Yang, who refused to look at it, turned his head away. Cutler stepped to his side, held the phone closer. Finally, Yang looked at it, before turning his glare on Cutler.

He spoke calmly in Wen's direction. Cutler didn't remove his eyes from Yang's own, locked there.

'Captain Yang says that if you do not leave the bridge,' said Wen, 'he will have to remove you, and place you under arrest.'

Now was the moment. 'Is that what happened to Bevan Whelan? Did you place him under arrest?'

Yang spoke rapidly to Wen. At Bevan's name, Li had turned from the wheel. He stood with his feet apart, pretending not to look at them.

'That photograph shows nothing,' translated Wen. 'Chief Officer Li is not a ... homo ... homosexual. You are trying to cause trouble with the crew.'

Cutler spoke out the side of his mouth. 'I'm not saying that Officer Li is a homosexual. I doubt that he is. I am saying that he is forcing a crew member to please him sexually, which is rape.'

Wen didn't translate. Yang glanced away from Cutler, barked an order. Slowly, the words trickled out of the engineer. Li tensed now, and when the engineer was finished, the first mate reached under the instrument dashboard, pulled out a billy club.

Captain Yang put out a hand. 'Get out of bridge,' he said again, but Cutler wasn't finished. He looked to Wen, who was staring at the floor, his posture defeated, trying to be invisible.

'Listen carefully, Engineer Wen,' said Cutler. 'Tell Captain Yang that if I see Officer Li go anywhere near the crewman in this photograph, then I am going to send this photograph to the PNA office in Palau. After the disappearance at sea of Bevan Whelan, my predecessor, and of the previous engineer, I think they will be very interested in a possible reason for the disappearance of those two men.'

Wen didn't yet know the circumstances behind his predecessor's disappearance at sea – the fact that he'd been thrown overboard and expected to hang on to an unstable buoy for eleven hours. Cutler didn't want to let Yang and Li know what he knew, because the information could only have come from the crew. The story would keep for a better time, and it wasn't needed to provoke the reaction Cutler hoped for, because Li was now in Cutler's face. He kept the billy club low, gripping the strap of Cutler's bag with his left hand. 'PNA don't care. We pay fine, so what?'

'Good. You understood me,' said Cutler. If Li tightened his grip on Cutler's bag, then he was going to have to act. 'But I am also going to send the photograph, and the video that I also took, to your company. To everyone in your company. I will say that Captain Yang knew about it and did nothing.'

Cutler expected Li to erupt, but he did something far more dangerous. He went perfectly quiet, and completely still. He smiled, then chuckled, pushed Cutler away, went back to the wheel. Cutler registered the surprise on Wen's face, but Captain Yang's expression registered the same quiet hatred as Li, burdened only with the silence of decisions made but unspoken.

Cutler was reminded of the chessboard beside them – Yang's

belief that he was always two moves ahead of Cutler, his pieces arrayed in a subtle but deadly formation, before the final move.

Just as Cutler wanted it to be.

27.

For five hours Cutler watched the fish come in. Seated in the shade against an equipment crate, where there was a power point which he used to charge his laptop, he observed Fernando work the gears on the winch drum behind Fazal, who expertly unhooked the fish and lines, placing the giant steel hooks in neat rows on the rack beside him while Aadam gaffed the larger fish and pummelled the sharks into quiet submission. Downstairs, Wayan and Budi took the smaller fish off the chute and killed them with a stab to the brain before gutting and transferring them to the blast freezer. Occasionally, when there was a larger tuna or a shark, they started up the chainsaw, removing the fins and tail of the latter, before putting the sharks over the side, where they landed with a splash.

This time, Cutler kept a tally of the sharks. Among the more than four hundred skipjack tuna, and the dozens of giant bigeye tuna, and a few larger southern bluefin tuna, the line dragged in several dozen silky sharks, and around the same number of oceanic whitetips, as well as seventeen tiger sharks and the same number of makos.

The only time he left his seat, making sure to take his shoulder bag with him, he went below to the processing station to document on film the practice of finning and tailing the sharks, before returning them alive to the ocean, to sink to the ocean floor and suffocate and starve to death.

None of the men seemed disturbed by his taking film of them at work, although Wayan concealed his face with his headscarf. As with previous hauls, the line collected a shark for roughly every ten tuna, as well as the odd unfortunate seabird, dragged under and drowned when the line was set. Oftentimes only the snagged head or wing of the bird remained, after its body was presumably taken by a shark.

The killing became monotonous under the boiling sun, none of the men speaking or breaking for water. Cutler had even given up watching Fernando for signs of harm, or an awareness that it was Cutler who'd seen them below deck. On the rare occasions that their eyes met, Fernando smiled shyly like he always did, before knotting his brow and tensing his body, returning to the seriousness of timing the intervals that relied on Fazal's expertise with the hooks.

While Cutler kept a tally with the ledger, he tried on many occasions to call Whelan on the satphone, to apprise him of the situation. The first two times the line lost its signal, up there behind the blue cloudless sky where the satellites swung in orbit. The third time the call connected, and he'd barely introduced himself before Whelan asked if he'd done as instructed, and shown the men the video, before the line cut out again, staying offline after that. He'd been relying on using the satphone in an emergency situation, but it was clear that it mightn't be of much use.

On the laptop Cutler flicked between screens that showed the *Shuen*'s transponder, turned on now that they were legitimately fishing, and the live footage from his bunkroom in the bridge. As he'd expected, not long after he left the officers, Li had entered the room and confiscated all of Cutler's gear. He didn't know where his suitcase and duffel were now, and was glad that he'd had the foresight to remove everything essential, especially the EPIRB and Glock, which stayed in the side pocket of his bag, where he could reach it quickly.

The only other time the camera in the bunkhouse had engaged was when Engineer Wen had entered, not long after the incident in the wheelhouse, and changed into his overalls, toolbelt and boots. He'd drunk a litre or so of water, sat disconsolately on his bunk for a few minutes, glancing nervously into the corridor before checking his watch, and returning downstairs to the engine room. Cutler wanted to speak to him again, but that could wait. Cutler didn't want to put the engineer in a difficult position, but the young man needed to know what had happened to his predecessor.

The line continued to roll in, singing under tension, spraying the deck with droplets of water that instantly evaporated in the heat.

There began a long run of billfish – two sailfish and more than a dozen swordfish – followed by the beautiful lime-green and blue colours of a giant dolphinfish. Fazal let them be bashed over the head before kneeling and extracting the hooks, placing them back on the rack before giving Fernando the signal.

The rotating wheel on Cutler's screen blipped and disappeared as the latest recording from the wheelhouse was sent to Whelan, to be translated and transcribed. Cutler was pretty sure that it would be fruitful – Yang's yelling at Li had been sustained and violent, and had gone on for near five minutes. Hopefully, in that period, the captain had brought up the ship's recent history of missing men, letting his anger overwhelm his regular strategic silence.

Li had argued back at first, but toward the end was largely silent. It was then that he'd gone down to their shared bunkroom and taken all of Cutler's stuff. Cutler had expected the first mate to try to get some sleep after that, assuming that to be part of Captain Yang's orders, but he hadn't returned to the bunkroom.

A baby dolphin came through the bulwark gate, already drowned. Fazal and Aadam looked at it for a moment, with its open eyes, baby teeth and stiffening body, before Fazal reached down and extracted the hook. Aadam shuffled it along the deck with his gumboot, nudging it back into the ocean.

'Jesus Christ.'

Cutler stood to get a better view. Fazal and Aadam turned to see what he was pointing at – the horizon to the north-west filled with hundreds of ghostly shapes, shimmering in the reflected light.

'Chinese,' said Fazal, unfazed, already signalling to Fernando to bring the line in. He paused when the bridge door opened, and Li came on deck toting the AK-47, sunglasses hiding his eyes, beads of sweat on his forehead. He glanced at them and saw that the fishing was halted, barked an order at Fazal, who nodded and flicked his hand at Fernando, the usual signal.

Cutler looked to Fernando for a reaction. The kid kept his eyes down, his hands tight on the winch-lever, engaging the gear and bringing in the next hook, this time attached to a small and flailing skipjack tuna, quietened with a thud from Aadam's club, its tail drumming on the steel.

The *Shuen* was stationary while bringing in the line, but the Chinese fleet were advancing rapidly, broaching the entire horizon.

There were too many to count. Cutler picked up his laptop and opened the AIS page, expecting to see the ships massing before them, but the screen was clear except for the *Shuen*, the Chinese vessels illegally maintaining visual anonymity.

Cutler saw Li staring at him or, more pointedly, at the laptop wedged inside the crook of his elbow. He closed it and placed it back in the bag. Li fingered the trigger guard of the automatic weapon, his face neutral, his eyes hidden. Fernando glanced in his direction, then turned his shoulder, staring down at his feet until Li returned to the bow, the weapon cradled against his chest while he watched the armada arrive.

Cutler took the opportunity to speak with Fazal. 'It's like something from fucking *Avatar*. There are hundreds of them.'

Fazal spoke out of the side of his mouth. 'Not hundreds. Thousands. Every year we see this. They are heading to the Galapagos Islands, to hunt for squid.'

Fazal was right. Now that the ships were closer, beginning to part around the *Shuen* like a slow-moving river, Cutler could see that behind the first row of ships was another row, and another behind that, and another behind that, stretching from horizon to horizon. Some of the ships were larger than the others, hundreds of metres long, the mother ships and factory ships, and there were dozens of them too.

'The Chinese work together, like a navy,' said Fazal. 'They have more big ships than the rest of the world put together. This is just some of the squid boats. The tuna boats are the same.'

Li was still occupied staring at the ships getting closer, the flags and ensigns visible now, but no people on deck.

'The Chinese and the Taiwanese,' said Cutler. 'Is there … conflict at sea?'

Cutler couldn't help himself; the sight made him nervous, more aware than ever that the *Shuen* was alone on the great ocean, distant from any form of law.

'Fishermen are their own country. Does that make sense? I have never seen fighting between Chinese and Taiwanese. Chinese are like proper gangsters.'

Fazal had laughed, signalling to Fernando while keeping an eye on Li.

'What do you mean?' asked Cutler.

'*Proper* gangsters. Fishing is a business. Why waste time fighting with Taiwanese people? The Chinese know they will win. Their fuel is paid by their government. Their government makes deals with every country, to make sure they get all the fish, the squid they need. You don't need to invade a country to take what you want. You just need to be richer, and clever. Lend other countries money, so they get in debt. Bribe some of their politicians. Get those politicians to make laws and business contracts that suit you. When you get caught breaking the law, the politicians you paid will protect you. Remind them that the country is in debt. Threaten to take away your aid. Just like proper gangsters do. Your government is your gangster. That is the way to do fishing business. Proper gangsters don't waste time fighting with boys who steal from shops.'

'Shoplifters.'

'Yes, shoplifters. That is what we are. *They* are like the mafia.'

The line began to whirr, and Cutler stepped back. 'How do you know all this?' he asked.

Fazal shot him a look. 'The young man before you. Bevan. And the ones before him. They tell me things. The real question is, why don't you know these things?'

A hint of a smile on Fazal's mouth, his eyes intent before softening with understanding. 'But now, let me work,' he said.

Aadam grunted and went to the bulwark, braced himself on it, swung down the long-necked gaff. His muscles bunched as he dragged up a three-metre mako, a slender, blue shark, its black eyes watching them as it leaked blood and began to thrash, Aadam punching out the great steel hook and reaching for his club.

Cutler stepped back into the shade. Every direction he looked, the Chinese ships were massed. Li's hands were no longer on the AK, which hung from his shoulders by a strap. He smoked a cigarette, pacing back and forwards on the stern like a caged animal. Even from a distance Cutler could see that his face was flushed, and that his shirt was soaked with sweat.

Cutler turned to the fishing line and cursed as another shark was brought aboard, this time a smaller tiger shark, already dead, worn out struggling against the impossible weight of sixty kilometres of floats and line, the hook improbably large in its mouth. By now he felt nothing when a fish, bird or shark was brought in – even in his short time aboard he had seen thousands of the creatures dragged onto the deck. He desperately wanted to speak more to Fazal, and to the others, but would have to wait. Despite everything they had endured, and continued to endure, the fishing must continue.

28.

Cutler badly needed to sleep. The burning in his eyes had been replaced by a dry pain lessened only by holding them closed with every blink, even as a dizziness came over him, a tumbling in his mind that sought to draw him down to the deck, where he might curl up and fall deeper.

He joined the men at the stern gate, where they washed in the yellow light from the bridge, pouring buckets of water over themselves, wincing as the scratches and cuts caught the salt. Cutler threw the bucket overboard and drew in the rope, poured the water over his head fully clothed, closing his eyes too long, almost falling asleep where he stood.

The *Shuen* was motoring to a new fishing position, and they had a few hours until the next line went out, and the cycle began again.

When they were clean the men sat and ate rice with peanut curry, made of fish sauce and Cutler's peanut butter, finishing the meal with the last of his muesli bars. Their fatigue hung over them like a shroud, and they barely talked.

Under the light of Cutler's headtorch, Fazal tended to the infected wounds on Budi's feet, before checking his own. The gash on his ankle now wept a clear liquid. The antibiotics seemed to be working, despite the poor diet and lack of time for their bodies to recover.

There would never be a right time.

Cutler opened his laptop, the brightness of the screen making his eyes water. Budi and Wayan were already arranging themselves against the bulwark, in preparation for sleep.

The *Shuen's* transponder was turned off.

Fazal knelt beside him, and Aadam stopped the laying down of his sarong and instead threw it over his shoulders. Fernando started to leave, taking only his tee-shirt.

'Fernando. Please wait. I want to show you all something.'

The boy paused, looked to Fazal, who nodded. He returned and stood behind Fazal as Cutler opened the video he had ready. Budi and Wayan came as Fazal waved them over.

'What is this?' Fazal asked. 'We see enough ocean.'

The screen was frozen on a frame of water. Cutler pressed play, and the camera jerked, and the hull of a ship came into view, before jerking back to the object of the video, the Indonesian men floating amid the wrack from their smashed boat, the sound of them pleading, and the hooting and abuse from the men on the ship.

Beside him, Fazal went very still, as stunned as the others. Cutler ran the twenty-nine-second video, the sound of the men screaming and the automatic gunfire, the shotgun blasts, the men sinking into the water beneath a slick of blood and oil.

None of the men spoke or moved away. They were communicating with one another, their eyes glancing left and right.

'Where did you get this?' Fazal asked. 'Why does it stop there?'

Cutler had expected the first question, but not the second.

'You were *there*? All of you?'

Fazal looked to each of them, read their faces. 'This is not your business. Where did you get this?'

Of course, the men wouldn't know. They didn't have access to anyone outside their world. No phones, or internet.

'I got it from YouTube. It's all over the internet.'

Aadam's eyes were closed, mumbling a prayer. Budi joined in, his head bowed. The two men prayed in unison. Wayan closed his eyes. Fernando made the sign of the cross, looked at his feet.

Fazal caught Cutler unawares, slamming the laptop shut, grabbing it and trying to wrestle it from Cutler's grip. He was stronger than Cutler, but didn't persevere when Cutler twisted it, pulled it free.

The two men stood facing each other, the others afraid but sensing their leader was in trouble. Aadam took two steps behind Cutler. Wayan and Budi stepped closer.

'Who are you?' said Fazal.

'I think you know. Why did you ask me, "Why does the video stop there?" Is there more video footage? Was the *Shuen* one of the ships?'

'No,' shouted Wayan. 'Not there.'

Wayan said something to Budi in Indonesian. Aadam nodded. The anger in their faces had gone cold, replaced by something else – the grim hatred he'd seen earlier. Cutler was surrounded. If they wanted to jump him, he doubted he could fight them off. Was this what happened to Bevan Whelan? Putting his nose in where it didn't belong?

'I'm not the enemy here,' Cutler said, trying to keep his voice even.

'You are more dangerous than the enemy,' said Fazal. 'You must keep away from us. From now, we don't talk to you. Understand?'

Fazal gave Cutler a shove, a single hand in Cutler's chest, but enough to put him off balance. There was nothing in the men's eyes except disgust, and anger, and a willingness to take it further, if Fazal so wished.

'I just want to know what happened to Bevan Whelan,' said Cutler.

'That is too much,' said Fazal. 'Now go.'

Cutler did as he was told. He knelt and packed up his laptop, stowed it in the shoulder bag. Aadam took a step closer, but Fazal stayed him with an arm across his chest.

Beneath the bridge, Cutler found a place behind the drum winch where it was dark, where even the weak light from the wheelhouse couldn't reach. He backed himself into the corner and took out his laptop again. He had never felt more alone. The men could do nothing to protect him, not even to bear witness.

Cutler opened the laptop and turned on the satphone, hotspotting the computer. He opened his email. He thought about the words he should write, but felt himself falling, his eyelids coming down. Cutler tapped out the message, pressed send. He stowed the laptop and phone, put the straps of the bag over his shoulders, ready to fight, or to run. He wedged the Glock behind him, leaning into the bag, now a pillow, and closed his eyes.

Minutes, hours, or days later, Cutler awoke. Torchlight in his face, so bright that it made him groan. He put his hands up but they couldn't stop the light, burning between his fingers, or the butt of the AK-47 that he saw too late, and then for a moment everything was light.

29.

The deck was inches from his face. It was grey and smelled of salt. He heard a sound, tried to move his head but couldn't, his body not obeying his thoughts. It was the drum winch – the line going out. He tried to turn his head and a shooting pain burst behind his eyes.

He came to again. It was still dark, but the skey was grey now, just like the deck. He took it easier this time. He could feel his body. His legs were bound. He lay on his right side, couldn't feel his hands.

Cutler breathed deeply for a minute, fighting off the panic that set in the moment he thought about his hands. He counted down from ten, then at zero rolled onto his back, freeing his hands. He lay there, staring up at the bulwark while the blood pumped into his arms in little jolts of nerve pain. He could feel tingling in his fingers, and then he could move them.

His hands were bound. He worked his wrists until he had full movement in his arms. He rolled forward onto his hands and used them to push himself into a seated position, the curve of the bulwark matching the curve of his back, his neck painful where the rail pushed on his head.

Cutler remembered the blow and put his hands to his face, his forehead, his hairline. He drew down his hands and saw the fresh and dried blood. His hands were bound with nylon rope, too tight. His legs were bound with the same rope, fixed to the bulwark with light chain. He was up near the bridge, the darkened windows of the wheelhouse above him.

Why was he alive? A question for another time. Li could have killed him, tossed him overboard, another one. That he didn't, meant nothing. He might do it soon, or tomorrow, it made no difference. He and Yang were the law, their powers godlike. Even if Cutler escaped his bonds, where could he run? Without his satphone, he had no way to communicate, or call for help.

Cutler turned his head to look down the deck. The sky was lightening behind the wheelhouse. The drum winch whined. Fazal placed hooks on the snoods then baited them and tossed the baited hooks over the edge. The drum winch whined again.

Cutler tried to shout but his voice choked itself. He had to swallow to breathe again, his throat so dry he had to keep swallowing. He concentrated on drawing spit into his mouth, to lubricate his tongue and lips, so that he might speak.

Wayan carried a fresh bucket of bait to Aadam, who saw that Cutler was awake. Aadam said something to Fazal.

Fazal looked at Cutler, but his expression didn't change. He turned his back to the winch and very quickly put a finger to his lips, to indicate silence.

Even so, it was too late.

The shadows behind Fazal moved, coalesced into the shape of Li, his automatic weapon slung on its strap, its muzzle aimed at Fazal, and then at Cutler.

He fired the weapon, a short burst, impossibly loud. The men dived to the deck. Li pressed the trigger again, the same terrible sound, the bullets heading out into the ocean, somewhere above Cutler's head.

Li stepped over the fishing line, staggering into the sunlight just breaking on deck. He shielded his eyes with one hand, the other still toting the AK. The crew began fishing again, their movements jerky and afraid.

Li shouted something and the engineer, wearing his overalls and cap, began to follow him, carrying Cutler's bag.

Li increased his pace as he approached, his eyes wild, sweating even in the morning cool. Cutler sat up straight. If he was going to be executed, he wasn't going to give the first mate any kind of satisfaction. At the same time, he stretched his legs along the deck as far as his restraints would allow. If Li came too close, he might be able to trip him, take him to the ground. The engineer wouldn't intervene, and Captain Yang was presumably still up in the wheelhouse, a half minute distant.

Li stayed out of range, as though Cutler was a mad dog on a chain. The man had cunning, and experience. He said something to Wen, who dropped Cutler's bag, went to Cutler and checked his restraints, held up Cutler's hands to Li and lifted his feet to demonstrate the intact knot. He looked Cutler in the eye, apologetic, ashamed, seemed about to speak then thought better of it, retreated back to Li.

Li spoke again and Wen knelt and opened the shoulder bag, tipped out the contents. Cutler was waiting for it, the sound of the Glock hitting the deck, polymer on steel, but the Glock wasn't there.

Cutler glanced at Wen, but his eyes were on Li, waiting for his next instruction. He took the laptop out of its sleeve and opened it, as ordered. The home screen of the Parties to the Nauru Agreement came up, its embedded oceanic blue circle containing globes of happy-looking fish.

'Password!' Li shouted at Cutler, the AK pointed at his chest. Cutler looked him in the eye, shook his head.

'Mr Paul, please,' said Wen, his eyes on the automatic weapon, his voice strained. Li hadn't slept for days as far as Cutler was aware. His pupils were dilated black, only a thin brown corona at their edges, meaning he'd just topped up on the *shabu*. Cutler could see the blood pressure in his face, the throbbing veins on his forehead, the pulsing jugular in his neck.

'What does he want to see?' Cutler asked, his eyes never leaving Li's face, taking the measure of how much he could be pushed. One mistake, he knew, and his life would be over.

Wen asked Li the question. Li nodded. 'He wants to see the video you showed the crew.'

Cutler spoke quickly, hoping that Wen would catch his words. 'Who told him about the video?'

Wen pretended not to hear, turning the laptop round to face him. 'The one from the northern islands.'

Fernando, from the Philippines. Cutler couldn't blame him. The information in exchange for extra food or being left alone for a few days – it didn't matter which.

The laptop was set up to delete its contents if a certain login code was used. Cutler thought about giving the code to Wen, but that might put him in danger.

'Pass the laptop here,' said Cutler.

Wen asked Li, who surprised Cutler by grunting, leaning closer, pointing the barrel of the AK directly at Cutler's head. If he came a foot closer, he would be in range, but with his finger on the trigger, the volatile chemical flooding his sleepless brain, it might lead to Wen getting shot in the struggle. Li would certainly empty the rest of the clip, out of reflex.

Wen passed the laptop to Cutler, who sat it on his knees, plugged in the numbers. He saw that he had an email alert from Whelan, a response from the message he'd sent last night. Li was leaning closer, could see the screen. Cutler opened the video instead, pressed play.

He didn't watch. Couldn't watch again. Wen's face hardened at the sound of the screaming men, calling for their mothers in a language he didn't understand, but understood anyway. Li's expression didn't change as the video played out its twenty-nine seconds of horror and tragedy.

When it was finished, Li spoke to Wen.

'Chief Officer Li asked,' said Wen, 'where is the rest of the video?'

It was the same question that Fazal and the others had asked.

'That's it. That's all of it.'

Li muttered, and Wen nodded. There were tears starting in his eyes. His voice trembled. 'Chief Officer Li asks where did you get the video?'

'It's on YouTube. I downloaded it before joining the ship. Anyone can see it, if they search *pirates murdered*.'

Li threw back his head and laughed. Cutler had spoken slowly and clearly, and he'd understood.

'Yes, *pirate*.'

Wen clearly wasn't convinced, shocked at Li's laughter. Cutler saw a bolt of anger in his eyes as Li muttered again, nodding toward the laptop.

Cutler closed the laptop and passed it to Wen, who passed it to Li, who flung it overboard, still chuckling. He stepped back and scratched his belly, putting the AK on safety.

'Tell Chief Officer Li that if I don't call the PNA every morning on my satphone, then they will begin to investigate.'

Wen spoke quietly but forcefully, his anger present in the words. Li stared at him and said nothing. He nodded toward the contents of the bag, and Wen began to stuff everything back inside, including the satphone.

The agreed-upon word was *cactus*. Australian slang with no room for ambiguity. Cutler just needed to say it on the satphone, and then they would be sent, whoever Whelan had in the area.

Wen followed Li back toward the crew, who were hooking and baiting the line that jerked out into the water, the sun already beginning to build a dome of heat above the ship, the deck baking as Cutler retreated inside the curl of the bulwark.

Cutler's handler, Khalil, was correct. He'd said, with his usual jovial cynicism, that history showed when you treated people badly enough, and were cruel enough, for long enough, then you could get them to do what you wanted, without complaint. Once the few who resisted were killed, made an example of, there was no limit to the power of those violent enough. Slavery had ended in the Roman Empire, and in the Americas and Arab world, not because of the resistance of the slaves, who often outnumbered their masters, but because of other interventions, other events.

It wasn't a hopeful view of human nature, despite Khalil's usual annoying cheerfulness, and was said in the context of Cutler's role in releasing a dozen trafficked Cambodian sex workers from an inner-city Brisbane brothel. His role had been minor, to act as muscle for an undercover buyer of women, but he'd been there at the end. The women were kept as prisoners in the brothel, had been tricked into thinking the Lucky Country would provide them with domestic work, only to be sold at auction by their traffickers to whoever wanted them.

That night Cutler and Khalil had gotten very drunk, but no matter how drunk he got, Cutler couldn't clear the memory of the women's faces, even after being freed. They didn't believe that they were free. They had marched onto the waiting bus with their heads low and belongings clutched to them, headed to a detention centre, from where they were going to be put on a plane home, broke and still in debt to the same people who'd trafficked them.

30.

Cutler must have drifted off, a product of his fatigue and the concussion that when he awoke caused him to scramble to his knees and empty his guts over the side of the ship. He felt better for a few seconds and then the headache kicked in. The railing boiled under his hands and his bare feet burned on the steel deck. He slid back down into the sliver of shade afforded by the bulwark, his legs exposed but his head protected.

Cutler heard panting, fast and regular like an overworked dog, and realised that it was him. He looked again to the fishing operations deck where Fazal had been studiously ignoring him, but where Fernando now glanced, before looking guiltily away.

From the shadows by the bait-freezer Wayan emerged with the bucket and rope, and the four-litre bottle of water. Because he was working in the freezer, as well as his usual sarong and headdress he wore an old sherpa trucker's jacket, the lambswool collar yellowed with age.

Wayan's face betrayed nothing as he approached – used to seeing men chained. He made to toss the bucket off the edge, but Cutler pointed to the water bottle. Wayan put down the bucket and unscrewed the cap of the bottle, passed it to him.

Cutler's arms were weak, barely able to lift the bottle. The knock on the head had rattled him more than he expected, on top of dehydration and sunburn, and possible sunstroke.

Wayan knelt and tenderly guided the bottle to Cutler's mouth, holding it there until Cutler had nearly emptied it. Wayan smelled of Cutler's tobacco and old sweat.

'*Terima Kasih*,' said Cutler. 'What happens now?'

'Don't know,' said Wayan. 'Maybe a boat come takes you. Maybe you stay here. For now, we fish.'

Wayan put down the bottle and tossed the bucket overboard. Someone whistled from over at the line, and Wayan began pulling the bucket in faster. He tipped the saltwater over Cutler's head.

Cutler rubbed the wound on his head and clots of dried blood slid onto the deck. The salt stung his wound and eyes, but the cool water on his skin felt wonderful. Wayan tossed the bucket overboard and drew it in again. This time he left it beside Cutler, returning to his work in the freezer, ferrying baitfish to Budi. Cutler dipped his hand in the bucket and cleaned the head wound, clearing the blood out of his hair before edging back into the narrow shade.

The nylon used to bind his feet and wrists would not swell in the water, and he doubted that he could slip the restraints otherwise. There didn't appear to be anywhere near him to abrade the ropes. Cutler looked up to the bridge. Everything he did was visible to the officers. He was going to have to talk his way out of this one, or else subject himself to whatever happened next.

It was a lie that if he didn't call the PNA headquarters daily then they would follow up by contacting the ship, and if not satisfied with an answer, an investigation would be launched. Li and Yang would probably know this, although he couldn't be sure. They had volunteered the information to the appropriate authorities when Bevan Whelan had gone missing, potentially days after it'd happened, rather than the PNA or Whelan Snr noticing.

Would the officers risk throwing another observer overboard, assuming that was what happened to Bevan? Cutler wasn't sure. It was highly likely that the officers would get away with it. After all, he'd done his research. Being a fisheries observer was considered by insurance companies to be one of the most dangerous employments possible. Across the globe, wherever observers were employed, they routinely disappeared at sea, or killed themselves when in port. The company would then be ordered to pay reparations to the observer's family, before a new observer would join the crew and fishing would continue.

Cutler didn't know how precarious or otherwise Yang's position was in the company, following the Whelan incident. His job as captain was to extract as many fish possible at the least cost. Was that cost measured only in dollars, or did it include fines levied by organisations such as the PNA, as well as reputational damage?

The treatment of the crew and the hours they worked suggested that the former was the case. If Yang's catch was consistent and made money for the company, then perhaps they wouldn't care about the treatment of observers, who according to the same logic would be considered an annoying bureaucratic burden placed upon them.

Cutler looked up at the empty blue sky. The ocean pitched gently beneath the hull, slapping and fizzing along its sides. Normally a restful sound, in Cutler's position it instead suggested the truth of Li's statement that the ocean didn't care, and that humans were merely tourists on the watery realm. Unlike in the forests, or on the shoreline, where it was possible for people to imagine themselves connected to a larger web of life, to a man like Li, despite his years at sea, he was merely the custodian of a machine that was part slaughterhouse, part refrigerated storage unit, connected economically to a longer chain of manufacturing and distribution, resulting in gaily coloured cans of fish on supermarket shelves. The fact that the same dolphins who excitedly rode the ship's bow wave, making eye contact with the humans aboard, were likely the ones subsequently hooked and drowned when the line went out meant nothing to Li. It was collateral damage and a waste of bait – the cost of doing business.

Cutler closed his eyes to the beauty of the sky and ocean. It was too painful to imagine floating in the ocean, witness to the same beauty while struggling to maintain buoyancy, futilely kicking his legs and paddling his arms until the weariness overtook him, and he sank, and fatally inhaled saltwater into his lungs.

31.

It took until nightfall for the line to go out and then be dragged back in, along with its string of hundreds of dead and dying fish, and dolphins and sharks. The men worked grimly under Li's surveillance. The first mate sat on an upturned bucket and smoked his way through two packets of cigarettes, the AK propped between his knees. Not once did he look at Cutler.

It was the engineer, Wen, that Cutler wanted to speak with. He only needed a few seconds to plant the suggestion, but the young man came and went from the bridge to the hatch stairs without looking Cutler's way, aware no doubt of Li's eyes upon him.

Short of the message he wanted to send Whelan, Cutler wondered how long it would take for him and Khalil to work out that something had happened, and what that would mean. Like all ACIC human sources, Cutler was known within the organisation by his codename only. Khalil's sources, he'd been told, were siloed from the sources of other analysts and project managers for the reason of plausible deniability, for those sensitive jobs where the rules needed to be bent. Cutler was effective, but effectively disposable. This had suited him thus far – he was well paid for his services. He took the work when it suited him. There was nobody telling him what to do.

There were no guarantees that Whelan would come to his aid,

if informed. There was little that Khalil could do, so far out of his jurisdiction.

Cutler hadn't identified Bevan's killer, if indeed there was one. This was both a failure on his part but also the ace up his sleeve, depending on how hotly Whelan's need for revenge still burned.

Either way, Cutler had to proceed as though he were alone. When he listed his advantages, they were considerable, although the irony of being bound while he counted his blessings wasn't lost on him.

He was alone. He wasn't subject to any oversight, or law. He would do whatever needed to survive. The threats to his survival were easily identifiable, and easily accessible, should he get the opportunity.

Leaving aside the fact that he was a prisoner, his vulnerabilities were also numerous. He was not alone. There was the crew to think of, and the young engineer to consider. He still felt a semblance of duty to Bevan Whelan's father, depending on the man's next actions, should Cutler be able to get a message to him.

His prison guard was a man who hadn't slept for days by Cutler's guess, fuelled instead by amphetamines. The man would be thinking clearly in his own estimation, the meth lighting up his head with a burning clarity, and yet in reality his actions couldn't be predicted – his impulse control was severely curtailed. He had already emptied one of the AK's clips in Cutler's direction, for the hell of it. Earlier, he'd killed one of his own officers by throwing him overboard, leaving him to the mercy of the ocean. He forced his men to provide him with sexual favours, and had probably done so to many men over the years. He had likely done far worse, too – his main role as first mate to keep the crew in line, to make sure they were at their stations, using fear as his motivator.

Fear breeds resentment and, ultimately, hatred, which in normal circumstances was something that Cutler might use, and yet Li's control over the men was so absolute that there was little they could do. No matter how badly they were treated, or how bad things got, things could always get worse for them, and very quickly. They were truly disposable.

Away from the dull lights cast by the bridge, its industrial shape outlined against the blaze of stars in the southern sky, the moon was rising, casting a silver sheen over the ocean and the deck.

Cutler was dry again, emptying his bladder throughout the day over the gunwale into the vast ocean, the swell clean and broad-backed, surface tension broken only by the ship's bow as it sliced its way forward.

Even from a distance he could hear the engine room when the door opened, the sound of a clattering valve train, pistons thudding in the heads in a controlled dance of fuel and air, the roar dulled as soon as the door shut.

The rest of the ship was silent, the men catching a few hours of sleep before the line was drawn in again. Even Chief Officer Li was gone from his post beside the drum winch, the smell of his cigarettes thick in the air.

Cutler hoped that Li was sleeping, but he doubted it. He hoped that Fernando was with the others.

Fazal emerged down the rail from the stern end of the ship, where the men were resting. He looked into the fishing area and saw that the deck was clear. He would still be visible from the bridge, but the look on his face as he approached Cutler was determined, and detached. Neither friendly nor concerned.

Actions louder than words, or expressions.

Fazal moved quickly, aware that at any moment the tannoy might burst to life, or the bridge door might open, revealing Li and his weapon.

He knelt beside Cutler and passed him a ball of compressed rice. He raised a small water bottle to his lips, angled it until Cutler had drunk it all.

'Eat. Quickly.'

Cutler was hungry and did as he was told. Fazal remained still, hoping that in the half light on deck he would blend with the shadows cast by the moonlight. The rice tasted stale and Cutler's throat was dry but he ate hungrily, savagely, until he had a small clump left. He closed his fingers around it.

Fazal made to leave, but Cutler put his wrists on his arm. 'What is going to happen, Fazal?'

The Rohingya man glanced at the wheelhouse, looming above him like a prison sentry-post.

'I do not know. My guess, he will have you transferred to the freezer ship, taken to port. He will tell the PNA that you were sick, or caught stealing, or something. That is what I think.'

'Fazal,' Cutler said. 'You were right.'

Cutler had known from day one that it would come to this moment, with this particular man. 'You were right that I am not here as an observer. Tell me. What happened to Bevan Whelan? I'm working for his father. He is paying me to find out.'

Fazal made to stand again but this time Cutler gripped the

taller man more forcefully, holding him there. Fazal could break the grip, his arms powerful with work, but instead he remained crouching.

'Why would I tell you this? Do you want to get me killed? I am in danger being here, now.'

'His father needs to know. That is all. Whatever the truth is.'

'That is a lot. It is too much. We are witnesses. They will separate us. Send us to different boats. Or worse.'

'So you saw something? Yes, or no? I don't need witness statements. I'm not a policeman. I just need to know what happened.'

'You know what happened. Why, you don't need to know. I am going.'

Cutler pretended to eat, leaning over his lap. 'Please, listen to me. Ask the engineer to call the satellite phone. The most recent number. Say one word—'

The door to the bridge squealed open. Li staggered out into the moonlight. He hit the safety on the AK and pointed it at them. Fazal made himself smaller, began to inch away as Li fired above their heads, the rounds hissing the air a metre above the bulwark, spraying the night sky until the clip was finished. Fazal scampered back to the main deck, a dark shadow finding the shadows along the side of the bridge, headed to the bow.

Li kept on coming, snarling in Chinese. Cutler stretched out his legs, his hands before him, ready to protect himself, or take out the man's ankles, drag him to the ground, but again Li sensed this and kept out of range, stepping to the side and delivering short, precise kicks to Cutler's torso. Cutler's back was wedged against the steel, and he couldn't turn, his hands unable to protect himself from the side, the kicks landing against his ribs, and then his head, cracking the other side of his skull against steel. He shielded himself as the blows rained down, waiting for Li to wear himself out, his neck jarring with every blow, and then it was over. Li was out of breath, still swearing between gasps for air. He wandered over to the stern and slung the AK over his back. He opened his fly and began to piss onto the silvered ocean, the swell lifting and releasing him, sucking at the hull. Cutler's vision blurred as the nausea in his belly rose again and he knelt and felt his body convulse.

32.

The ship had been pushing hard for nearly two hours, a strengthening wind keeping Cutler awake. He was almost cold, for the first time since he'd joined the boat. The moon was full above him, bleaching out the sky, lighting his wrists as he worked the nylon binds against the deck. There was nothing to cut the binds with, but the deck was pocked with nubs of painted-over rust. He sawed the edge of his wrist against the deck, the nylon heating with the friction, a few small twists of the rope now abraded enough to be pulled apart, although to complete the action would take another twelve hours at this rate.

It didn't matter. He had the time. In another couple of hours the fishing operation would commence again, which would provide him cover.

There was no sign of Li near the killing floor, and nor could Cutler smell his cigarettes. Cutler kept abrading the rope, keeping the heat up, his wrists aching and his fingers deadening from the constricted blood.

He heard a clatter. From the shadows behind the bridge, a silver shape skimmed across the deck toward him, spinning and rolling.

As its momentum died, he saw that it was a small filleting knife, sliding right to his feet, within reach.

Cutler looked over to the shadows, but there was no sign or signal there.

He could draw the knife toward him with his feet. It lay there, the blade reflecting the moonlight, sharp and inviting. Large enough to do the work of cutting his binds, small enough to be concealed, for later.

Cutler looked into the shadows. Still no signal. An anonymous good deed from one of the crew? Perhaps. Or the engineer? Maybe.

Cutler looked at the knife, his eyes drawn toward its silvery blade, reminding him of the knife that he'd carried as a kid, in the group home where he lived, before the sergeant and his wife had taken him into their home.

He carried the knife everywhere – at school, to the shower, sleeping with it under his pillow. It was a blunt fishing knife with an old wooden handle and a broken blade that he worked back into a point against the concrete floor of his room.

The knife went everywhere with Cutler but it didn't make him feel safe. Safer, perhaps, but not safe. He knew that if he drew it in a fight he wouldn't use it – overcome by fear and paralysed, as always, unable to escape or fight or even shout at his attackers.

The fear that paralysed him made him despise himself even more. He was an orphan. Nobody wanted him enough to call him their own. The social workers and the foster carers tried their best, but even as a child he could see that a kind of scale had grown over their eyes, reflecting back the image of himself that he least liked – sitting in a chair, trying to be the good boy that they needed him to be, to make everything easy and smooth.

The paralysis wasn't only a physical thing that stalled his body and froze his tongue. It also deadened his memory. As a boy he could barely remember where he was last year, let alone his early years. His feelings were too big for words and smothered everything.

Cutler said the name quietly to himself, and to no-one else, not even the moon above him or the ocean around him. He hadn't said his name for many years – his birth name, given to him by some nurse or doctor or orphanage manager. It was as fictional as all the other names he'd taken on and discarded, the identities he'd inhabited and believed enough to make others believe. Then he would return to Khalil, the only man alive who knew his birth name, and his identity, which was a story like all of the others. Who gave him a new name and new papers and a new identity to suit his purposes, and which Cutler was always grateful for. Who told him that he never need return to his original name, if that's what he wanted.

Cutler could shed the names and the stories, but Khalil was right. He could only do that because of the one story that he couldn't shed, which wasn't a fiction, which was the story of the frightened boy who slept with a blunt knife under his pillow. That boy no longer existed on paper, but he was very real. Cutler thought of him now, saw the eyes burning in the darkness, diamonds of light where the tears had started, but never fell.

That boy had learned some things about people. He carried the knife because he was determined to never let anyone sneak up on him, or betray him, or trick him again.

Fool me once, shame on you; fool me twice, shame on me.

Cutler bunched his knees and hardened his heels against the deck. He kicked the filleting knife away, clattering against the painted steel, sliding across to the bulwark opposite and through a scupper into the ocean.

Over by the darkness enveloping the killing floor, Cutler heard Li's laughter, feathered by the wind. The red eye of a cigarette lit and drawn into lungs, the smoke catching the breeze, tugged out of the shadows and spiralling toward the moon.

33.

One by one the crew arrived on deck, weaving past the bridge from the bow, where they'd been sleeping. Fazal led the way, Fernando behind him, guided by the spotlight above the wheelhouse which had located the GPS marker buoy. The two men were five metres from Cutler, but neither of them looked at him. Li was seated again at the drum winch, chain-smoking and watching them work. He didn't look like a man who hadn't slept for nearly four days. He looked like a man who was accustomed to going without sleep for weeks. His tee-shirt was stuck to his skin and his belly hung beneath it, pale and soft. He was looking at Cutler, or perhaps at the vast ocean behind. He shifted only when Budi shuffled toward the crate that contained their gumboots and plastic aprons, in preparation for heading below deck.

The engineer came out of the bridge door, wearing his overalls and boots. The engine would be turned off while the line was brought in, and he could do his maintenance work.

The moon had sunk to the horizon and the night sky was studded with stars, some so bright that they hurt Cutler's eyes. The generator whirred and the deck lights turned on and then the stars were gone, replaced with a milky halo around the ship that gave the deck a fairground atmosphere, reflecting off the inky ocean that slapped against the hull. There was a choppiness to the waves that was different to the usual open-ocean swells. Cutler crawled to his knees and looked over the rail. In the distance, against the dark horizon there were a few lights, belonging to other fishing vessels.

He turned, and Li had wandered over to him, standing only feet away. Cutler could smell his rancid sweat over the pungent cigarette smoke soaked into this skin and hair. His eyes were slightly unfocussed. He'd been drinking.

'Your home that way, south. PNG. We take you home, ok?'

Cutler pretended to believe him. 'Yes, take me home. Thank you.'

Li muttered to himself and belched, shouldered the AK and scratched his belly. 'Fuck you,' he said quietly. 'You must swim. Swim, yes? Like a fish.'

The engineer appeared behind Li, making him start. He stood away, suspiciously regarding the younger man, who held up a plastic bottle of water, and a paperback. Wen spoke to Li in Chinese, his voice deferential, his head bowed a little. He made a neat little package of the book and bottle and pretended to present it to Cutler, like an offering.

Li snatched at the bottle, twisted the cap and took a mouthful. He spat out the water and tossed the cap overboard, threw the bottle underhand onto the deck beside Cutler, who scrabbled for it, brought it to his lips, gulped it down.

Li demanded to see the book. Wen held the copy of *Travels with Charley* open for him, flipped through the pages, his thumb gripping the spine. Li grunted, and Wen knelt and presented the book to Cutler.

'Cactus,' said Cutler.

'You're welcome,' said Wen.

Wen stood and took out the gloves from his toolbelt, turned and headed below deck.

Li grinned and pointed to the south. 'You swim home? Swim home, ok? Make new home on top of FAD?'

Cutler didn't give him anything, waiting for him to get bored and leave. He slid the book beneath his hip and looked down at the deck, as though defeated. He could hear Fazal and Fernando struggling with the marker buoy, dragging it up carefully, the choppy water making it difficult.

If the *Shuen* was near PNG, then it was also near the area Whelan estimated that the so-called pirates had been murdered, after their *prahu* had been smashed under the bow of a fishing boat. Indonesia, the Philippines not far to their east, the territorial waters of Palau to their north. Cutler had looked at the maps. There was a narrow band of international water between the territorial waters of PNG and Palau, where the *Shuen* had spent its time the past days. Whelan believed that the international water was where the Indonesian vessel had been destroyed, and its crew murdered. It was a place fishing crews went when their fishing day quotas had been met, to continue fishing. A lawless terrain, beyond the jurisdiction of any country, where the boats of a dozen countries competed for the fish, but that wasn't what Cutler was thinking about.

Whelan had OceanFresh boats fishing in PNG waters. O'Reardon had talked about fishing the international waters between PNG and Nauru. If only Cutler could get a message to them. The fact that Wen had given Cutler the copy of Steinbeck's novel meant that Fazal had spoken to him, given him the book. It was the only explanation. Wen hadn't blinked when Cutler had said *cactus*, instead of thanks. Perhaps he had heard 'cheers' instead, Cutler didn't know. He had to hope that Fazal told Wen what to do. No small thing for the engineer to betray his officers, the company he worked for. The chances were good that Cutler was getting ahead of himself. The *Shuen's* transponder was likely turned off, which meant any help locating him was unlikely.

Cutler watched the men work, the automation in their movements a product of fatigue and repetition. He took up the copy of Steinbeck's novel. He wanted a sign from Fazal that he wasn't mistaken, that the book was itself a message that he was going to help, but Fazal wouldn't meet his eye.

Cutler opened the book and laughed. He was too worked up to read the words, but he imagined O'Reardon's face at the journey the book had taken since leaving his library. Cutler opened the book in the middle and, like Wen had done, flicked through the pages, hoping for a message. He found it on page forty-five. A small steel rectangle, taken from an old razor, rusted in its centre but its blade glowing in the deck lights. Cutler opened the pages wider and slipped it into his fingers. Making sure that Li wasn't watching, Cutler brought his hand to his mouth and slid the razor blade onto his tongue, closed his mouth around it.

34.

The sun rose hot and red over the *Shuen*, blasting Cutler's position at the bulwark with both a force and a weight that made him shift in his restraints, but no matter where he moved or how he positioned himself there was no shade. He watched the skin on his already tanned arms and feet redden and felt his lips crack and his scalp fizz. He was so dehydrated that he was beyond sweating. Sunstroke wouldn't be far off, he knew, unless he could find some shade.

That wasn't likely, for some time. The *Shuen*'s operational deck faced the line coming in from the west, the boat drifting in the chop where oceanic swells that had likely crossed the entire Pacific met with local windblown waves, originating in the weather system to their south, whose black and grey clouds were dense and shaped like a blunted mountain range. If Li was correct, and PNG was to their south, it was too distant to be visible, although the clouds that didn't appear to move suggested a land mass sufficient to create its own weather.

Cutler couldn't begin to use the razor blade to work on his bonds, not yet. Chief Officer Li had taken his position on an upturned bucket in the shade beside the men bringing in the line – Aadam bludgeoning fish and sharks, and Fazal removing the hooks and placing them on their racks. The drum winch whirred and stalled as more fish were brought aboard.

It was early morning but the direct sun on Cutler's face and the reflected heat off the deck made it feel like he couldn't breathe. He was panting again, couldn't get comfortable on the heated steel, it felt like his brain was being broiled inside his skull.

He noticed the reaction to the voice before he realised it was his own. 'Water!' he'd shouted. 'Please.'

Fazal placed a hook on the rack and raised a hand to Fernando, to hold up the production line, but Li stood and pointed the AK at the taller man. Fazal put his hands in the air, the line began to whirr and another fish was dragged aboard.

Aadam went to bludgeon it, but Li barked an order. Instead, Li slung the automatic weapon over his shoulder and, laughing, bent to the task of subduing the fish. He picked it up, and even from a distance Cutler recognised the lateral tail-flukes. Li hoisted the immature dolphin and began to approach. His thongs squelched with blood that ran from the dolphin's mouth down Li's legs and onto his feet. The dolphin was still alive, trying to swim its body in the hard gravity of the heated air. Li smiled behind his grimace, keeping a grip on the mammal's tail as he began to swing it, releasing it on the third swing so that its momentum carried it tumbling and skidding across the deck until it hit Cutler's legs.

Li wiped the blood and slime off his hands on his shorts, staying to watch Cutler's reaction. The dolphin squirmed onto its belly, its black eyes strangely calm, its blowhole opening and closing, the blood coming from its mouth red and aerated with bubbles. Cutler knelt, keeping the razor blade pressed flat on his tongue, taking up the dolphin's tail. It was heavier than he expected, maybe forty kilos. The weight made his wrists burn as he staggered to his feet.

There was no graceful way to do it. As Li had done, Cutler swung the dolphin onto the bulwark, its belly landing hard. The anger blossomed behind the dizziness in Cutler's eyes, making him feel faint. He braced his belly against the bulwark and slid the dolphin forward, its weight sending it vertically into the ocean, its tail slapping the surface as it disappeared into the blue. Cutler caught his breath as the dolphin began to float back to the surface, belly up, making tired movements with its tail. It rolled and tried to swim, back onto its belly and flapping with its tail. A small hiss of steamy breath from its blowhole, and then it dived and swam in a frantic circle through the water, before spearing away beneath the shadowed surface under the bow.

Cutler sank to the deck, put his head in his hands. He felt like screaming, or breaking something, could feel the hot tears behind the lids that he clenched shut. He wouldn't give Li the satisfaction, but that was only because he retained some little strength, some little pride.

He knew, however, that his strength and pride were diminishing, almost gone. What would be left when he finally broke? And what wouldn't he do to survive?

He'd thought himself strong, and capable, forged by his experiences, but now he saw how distant he was from a man like Fazal, who'd endured five years of this, and worse, and somehow kept his dignity. What kept Fazal going was his responsibility toward the other men, and the hope that one day his opportunity would come – his chance to escape.

Was revenge part of his plan, too, when the moment was right?

Cutler heard footsteps, not the squeaking of Li's flip-flops, but the creaking of old rubber boots. He looked up and Aadam was offering him the water bottle, its lid unscrewed.

He must have seen Cutler's tears but said nothing.

'Drink. You must drink. Soon he change his mind.'

Cutler slid the razor blade off his tongue and tucked it against the inside of his cheek. If he'd been cut, he didn't feel it. He yanked the bottle out of Aadam's hands, tried to raise it to his lips, but realised that his bound hands couldn't grip the heavy bottle.

Aadam took its weight with a hand at the base of the bottle, tilted it as Cutler drank, more water than he'd ever drunk. The sunlight on his eyelids burned right into his head, throbbing with both a dull ache and a sharp pain every time he moved his neck.

He drank the bottle dry, let his hands go.

A sound, like a mosquito coming from the south, getting louder. Cutler leaned back onto the steel rail that angled his head. Something about Aadam's legs, turned to the south, not moving or returning to his post.

The sound was getting louder, coming low and reflecting off the water. Unmistakably a light aeroplane, the pitch changing the air around them as it rose higher, distorting as its wings tilted and corrected, closer than Cutler had first thought.

He clambered to his knees, watched the white speck glowing where the sunlight sheared off its fixed wings and fuselage. Cutler scanned the horizon. There were no other ships in the area that he could see. The plane slowed, and dropped, the single propellor strafing the ocean with revolutions of sound, familiar and yet alien, the first sounds from the world outside the ocean since Cutler had come aboard.

He heard a shout behind him as the light aircraft continued to descend, coming alongside them now, only a couple of hundred metres above the surface to their port side. It was clearly visible, unmarked except for some lettering behind the cockpit, a plane with a small range far out in the open ocean. He could see the pilot's sunglasses, a cap on his head.

Li was shouting louder, but not at the plane, herding the men below deck. Up in the wheelhouse, he assumed that Captain Yang would be similarly distracted. Cutler curled up in the foetal position on the burning deck, hid his face from the bridge. He could hear the plane circling back. He slid out the razor blade into his cupped hands, placed it back in his mouth, fixed in his teeth. Very slowly, he began to cut at the ties on his wrist. The blade wasn't sharp or strong. It bent on the nylon strands, the cuts not clean or even but he was making progress. He only needed to cut one strand of the rope, working quickly now, Li's shouting hoarse and increasingly lost to the sound of the aircraft coming alongside them again, a burst of automatic fire from the AK, the ship's horn blaring three times. Cutler didn't dare look. He cut and sawed, could taste blood on his lips, and then he was through. He spat the blade into his hands and crawled back onto his knees, fell against the bulwark, lifting his hands to the plane that was climbing above them, Li firing the AK until the clip was empty, Yang blowing the ship's horn while the passenger in the cockpit kept a camera at his eye as the plane rose into the great orb of sun and then was invisible.

35.

The deck swarmed with activity, the drone of the plane lost to the clouds massing to the south. Li disappeared into the bridge while Fazal and the others resumed fishing. There was no option but for them to bring the line in, or cut it. By Cutler's estimation, there were another fifty or so kilometres of line to retrieve, or another five hours of fishing before they could move.

Li emerged with a new clip in the AK-47. He'd clearly topped up on the *shabu* as well, shouting and ordering the men to work faster, his jaw gurning in between barked commands, his limbs twitching involuntarily like a demented marionette, knees popping out at the sides, his feet stepping to recover his balance, his back arching and straightening, his arms jerking despite the weight of the heavy weapon.

Fazal ripped the hooks from the mouths of the tuna and tossed them to Aadam, who either clubbed them or put them straight down the chute. Li stood next to Fernando and shouted at him to increase the pace of the winch, despite Fazal working at full speed.

Cutler didn't know who was in the plane that had flown north to observe them, before returning to the land of clouds, but he had to hope that somehow Whelan was working to retrieve him. The *Shuen* wasn't doing anything illegal, fishing in what he assumed were the international waters, where in any case no law could touch them. Cutler didn't know whether the plane had tried to communicate with Yang in the wheelhouse during the flyover, or whether the captain was just taking precautions by preparing to move.

Cutler looked down at his bonds. He'd tucked the severed ends of the rope back into the remaining five turns of rope that fixed his wrists. He could be out of his bonds within a minute, but the time wasn't right. There wasn't any place to hide on the ship that he was aware of. He needed to conserve his strength and wait. He couldn't risk trying to overpower Li when the crew were around. He wasn't sure whether they would help or hinder him, for a start, having nothing to gain by mutinying, when they had plenty to lose if Cutler wasn't successful. The chances of stray bullets from the AK hitting those on deck were high unless Cutler could disable Li immediately. Cutler's head still ached, despite the water he'd drunk, and he felt dizzy and nauseous – he wasn't sure he had the strength to go one-on-one with the wary first mate, his muscles rigid with anger, his eyes looking everywhere for an opportunity to punish.

The bridge door squealed open. Everyone turned to look, including Li. It was Captain Yang, dressed in shorts and a tight white singlet. It was the first time Cutler had seen the captain outside of the wheelhouse since he'd arrived on board. Yang raised a hand to protect himself from the sun, his skin pale and sweaty, dark bags under his eyes.

He held Cutler's Glock pistol in his right hand. He looked down at it, and turned off the safety, and then he was moving toward Cutler, pointing it at him.

Cutler watched him come, tried to look unconcerned. The captain caught something in his eyes and raised the pistol and fired it above Cutler's head.

That got Cutler's attention. The man didn't know what he was doing – the recoil sent his arm wildly to the left, his finger still on the trigger.

Fourteen rounds left in the clip.

Cutler twisted his wrists a little. If this was to be his execution, he wasn't going to go quietly. He rolled forward onto his knees, climbed to his feet, held up his hands in surrender, loosening his wrists a little more.

It wasn't to be an execution. Yang kept his distance, outside the range of any swing, pointing the pistol at Cutler's chest. There were bootsteps on the hatch stairs, and Engineer Wen's flushed face rose from below deck. He hurried over to Yang's side, ducked his head in a little bow.

Yang's eyes blinked in the harsh glare off the steel, but his voice was calm. He spoke for nearly a minute, Wen nodding.

'Captain Yang wants to know why an aeroplane has come looking for you.'

Cutler nodded. 'I told the captain that the PNA authorities would begin to look for me if I didn't contact them every day.'

Wen translated, the captain never taking his eyes off Cutler. His eyes carried the expression of a policeman, hearing a tired old lie. He shifted on his feet. Finally, he took his finger off the trigger, and placed it over the guard. He spoke directly to Cutler, while Wen listened.

'The captain says that you're lying. The plane came north from

PNG, your home, not from Palau. How did you get a message to your family?'

Cutler held up his wrists, looked down at his bound ankles and back at the captain. 'How could I? I've been chained like a dog for days. I ask the captain to release me, let me leave the ship, or let me continue to do my job. Tell him I don't care that he's catching sharks. Tell him to look at my legs. I have no love for sharks.'

Wen began to translate, but Yang stopped him with a grunt, began to speak. Very carefully, Wen reached behind Yang's back, and extracted the satphone from his belt.

Captain Yang put his finger back on the trigger. Despite himself, Cutler flinched. Even a novice couldn't miss from that distance.

'Captain Yang says to call PNA. We will listen.'

Wen turned on the phone. There was only one number in the contacts. He pressed dial and turned the speaker on. The phone dialled but nobody picked up. Cutler cursed under his breath, Yang's eyes sharpening.

On the twentieth ring somebody answered but didn't speak. Cutler leaned forward. 'PNA. This is Paul Cutler, observer on the *Shuen Ching 666*. I am here with the captain and engineer. I think we are in international waters north of PNG—'

'Mr Cutler. Are you OK?' said Whelan. 'Did you receive our recent messages, dated yesterday?'

Wen quietly translated. Yang looked pleased.

'No sir. My computer is … broken. But did you receive my message of a few days ago? That information is still current. What is your response, please?'

Cutler didn't know what Wen was saying, his voice barely audible, but Yang's suspicions hadn't been aroused.

'The answer is *no*, Mr Cutler. No is the answer, understood?'

Cutler tried not to look shocked, but Yang caught something in his stalled breathing, the subtle shift of his shoulders. He gave Wen a hard look, barked a question.

'Captain Yang wants to know what you asked?'

Cutler nodded. He spoke extra loudly, for Whelan's benefit. 'I asked PNA if I could leave this ship. I want to go home. The answer is no.'

Yang understood, grinned. He nodded toward the phone, a signal for Wen to hang up.

Whelan spoke loudly. 'In my last message I asked you an important question. I haven't received an answer. Do you remember my question, and if so, what is your answer?'

Yang didn't understand, a look of confusion in his eyes, but neither did he care. He nodded toward the phone again, and shouted an order at Wen, whose thumb moved toward the phone's red button.

Cutler didn't have time to think. 'Yes,' Cutler shouted, 'the answer is yes.'

Whelan's question had involved the existence of the film of the *prahu* being sunk and the men murdered.

The urgency in Cutler's voice spooked Yang. He braced his arm and pointed the pistol at Cutler's face. Cutler kept himself calm. He'd snatched a glance at Wen, who had merely pretended to hang up the phone, which was still live.

Cutler had to hope that his voice was loud enough to carry. 'If you shoot me, they will find out. What are you going to do with me?'

Yang's smile widened. He spoke calmly and clearly, the cruelty kept to his eyes.

'Captain Yang says he gives you a choice. He can either put you on a FAD, with a bottle of water and a knife, give you a … a sailor's chance, or call the Palau coastguard, tell them that you raped a young boy from the crew, have you arrested. What is your choice?'

Cutler looked at Wen, who held the phone down low.

'Tell Captain Yang to go fuck himself.'

Wen didn't need to translate that. Yang's eyes hardened, but there was mirth there too. He spoke loud enough for Li to hear, away by the bridge.

'Captain Yang says that you just killed yourself. You told PNA you were sad, wanted to go home. They said no. So now you kill yourself. Tonight, when it is dark, you are sure to fall overboard. You live your life like you play chess. You are reckless and a … stupid fool.'

Cutler glanced at Wen again, saw his thumb end the call. Yang muttered something through his smile. Wen shrugged, looked at Cutler as he threw the satphone overboard, stepping back in time with Yang, occupied now with engaging the safety on the Glock. He said something to Li, who smiled and unslung the AK, leaned it against the bridge. From the sheath at his belt he took out a large knife, held it shaking in his hand, his neck twitching, the smile never leaving his face.

36.

Cutler pinched his wrists together while Li knelt over him and retied his feet to the pipe beside the bait freezer, out of sight if the plane returned to observe them.

Cutler looked down at Li's sunburnt neck, the dandruff in his hair, thought about knocking him off balance, laying a choke on his throat, the pleasure he'd feel as breath left the older man.

The knife was back in its sheath although within easy reach. If Li checked the bonds on Cutler's wrists, then he would be forced to act, but the first mate's hands were shaking so much that he'd struggled to tie even a basic knot. As soon as it was done, he tried to stand and staggered, had to brace himself on the wall, his groin inches from Cutler's face. Li pushed himself off the wall and went back to his upturned bucket beside the winch, watched Cutler while he lit a cigarette, sucked deeply on it. The manic energy that had animated Li when the plane had flown over was gone. He sat on the bucket and, apart from the shaking of his hands and the odd jerk of his foot, he was still, his back hunched and his head heavy.

Cutler had worked with serious meth users over the years, and so knew the signs. He'd rarely met anyone who stayed awake as long as Li, but even he must sleep sometime, or top up. He looked like an old man, propped there on his knees, dried out and ruined.

If Fazal, Aadam or Fernando knew what Captain Yang had threatened Cutler with tonight, they gave no sign. Beneath the overhang of the bridge the air was stultifying. Now that Li's demands to work faster had tailed off, the winch moved at its regular pace, the skipjack tuna and occasional shark or billfish dragged on deck and clubbed then sent down the chute.

Cutler kept his eye on the skies, hoping that the aeroplane would return, but the clouds to the south became ever distant as the *Shuen* drifted north.

He closed his eyes, to rest them, felt himself drifting off, but the sound of the ship's horn startled him awake. Li jumped to his feet, reaching for the AK. Yang's voice came over the tannoy, speaking in rapid Chinese. Engineer Wen appeared from below deck, and Cutler looked to where he was pointing, guiding Li's eyes toward the liquid horizon.

It was a giant fishing vessel, the largest Cutler had ever seen. Beside that was another one, and another one beside that, directly to the west.

Wen turned to Fernando, ordered him to bring in the line. 'Don't worry about fish. Just bring it in. Remove the fish any way. But quick.'

Cutler could see the problem. The giant orange vessels, flying Panamanian flags, were trawling in a row, directly across the floats of the *Shuen*'s longline. Sure enough, the longline tautened and began to lift out of the water.

'Spanish ships. Supertrawlers,' Wen said. 'We're in international waters, nothing we can do except—'

Fernando engaged the winch, but it whined, shuddered, began

to smoke. The longline was tailing after the Spanish ships, had been caught in their nets.

The *Shuen's* engines engaged, the ship vibrating angrily as the big diesel engine drove the propeller hard. The *Shuen* began to try to turn in the direction of the Spanish ships, but that only angled the line around the gate, taut on the rusting steel.

The *Shuen* was hooked like a big fish, the propeller churning but no match for the power of the supertrawlers that'd snagged their longline, dragging them at the stern.

The line was so tight that it began singing. If it snapped further out than the gate, line laced with hooks would spring from the ocean and rake the men at work. Cutler made himself small, as Aadam and Fernando ran for cover. Fazal did the same, pushing past Li, who was frozen, his AK aimed out at the ocean.

Wen took the knife from Li's sheath and, crouching beside the gate, began to saw at the line.

Li began to shout, suddenly aware of what Wen was doing. He snarled at the engineer and when it was clear that he wasn't listening, occupied with his task and protecting his eyes from the inevitable break, Li fired a round into the gate door, missing Wen by a foot.

Cutler stood, began to work the rope at his wrists. Beside him, Fazal had appeared, the same thought in mind. He said nothing as he watched Cutler begin to loosen the ropes at his ankles.

Li fired another round, his voice lost in the deafening noise of the AK at close range, ringing off the steel around them.

Wen continued to saw, and the line cut, whipping across Li's legs, slashing into the steel above the winch. Immediately the *Shuen* righted, causing Li to stagger, and Wen to nearly fall overboard.

A bloody lash appeared across Li's thighs, but he didn't appear to notice it. He was still shouting, and Cutler was still deafened. Engineer Wen stood, no longer passive, overcome with adrenalin or something else, shouting back at Li, walking directly onto the barrel of the AK, shouting and shaking a fist in Li's face.

Cutler didn't understand Wen's words, until he heard Fernando's name.

Li went very still. He took a step back and swung the AK toward Aadam and Fernando, who were cowering beside the winch. Cutler moved as Fazal moved, but it was too late. Li fired a single round into Fernando's chest, sending him sprawling against the wall, dead as he slumped to the ground.

Wen shrieked, swung the knife at Li's neck. It lodged in his shoulder, stayed there. The man didn't seem to notice, took aim on Aadam just as Fazal tackled him from the side, the AK on semi-automatic mode loosing another shot into the steel above the winch. Fazal rolled off Li, who bellowed, reached for his missing knife, plucked it from his shoulder just as Cutler's kick struck his head, as Fazal reached for the clattering knife and plunged it into Li's chest.

Cutler and Wen stood back as Fazal continued to stab Li in the chest, the knife striking bone and breaking through, Li long since dead.

Neither man intervened, the years of stored anger welling up until Fazal's arm slowed, and the wails began to quieten, and the tears began to fall.

The bridge door squealed open. Cutler took up the AK-47.

Captain Yang emerged with the Glock in his hand, saw in an instant what had happened, jumped back inside the door, locking it behind him.

Cutler put a hand on Fazal's shoulder, the man shocked into stillness at what he'd done, his head bent as if in prayer. Aadam lifted him off Li's corpse, sat him on the bucket. Aadam took Chief Officer Li by the ankles, began dragging him toward the gate.

'No,' said Wen. 'He has family. A wife. Children.'

Aadam showed no sign that he'd heard. He slid Li to the edge of the gate, nudged him overboard.

The splash was loud.

Wen stood in front of Cutler, tears in his eyes. 'Now what happens?'

Cutler slung the AK over his shoulder. He patted Wen on the arm. 'First thing we need to do is tie you up. You understand why?'

Wen nodded, went without being asked to the rope that Cutler had left, curled against the wall. He sat down, and held the rope up to Fazal, still mute with shock.

'I'll do it,' said Cutler, and knelt to the task.

37.

Budi and Wayan emerged from below deck, fear on their faces. Budi took one look at Fernando, laid out now in the shade, his eyes closed and hands crossed across his chest, and wailed. He knelt beside the boy and began to pray.

Wayan stayed where he was. 'Where is the pig?' he asked Aadam.

Aadam indicated the ocean with a flick of his head.

'Why? Why does he kill the boy?'

Aadam looked at Fazal, whose eyes were still on his bloody hands. 'The engineer. He say something to the pig, about the boy.'

All eyes turned to Wen, seated against the crates, his hands loosely tied. Wen looked at Cutler, who delicately shook his head. Wen looked at the floor, said nothing in his defence.

Wayan took Cutler by the arm, turned him. 'Why does the pig shoot the boy?'

A glance at Aadam, and Fazal, told Cutler that they knew, even if the others didn't. 'He was crazy. The *shabu*. He even shot at the engineer, for cutting the longline. He was going to kill us all.'

Wayan looked doubtful, his dark eyes full of anger, and grief. 'What we do now?' he asked Fazal.

Wen cleared his throat. 'Captain Yang will call the Palau coast guard. I will tell them what happened. I promise.'

This sparked Fazal into life. He laughed bitterly. 'No, that is *not* what is going to happen. The other boats in the fleet. Any nearby. They will come and kill us.'

As though the captain had been listening up in the wheelhouse, the *Shuen*'s engine roared louder as the ship slid into gear. The bow lifted under the maximum thrust, the propeller churning a turbulent wake as the ship turned to the east.

'See,' said Fazal. 'He is going to meet them now. We must stop the engine. Block the door below deck.'

'You're right,' said Cutler, not wanting the *Shuen* to depart further from its position, sighted by the aeroplane. 'Engineer Wen. If I turn off the fuel line, is that safe with the engine running?'

Wen nodded. 'It will starve the engine.'

Cutler put a hand on Wayan and Aadam's shoulders. 'Come with me.'

The two men followed as Cutler climbed down the hatch stairs. He waited until they joined him, below deck, and pointed to the heavy steel door that led to the bridge.

'Block it shut. Something big.'

The two men understood, the ship slamming into swells and rolling, the hull groaning with every pitch, the propellor squealing when it left the water.

Cutler left them dragging a crate toward the door. In the engine room, he retraced his earlier steps, when he'd identified the working parts but also the valves and meters. He found the brass fuel line valve that switched between the main tank and the reserve, turned it fully to the off position. He listened to the pistons in the engine continue to pump in the heads as diesel was injected, compressed and exploded. The engine continued to run. He checked the valve again and waited. The engine began to struggle as the diesel in the line became depleted, eventually cutting out, stalling completely, the mesh floor beneath Cutler's feet juddering.

The crate by the bridge door was jammed with food cartons and weights, jerries of kerosene and propane tanks. Cutler tried the door – it didn't budge an inch.

When they came back on deck Cutler saw that the *Shuen* wallowed in the swells, the spume from the transverse choppiness leaping from wave to wave. The wind was slight, the waves originating far to the south, bearing north from PNG.

Over by the gate Fazal and Budi had stripped Fernando naked, laid him on his side. The boy's back was ripped open where the round had exited, a mess of bone and meat. With the bucket tied to a rope, Fazal washed the wound of blood, praying all the while.

In the whole time he'd been aboard, Cutler had never seen the men formally praying, or noticed any evidence of prayer mats. Budi and Fazal's words wafted about the deck in the slight breeze as they washed Fernando's body and hair, laying him on his back and sliding him onto a canvas tarp. Aadam joined them, saying the same prayer, began to stitch the canvas shroud with a fishhook and monofilament, from Fernando's head to his toes. When the stitching was complete, Fazal stood and washed the knife he'd used to kill Li, made sure that it was good and clean before he trimmed off the edges of the tarp. He nodded to Budi and Aadam, who tenderly lifted the boy. Wayan met them at the freezer door. He bowed his head as the two men carried in the body and placed it among the fish.

Fazal washed the blood off himself with buckets of water, none of the men saying anything until all traces of blood were gone, sluiced out into the ocean, the deck drying before their eyes.

'What now?' Wen asked weakly from his position in the shade.

Fazal spoke to the men. 'We eat, to celebrate Fernando. He was a Christian.'

Cutler knew to keep quiet, but Wen didn't. 'This is a mutiny. Shouldn't you try and capture Captain Yang, as a hostage? There is an oxy-acetylene torch below deck. You could cut the door open.'

Fazal didn't look at the engineer, instead speaking to the others. 'What good will that do? We have one machine gun. We eat and celebrate Fernando. We prepare ourselves to fight, and to die.'

The men began to climb down the stairs. Fazal stepped close to Cutler and muttered as he passed him. 'Are you happy now? This is all your doing.'

Cutler didn't reply. He watched the men emerge from the gloom below deck with cartons of the officer's food – white beans, soups, green vegetables. Aadam brought up a juvenile skipjack tuna, which hadn't frozen completely. He took it to the bulwark and began to cut it into steaks. Budi returned with their cooking equipment. The men knelt in a circle and added canned food to the pot, while Budi began to fry the steaks in red palm oil.

Cutler didn't offer to help, not wanting to intrude. Fazal was right – everything that had happened, and would happen next, was a product of his questions, and his revealing to Captain Yang about Li's abuse of the boy. Cutler took a seat on the wall beside Wen. Aadam brought him a carton of cigarettes he'd found below deck – Mevius – a brand he didn't know. He peeled open the carton and knocked out a packet, tapped out a cigarette. Aadam tossed him a packet of matches.

What Cutler really needed was some electrolytes, and something to clean his head wound. Antibiotics perhaps, and certainly some codeine, but the cigarette tasted glorious, sating the withdrawals that had added jitteriness to his pain of the past days.

The food was prepared, and the men sat in a circle, away from the stove, uncaring of the sun that beat down on them.

'Join us,' said Fazal, spooning the stew into plates. 'Please.'

Wen shrugged off his binds, and squat-walked across the deck to join the men. Cutler did the same, accepting his laden plate with thanks. His stomach growled and his mouth salivated, despite himself.

He hadn't realised how hungry he was.

The sun and the chilli made him sweat, but it was the best meal he'd ever eaten, mixing the rice with the curry and flakes of fish with his fingers and scooping it into his mouth.

'Budi,' said Fazal. 'You are the oldest. You begin. Tell us a story about Fernando.'

The men listened as Budi began to speak, tears in his eyes but laughter in his voice.

38.

The two ships came from different directions, but appeared at the same time, silver reflections on the oceanic horizon that hovered in the mirages wavering along the deck surface before them.

Fazal passed Cutler the binoculars, looking at the ship to the north. As the ship passed beneath the midafternoon glare its outline became clear. Cutler passed the bins back to Fazal.

'Longliner,' Cutler said. 'Can tell from the bridge.'

Cutler and Fazal walked the deck to the east, where the second ship was still lost in the dazzle of light.

'Might be freezer ship, might be another longliner,' he said.

'You're sure Captain Yang wouldn't have put out a mayday call?'

'Yes, I'm sure. When mutiny happens, it always ends this way. The company ships come. The problem is finished. I never heard of a mutiny ship making it to port.'

They went back to the operations floor, where the men were resting around a pile of rudimentary weapons – a cane knife, a wrench pipe, two gaffs and miscellaneous knives. Fazal went and tapped each of them on the shoulder, including Engineer Wen, who held out his wrists to be bound again.

Fazal put his hand on Cutler's shoulder. His expression was grave. 'Mr Paul,' he said. 'This is your chance. I can tie you up too, make you a prisoner. They will think you took no part.'

The thought had crossed Cutler's mind, but he'd dismissed it, reminded of Captain Yang's promise to have him killed. He didn't doubt the sincerity of those words when they were spoken, and even less now.

'Thanks, but no thanks. I'm not going to let you die. And I know how to use this,' he said, tapping the AK.

Fazal gave Cutler's shoulder a squeeze, nodded and bent to tie up Wen.

The ship to the north was coming fast, ploughing through the swells. The *Shuen*'s horn began to blow, and a red flare burst from the open window on the side of the wheelhouse.

Captain Yang must have turned his transponder on, or at least Cutler hoped so.

Cutler held the bins to his eyes again. The Chinese script and the fleet name were visible in the moments when the ship levelled out between swells. This one was the *Shuen Ching 588*, flying the Taiwanese flag.

The ship slowed and turned sidelong as it approached.

'Other ship here,' shouted Aadam from the starboard side. Cutler heard a shot, saw his Glock aimed at Aadam from the wheelhouse window, Yang emboldened now that reinforcements had arrived.

Thirteen rounds left in the Glock.

Aadam scuttled toward the bridge, out of Yang's line of sight, as the second *Shuen Ching* arrived, turning its flank to them a hundred metres away.

It was easy to see how they would approach this. Two ships, attacking different sides of the *Shuen*. Yang would have told them that there was only one automatic weapon, with one clip of ammunition.

What he didn't know was that Cutler was trained to use it. He kept the weapon on semi-automatic mode, knelt and braced his elbow on the bulwark gate. An armed officer appeared on deck opposite him, waving at some crew, who were carrying fenders and ropes. They were close enough that Cutler could hear their voices.

'You should do it now,' Cutler said to Fazal, who'd gathered Budi and Wayan beside him.

The three men made themselves visible, began to cheer, waving at the ship opposite, drifting toward them.

The moment that Cutler saw the officer raise his AK he fired a single shot, aimed a metre above the man's head, the ricochet loud on the other deck. The crew beside him dropped below the bulwark, except for a lone man in a blue singlet, hatless, who pumped a fist toward them in solidarity.

Li had fired two bullets at the engineer, then another that killed Fernando. A loose round had fired when he was tackled.

Following Cutler's single shot, there were twenty-five rounds in the magazine.

Cutler ran to the other side of the ship. Keeping out of Yang's sight, he took aim on the officer there, armed with a shotgun, then scuttled back to the other side. The shotgun was still out of range, and would be for a while.

The ship had drifted closer. Fenders had been deployed along its flank. They were going to drift until they were alongside, and close enough to board.

Fazal and the others were still cheering, waving their weapons. The officer across from them kept below the bulwark. He probably had unlimited ammunition but couldn't risk a firefight from the ship's deck in case the bridge was pierced, or the hull.

Cutler thought about giving the wheelhouse a blast, to get them to move, and so switched the mode to automatic. He needed to push them back. Yang was no doubt communicating with them on the short-wave. He didn't have a clear shot to the top of the wheelhouse because of his angle of fire.

He wished he had a megaphone, or something large enough to write on. He would offer to let Captain Yang and Engineer Wen leave the vessel, to be lowered down on the liferaft, as long as the ships left them the *Shuen*. But he didn't have a megaphone, and he couldn't communicate with Captain Yang either.

He had no choice. He switched back to semi-automatic mode and began to take out the first ship's windows, aiming high into the glass to minimise hitting an officer.

He didn't want to kill anyone, not yet at least, not until it was kill or be killed. He scuttled back to the starboard side, did the same to the ship there, the heavy glass imploding into the wheelhouse.

Six more shots used. Nineteen left in the clip.

The action had the desired effect. The two ships' engines throbbed as they motored forward, turning to distance themselves.

It would be dark in a couple of hours. Nobody knew that the three ships were there. The two other ships could be patient, wait for others to join them.

'Another ship,' shouted Aadam. 'Coming from south. Small one.'

Fazal put the binoculars to his eyes. 'Aadam is right. Smaller ship. Not a longliner. Maybe purse seiner.'

Cutler dared to hope. 'What flag is it flying?'

'You must see this,' said Fazal, passing him the bins.

Cutler smiled so wide his lips cracked. '*Ouch.* The Jolly Roger. I know that ship.'

'The captain has a sense of humour. The one that brought you here, yes?'

'Yes. The *Monterey*. American captain. Fijian crew.'

The *Monterey* looked small in the big swells. Cutler said a quiet thanks to himself for Yang turning the *Shuen*'s transponder on. No doubt they'd drifted some distance from where the aeroplane had spotted them.

Cutler wished he could hear the comms between the four ships. Wished he could hear Captain O'Reardon's voice. No idea how the American was going to extricate them from the situation they were in but was confident that the old war veteran would try.

The *Monterey* slowed as it came at them, turning sidelong. They wouldn't know that the engine had been disabled – they were blocking the ship in.

Silence as the *Monterey* sat there, rolling in the swell. After a few minutes the *Shuen*'s tannoy crackled, Yang's voice angry, speaking rapidly in Chinese.

Cutler looked to Wen, who nodded. 'Captain Yang says that the American ship is here to collect you. He will not try and stop you leaving. The American ship is going to drop a smaller boat, to come and pick you up. None of the other ships will stop them.'

The smile on Fazal's face fell away.

'What he means?' asked Budi. Fazal shook his head, laid down the gaff in his long arms.

Cutler looked to each of them in turn. The defeat in their faces, and disappointment. Near the end now.

'Fuck that,' said Cutler. 'Wen, go and stand beneath the wheelhouse. Shout to Yang that we are *all* going, or none of us are going.'

Wen stood but shook his head. 'Captain Yang, he will never

agree. The other ships, they will never agree.'

Cutler had no way of communicating with O'Reardon. He looked Wen in the eye. 'Then you tell Captain Yang that we will sink her. We will sink the ship. We have nothing to lose.'

Wen nodded, went over to the wheelhouse, showed his restraints and started translating, his voice trembling. When he'd finished, he stood there and waited. The minutes ticked by, nobody speaking until the tannoy crackled once again, and Yang spoke to the young officer, what sounded like a single sentence.

Wen shrugged at them. 'Captain Yang says that the American is refusing to take the crew. Only Mister Paul.'

Cutler felt a nudge in his side. He looked down to the smartphone in Fazal's hand. The tall man passed it to him, wrapped it in his fingers. 'Then I think you are going to need this. It is what you came here for, I think.'

Cutler didn't understand. He didn't know who the phone belonged to. He assumed that the phone contained evidence of how Bevan Whelan had died. 'What is this?' he asked, opening the phone, tapping through to the photo library, which contained dozens of images of a young Chinese man he didn't recognise.

'Who is this?' he asked.

Fazal took the phone from him, opened a video. Cutler looked to the others, but they looked away. It was a three-minute video. As soon as the first images clarified out of the jumbled movements of the camera, he recognised the same voices, the screaming of the men in the water. He had only seen the first twenty-nine seconds. The shotgun was fired and the man's head exploded in the water.

The laughter followed, the sound of cheering. As the video continued into the second minute the camera swung across the deck to the ship opposite, the *Shuen Ching 588*, and then further to a ship Cutler didn't recognise, except for the blue logo painted on its bow, the company brand of Whelan's OceanFresh.

'Fuck me,' he said. 'Fuck *me*.'

None of the men said anything. Fazal passed the phone back to Cutler. 'The film was taken by the engineer of another *Shuen* company ship, maybe this one next to us. He was transferred onto this boat. He trusted me with the phone. The Captain and Li had him killed, put on the buoy as punishment for complaining about what happened, for not reporting it. He was a broken man. His mind had broken, but it was me who got the boy, Mister Bevan, killed. He asked about it, and I showed him. He copied the film from this phone. He said that he was going to send it to his father and to journalists. I warned him not to. Li must have found it. I didn't see what happened. I think you know.'

'Did Bevan send the video?'

'I don't know. I think this is the only film of what happened. I've kept it hidden.'

'Why didn't you show me this before, when I asked about it?'

'Why do you think? Everybody who touches it dies. It is a thing of evil. All of us will die now.'

Cutler called Wen over, whispered in his ear. The engineer went back and stood beneath the wheelhouse, shouted up the translation of Cutler's words.

Another long silence followed. Cutler stood out in the sunshine, where he was sure that O'Reardon could see him. He held the phone up for a few seconds, then returned to the shade and put the phone in his pocket, waited along with the others.

The tannoy hissed, and Captain Yang spoke a single word. Wen held up his thumb, above the binds on his wrists.

'I'm not sure what happens next,' said Cutler. 'I don't trust the other ships if we get in the skiff.'

'I don't think that will be a problem. I think their problems are bigger.'

Cutler didn't see what Fazal meant. He could see the officer on the ship across crouching at the bulwark, could see shadows moving in the wheelhouse. Then, along the sides of the ship he saw the crew, creeping forward. One of them reached the officer with the AK. There was a struggle, a burst of machine gunfire into the air. The AK was brought down on the officer's head, then thrown overboard. From the ship on the other side Cutler heard the sound of shouting, and a shotgun blast.

Men began jumping into the water simultaneously, from both sides. Six men from the ship opposite, four from the ship to their starboard, swimming toward the *Monterey,* just as O'Reardon had warned Cutler would happen.

'How did you know?' said Cutler.

'It's what I would have done.'

The two ships beside them started their engines, began to inch forward, to run the men under. Cutler turned and fired another shot up at the wheelhouse, but the ship didn't slow. More rounds followed, but they weren't fired by him.

On the deck of the *Monterey,* he glimpsed the muzzle-fire of one weapon, and then another. He took the binoculars off Fazal, swept the deck and saw Joseph on the stern, firing his sniper's rifle propped on a winch, emptied at the wheelhouse of the nearest *Shuen*, which slowed, began to reverse. Cutler took aim at the ship on the other side, but he needn't have. It too was reversing out of harm's way.

The ten men swam across the ocean, their arms chopping the surface even as David began the process of lowering the *Monterey's* skiff into the water. When it was leashed to the stern he waited for the first men to reach him, began to lever them out of the water, pushing them behind him as he reached for the next man, and then the next.

39.

The ten crewmen sat dripping on the stern deck, their faces alive with excitement. Cutler and Fazal lifted Fernando's body, wrapped in its shroud, from Budi and Wayan's arms. The skiff pushed back a little, and they grabbed its sides before climbing aboard the *Monterey*.

The Fijian crewman, Joseph, took the skiff's rope and hitched it to the winch chain. David climbed out of the skiff and joined them on deck as the skiff was dragged onto its slide. He collected the sniper's rifle and Cutler's AK, slung the latter and hefted the former, took them forward on the deck, somewhere out of sight.

'Andika!'

Budi had seen a familiar face, a boy not much older than Fernando. He had open sores on his knees and arms. Budi embraced him, ruffled his hair, embraced him again.

Joseph began handing out packets of biscuits, and sharing around bottles of water, the men thanking him with smiles and simple English.

Fernando's body was light on their shoulders, and Cutler and Fazal moved along the deck, toward the blast freezers near the mound of purse-seine netting, beside the great power block. David opened the freezer for them, and they placed Fernando on the icy floor.

Outside, David turned to Fazal, thrust out a hand. The two men were roughly the same height, but Fazal was thinner, hollowed out by years of poor eating and hard work. David's eyes weren't friendly, however, unlike Fazal's. 'You go back with the others. Captain says you stay on stern deck. We have to feed you, make sure you aren't sick with disease.'

'What disease?' Fazal asked quietly.

'You know. Dysentery. Covid. Other things.'

'How are you going to know those things?'

David shrugged. 'You ask *them*. Tell them to be honest. If they are sick, we can help them.'

'Are we ... safe here?'

For all of Fazal's strength of character, the question betrayed what each of the crewmen must be feeling. Was this real? Were they safe?'

David looked Fazal in the eye, put both hands on the other man's shoulders. 'Brother, I can see that you have suffered. You are safe here. The captain is angry, but he is always angry. Rest. Sleep. Eat.'

Fazal looked at Cutler. 'The thing in your pocket. Be careful with it. You are in danger.'

'What does he mean?' asked David. 'Aussie, if you have another weapon, you need to give it to me. The captain wanted me to search everyone, but I can see those men have only the clothes they are wearing. Not even any shoes.'

'I don't have a weapon,' said Cutler. 'I have a phone. A phone that can't make calls.'

'Follow me,' said David, turning toward the bridge. The deck was clean and everything was strapped down. Cutler didn't know how far the *Monterey* had come for them, but it was clear that they hadn't fished for some time.

The cook was busy in the galley, didn't look up from his pots as Cutler passed, the smell of tomato broth and rice, and grilling fish.

Casey's room was empty, higher up in the bridge. Her gear was still strewn across the little desk and bed, her laptop open to the AIS page, where the three *Shuen* vessels blinked on the screen.

Cutler found her in the room at the base of the stairs, her back to him, removing shells from a pump-action shotgun that she placed in a steel locker. David knocked and she turned and took the weapons from him, smiling at them both before returning to her work.

Captain O'Reardon wasn't at his wheel, staring out at the ocean. David opened the door to the wheelhouse and stood back, closed the door behind Cutler.

O'Reardon, dressed in denim shorts and a singlet, strode across the room from the window where he'd been observing the *Shuen* fleet, the heavy binoculars bouncing on his belly.

'Why aren't we leaving?' asked Cutler.

O'Reardon looked at Cutler like he was stupid. 'David told me on the two-way that you don't want me to sink the vessel you were on.'

'Yes, that's right. I was there when he told you.'

'Why not? It's immobile.'

'The man who killed Bevan is already dead. There's a crew member, the engineer. He helped me ... us.'

'What about the captain? Joseph could have taken him out with the sniper's rifle. He had a clear shot.'

'He deserves it, but I suspect he's got it coming.'

'What do you mean?'

'I need to use your satellite phone.'

O'Reardon looked Cutler up and down, observing the sweat on him, the mess of his hair where he'd been injured. 'Good. Because someone wants to speak to you.'

O'Reardon reached for the satphone buckled to his hip.

'I don't want to talk to Whelan. Not yet at least.'

'Whelan, I never liked that guy, but he's the reason we came to get you. He's the one who talked me into letting those men aboard. Men, who're now my responsibility. It's a fucking mess, son. I warned you about that. What am I supposed to do with them?'

'I'll speak to Whelan, after I've spoken to someone else.'

O'Reardon's blue eyes were shot through with manufactured anger. There was concern for Cutler there too, and something else. 'Do that,' he said. 'And then get yourself some chow, a shower, and some sleep. You look, and smell, like shit.'

Cutler smiled and accepted the phone. He walked to the corner of the room furthest from the captain, turned his back. He punched in the numbers, hoped for the best.

'Hello, Newtown Florists. How can I help you?'

'Neve, it's me. I need to speak with him. The number is ...'

Cutler turned and O'Reardon called out the numbers. Cutler repeated them slowly.

'Yes, I'm fine,' she said. 'Doing very well, thanks for asking. The native flowers are hot at the moment. Kangaroo paws, all the way from Western Australia, really brightening up the place.'

Cutler smiled down the phone. 'Thank you. It's good to hear your voice.' He hung up, looked over at O'Reardon behind his wheel. Cutler hadn't even noticed that the engine had started, and that they were now moving north, away from the grey bank of terrestrial clouds.

The phone rang, and he answered it immediately.

'Son, I've been waiting on your call. Whelan told me what happened. Some of it, anyway.'

'You were *worried* about me, and yet it was you who trained me up.'

'Very funny. I'm assuming that you've spoken to Whelan?'

'No, I haven't.'

'He's the … client, son. He's the one paying the bills.'

Cutler didn't reply, waited for the penny to drop.

'What do you have for me?' asked Khalil.

Cutler described the recording of the massacre at sea. The presence of the *Shuen Ching* vessels, another unknown vessel, and the Australian ship belonging to Whelan's company. He told Khalil that the video was what led to Bevan's murder, and the murder of the Taiwanese engineer who'd filmed it.

'*Ya salaam*, son. What a mess.'

'Is it useful to you? I know it is to Whelan. He kept asking me about it.'

'Why has he only seen the first thirty seconds?'

'That I don't know. Those who know are dead.'

'Yes, it's useful to me. And yes, you need to be very fucking careful. Do you trust the American captain?'

'I think so.'

'Good. Because I need to tell you something. It's the kind of shit you can't make up.'

Cutler listened while his handler outlined the state of play. He could see why Khalil though it so improbable, and yet important. The Taiwanese company that owned the *Shuen Ching* fleet, and many others around the world, had bought a large stake in Whelan's OceanFresh company, backed by significant finance capital, the kind that only invested money where short-term profits were expected. The Taiwanese giant wanted access to Whelan's lucrative Southern Ocean yellowfin and toothfish quotas, and his quotas elsewhere in the world. Whelan wasn't happy about it, but there was little he could do. It would likely mean an end to his regular way of doing business. In other words, Khalil explained, Whelan's company stocks had gone up, but his own had gone down, in terms of influence. The release of the full video would see him further marginalised. It would make securing finance difficult, if not impossible, from his usual institutional lenders. It would destroy his personal reputation as a man who wanted to improve fisheries, and the way that things were done.

'In other words,' Cutler said. 'You want me to send you the video, and not Whelan.'

'Correct. We won't be able to do anything about the murders, or anything else you've seen, because they're beyond our jurisdiction, but—'

'He's a good man to have on the hook.'

'Very clever, but yes. The number of drugs and weapons coming in on fishing boats is ridiculous. Tell me what you want, and I'll make sure you get it.'

'Getting a hook into Whelan – is that why you made the introduction between me and Whelan in the first place? Why you recommended me for the job?'

'You're too smart for your own good. I've told you that before. But yes, sometimes dreams really do come true. I assume that you've figured it out?'

'I think so, but not me. Fazal, one of the crewmen, who gave me the phone.'

'And?'

'Whelan was lying when he said that his Spanish PI had only just sent him the video, the day he sent it to me. It was sent to him a long time before. Whelan said that the Spanish PI was tracing it back. He must have found out that an OceanFresh ship was there. He must have traced the video right back to the engineer's phone. In other words, I wasn't on the *Shuen* just to find out what happened to Bevan Whelan, but also to locate the phone, or any other record of what happened.'

'That sounds about right. Human nature, eh? Now—'

Cutler smiled. 'You got a pen and paper? What I want – it's a long list.'

He hung up when he'd finished. O'Reardon was still at the wheel, staring out at the ocean, the bleached white hairs on his arms and shoulders catching the light.

'You're not as stupid as I thought, Aussie. Now go and get some chow, and a deck shower at least. We got a long way to go.'

'Yes, Captain. And thanks.'

'You're welcome, son. It's good to get the blood up every now and then.'

40.

The video was proving to be very persuasive, and the private jet Whelan had chartered from his wealthy mate was getting a workout.

Cutler and Casey drove their dirt bikes along the dusty access track that entered the Guam international airport via a back entrance, accelerating along the minor runway before angling into the hangar where the crewmen from the three *Shuen* vessels were quartered.

Casey removed her helmet and shook out her hair. Cutler took off his own helmet and slung it on the handlebars. The day was hot and cloudless, and out of the wind generated by their bikes, spearing along the coastal roads, Casey pointing out the spinner dolphins hunting and playing inside the fringing reefs, Cutler could already feel the sweat coming to the surface of his skin.

Nine of the Indonesian and Malaysian men had already gone out, wearing money belts stuffed with a mix of American dollars, rupiah and ringgits. Cutler had been there late the previous evening along with Fazal to see off Budi, Wayan and Aadam. The men embraced Fazal, and shook Cutler's hand, excited but still not quite believing that they were headed home, back paid for their years on the ocean, at the Australian minimum hourly rate, as Cutler had demanded of Whelan.

Cutler knew the feeling. Many things could still go wrong, and they wouldn't quite believe it until they reached home, were in the arms of their loved ones. Even then, they would need to be careful, keeping away from the spies of the fisheries agents who'd employed them, who'd tricked them into a life of servitude and debt.

The men had no papers, for a start, their passports confiscated by the fisheries agents in Singapore and Manila, or by the Taiwanese captains. O'Reardon had chosen Guam not only because it was close to where the men had been liberated, but also because the *Monterey* was flagged to America, and was less likely to arouse suspicions as it entered the territorial waters. Even so, the Fijian crew had remained on the *Monterey*, while O'Reardon brought the men ashore in three separate trips in the skiff, late at night, to a quiet beach on the south of the island. Casey's mother met them with a minibus which took the men to the airport hangar, where they'd remained ever since, hidden from the American authorities.

Cutler had waited nervously into the early hours for news of the Indonesian and Malaysian crew's arrival in Surabaya, the airport chosen because it was familiar to the Australian pilot, but who assured Cutler that he'd get the men off the plane and through the fence and into the city. The call came through at five in the morning from Budi that he was safe, with the others, in a taxi to the central bus station, where the men would go their separate ways.

The three Filipino men roused themselves from their positions in the hangar, where tarps had been folded to form beds, and a nearby table was laden with food and drinks. They didn't have any luggage, and each stuffed two plastic bags with the American snacks and drinks in preparation for the flight, and then the long journey home.

Cutler had bought each of the men mobile phones, and international cards. Their families knew that they were coming home, knew to be discreet about it too.

Fazal was still talking on the phone when Cutler entered the hangar, where the air was thick and still. He looked at Cutler and put up a finger.

While Casey guided the three Filipino men to the stairs of the jet, Cutler went to the coffin on a trolley that waited near the entrance. The coffin had been hastily secured from a local undertaker, and it was too large for Fernando's small body, but it was nicely appointed with silver-plated handles and a large silver cross on its lid. The money owed to Fernando had been nailed inside the coffin, along with a tropical wreath made by Casey's mum, out of dried reeds and bamboo, and some flowers that Cutler didn't recognise. There was nothing else of Fernando to include inside the coffin – no passport, photographs or possessions, except for the letter to his parents written by Fazal, which told them in broad terms what had happened to their son, warning them to keep quiet about the money, and an apology that he couldn't protect him.

Fazal was on the phone to them now, organising them to be at the remote airport to collect the body, and from there to take him home.

Cutler put his hand on the coffin, which was oddly cold. He thought of the boy's parents, and their misery and grief, written now across Fazal's face as he broke the news. It had taken him all night, and many calls to locate them, in a small fishing village outside of Sorsogon City.

The Rohingya man wiped tears from his eyes as he spoke, his English plain and exaggerated, spelling everything out. He nodded and hung up, took a deep breath.

Cutler still had no idea what Fazal was going to do. He had no home to return to, his village erased from the map, his family scattered across Bangladesh, and in refugee camps across Southeast Asia. The only win Cutler had been able to secure from Whelan for Fazal was to begin proceedings to have his cousin removed from Australian detention. Whelan didn't have that kind of juice with the federal minister, but Khalil had clearly been able to demonstrate the usefulness of Whelan's potential information to the politician. The aim was for Fazal's cousin to be released into the community on a visa.

When Cutler had offered to get Fazal into Australia, the tall man had spat on the floor. 'I don't want to go to your country,' he hissed, and Cutler left it at that.

The Australian pilot didn't know any suitable airports in Bangladesh but was working on it.

Fazal crossed to the other side of the coffin, took the handle. He moved stiffly, uncertainly, unused to walking on land. Cutler took a handle, and the two men wheeled it out into the sun, a heat mirage building on the runway behind the jet, the dark green of the tropical forest on the ridgeline across from them softening the brightness of the city behind the walls.

The cargo area of the jet was small. The pilot had secured some scaffolding from the hangar. Cutler and Fazal took up the coffin, which was surprisingly heavy, lifting it onto the scaffold where the pilot was waiting, his eyes hidden behind sunglasses. He'd obviously been ordered not to converse with them, because he hadn't said more than a handful of words to them throughout the whole operation. His aloofness had made the crewmen even more nervous, but even now he merely grunted as he pushed the coffin off the scaffold and into the bay.

Cutler and Fazal climbed down, followed by the pilot. Cutler unlocked the wheels of the scaffold while the pilot began to remove the chocks at the front and rear wheels of the jet. He said nothing as he climbed aboard and pulled up the ladder-door. He was clearly used to transporting captains of industry, and not fishermen. He was breaking the law by doing so, was in a hurry to leave. Cutler and Fazal pushed the scaffold back toward the hangar, while the jet engines roared to life, the air whistling around them as it taxied away.

Cutler and Fazal watched it roll onto the runway, pausing to await permission to depart.

'Have you thought any more about my offer?' Cutler asked out of the side of his mouth, not daring to look Fazal in the eye.

'Yes, I have.'

Fazal didn't want to live in Australia, but Cutler was pretty sure he could secure an Australian passport for the stateless man.

'And?'

'I accept. With thanks. Is your benefactor genuine about the offer? He won't cancel it in a year from now?'

'He doesn't have much choice, and no, he wouldn't dare. We just need to organise an exit stamp. It'll take time, but it'll happen.'

'Money talks, as they say.'

'Yes, but it's also money that's motivating him. If that video ever comes to light, he will lose millions, maybe tens of millions.'

'Maybe it should come to light.'

'I agree. But not now.'

'Yes, not now.'

'What are you going to do with the money? How are you going to start?'

As well as Fazal's years of back pay, which amounted to nearly a quarter of a million dollars, a fortune in Myanmar, Cutler had demanded that Whelan provide Fazal with a matching amount. It was Fazal's dream to contribute somehow to the sailor organisations that existed in countries like Singapore and Malaysia, or to set up his own, specifically to help rescue trafficked Rohingya men and women. He planned to begin by getting word out to the villages that remained in Myanmar, and in the refugee camps in Bangladesh and elsewhere, that all that glitters is definitely not gold. It would be highly dangerous work, and it would take money for bribes, and to pay the manufactured debts of those already enslaved.

The question was where he'd base himself. He liked Malaysia, felt comfortable there. When the passport arrived, he'd be able to travel to KL and set up, start a new life.

The jet jolted, inched forward and began to roll, its sleek wings bowing under the weight of the thrust from the twin engines as it cruised now, picking up speed and lifting, soaring into the air and away to the ocean across the hills.

Casey was already astride her bike. She passed her helmet to Fazal, who fitted the straps. They were staying with Casey's mum, in her house overlooking the bay. Cutler and Fazal were going to bunk together in a shipping container turned into a room in the back yard, among the banana and pawpaw trees.

Cutler sat on this bike and waited for Fazal to slide on behind him, place his hands on Cutler's hips. Casey turned on her seat to smile at Cutler, its meaning hard to read. Her mother had been wary of him when he'd first arrived at their house, until mother and daughter shared a glance, after which she relaxed a little, which told Cutler that he and Casey would be friends, and nothing more. That was fine with him. He loved being in her company, but she was going back to sea with her father until the American semester started, and Cutler was returning home to Australia, to what exactly he didn't know.

One day he would receive a call from the florist, and then it would all start again, under a different name in another city and with a different group of men and women. He would befriend them, and then he would deceive them, and then he would disappear.

Where it stopped, he didn't know.

He switched the dirt bike on, revved the engine. The tall man behind him lifted his legs and gripped Cutler's waist, Casey already rolling on the tarmac toward the track that led into the fields, and from there to the coast roads south.

Cutler lifted his feet and felt the bike surge, eager to feel the wind on his face.

Author note

What motivates a writer to tell a story of course varies from writer to writer, and story to story. My early crime novels purposefully set out to entertain readers but also to use the medium of crime fiction to represent Western Australian stories around which enduring mythologies and enforced silences had accrued. I was lucky in that the more I looked at those silences, the more stories I found.

The motivation for writing *Cutler* isn't hard to identify. One of my great loves has always been the ocean. I was rarely happier as a kid than when I was either surfing or diving on the local reefs. As the father of three children, I of course want the same for them, and for any generations to come, despite the broader effects of our rapaciousness on a warming planet.

As I stand on the beach before entering the cool clear waters of the Indian Ocean where I dive with my family, the reefs in the national park alive with endemic and resident fish, crayfish, octopi, sea dragons and numerous other species, it's easy to imagine that all is well with the world's oceans. As recently as fifty years ago the common belief was that the global ocean contained an unlimited and eternally replenishing resource in the form of marine animals to be harvested. This belief has been devastating in its impact. While the public perception of the artisanal fisher aboard their small boat, motoring gamely into the infinite distance has been cleverly framed in commercials put out by brands such as John West et al., the reality of modern industrial fishing couldn't be more different. As with every industry in the latter part of the twentieth century, technological improvement, economies of scale and in many cases government subsidies have been game-changers, leading to the rapid depletion of fish stocks across the globe. Many have crashed beyond recovery, most famously the once legendary cod fishery off eastern Canada (according to the World Bank, an estimated 90 percent of the world's fishing stocks are already fully exploited, overexploited or depleted.) Fisheries scientists and conservationists have spoken to me of the ongoing 'race to the bottom' and of 'fishing down the food chain' as the number of adult fish belonging to apex species are diminished, and either juveniles of those species or less lucrative species are harvested instead, often for fishmeal. Even where the catch focus remains on apex or prestige fish such as bluefin tuna, marlin or swordfish, a perverse economy is at work whereby the more 'fished out' a species becomes, the higher its value on the open market, leading to increased effort for an ever-diminishing catch and an even more rapid decline in stocks.

Rising costs and increased competition, both within national Exclusive Economic Zones and in international waters, has also led to a particularly repugnant means of reducing the one aspect of expenditure that is often within a captain's control – that of the cost of labour. Maritime slavery is the result, with workers commonly underpaid (or not paid at all), routinely abused and in many cases murdered. It was recently estimated by Global Fishing

Watch that the number of forced labour victims (using a data set of 16,000 vessels) likely exceeded 100,000 souls, operating across all ocean basins.

The understandable focus of NGOs seeking to limit this global damage has been upon IUU (illegal, unreported and unregulated) or pirate fishers, registered under 'flags of convenience', for whom quotas and working conditions are unimportant, to say the least. What is becoming apparent, however, is that legitimate fishers are in fact the largest contributor to the environmental pollution (discarded fishing lines and nets) and diminishment of fish stocks around the globe, because of the sheer number of vessels, the scale of their operations and poor or corrupt monitoring of catch against quotas. Billions of humans depend upon fish protein for their sustenance, and fishing will always continue, but the remorseless logic of technological improvement and unfettered competition beyond the horizon, and therefore 'out of sight and out of mind', can only lead to increasingly empty oceans, unemployed fishers and hungry people.

The global ocean has not only protected us from the worst effects of climate change thus far, acting as a huge heat sink, but its creatures too have shown resilience in the sense that when given a chance, stocks of many species have shown an ability to recover when left alone. While the very idea of sustainable fishing is hotly contested, given the criminogenic nature of the industrial fishing business and the power of its lobbyists, there have been some minor success stories, such as the sustainability goals of the PNA tuna cartel (the eight countries' EEZs contain 25 percent of the world's tuna stocks) and its management, MSC certification and

Pacifical co-branding of the resulting Pacific tuna catch, which has seen skipjack tuna and yellowfin populations in the region stabilise.

More broadly, common suggestions for remedial action to make industrial fishing more sustainable in the short term include the removal of subsidies that enable the otherwise economically unviable distant water fishery, and the redeployment of those subsidies toward broader enforcement measures. Other measures include better enforcement of supply chain, and monitoring procedures to diminish the capacity of illegally caught and 'forced labour-caught' fish to enter wealthier markets (an estimated 20 to 34 percent of fish imported into wealthier countries is illegally sourced and 'laundered' with legally caught fish), together with the total cessation of industrial fishing in international waters. The common theme among all of these proposals is improved monitoring and enforcement for the benefit of fisheries workers, global fish stocks and the long-term health of the ocean itself.

—

I recently had the pleasure of sitting quietly next to a giant potato cod, nearly 14 metres down on the clear ocean floor at the entrance to Exmouth Gulf, adjacent to World Heritage–listed Ningaloo Reef. I watched as it opened its mouth to enable cleaner wrasse to go to work removing lice and other parasites. While the cod was being serviced, she had nothing to do except watch me, both of us motionless in the cool waters as the wrasse darted in and out of her cavernous mouth. This particular cod was safe from being caught due to her existence within the marine boundaries of a military facility, but even so the time we spent together and the curiosity and interest in her eye made me reflect upon my childhood, when I'd been a keen fisher and spearfisher, killing thousands of fish – usually dispatched with a knife to the head or a quick snapping of the neck. I'd been brought up to be respectful when taking a life, and yet even so, fish were generally considered to be different, and less worthy of such respect, perhaps because they lack the expressive features associated with more 'charismatic' marine megafauna and cetacean species. It's easy to not think of fish as intelligent creatures with complex social lives, although any time spent watching them closely will soon shift this perception.

The cod continued to wait patiently for her service to be completed, the electric colours of the wrasse in contrast to her warm brown skin. She was estimated to nearly fifty years old, roughly the same age as the 500-kilo Queensland grouper that lingered above us. The wrasse finished their work and the cod turned her flank to me, moving off into the deeper gloom. My brother signalled to me from further away, where he was watching two reef sharks resting on the sandy bottom. It was nearly time for us to return to the surface, my reluctance coloured by my wonder at the world beneath the waves, and a strange anxiety that this particular reef might not exist when next I return – an apprehension that I couldn't shake when I returned to the surface.

Not far from us, the oceanic horizon was littered with encroaching oil and gas rigs, and several industrial proposals have been mooted for the waters and wetlands even closer to where we're diving – schemes that only the intercessions of concerned citizens have to this point kept at bay. *The process is made by the people who are made by the process* said Bloch (albeit writing about utopian thinking), something never truer than when looking at the ability of fishing companies across the globe to subsume themselves within narratives and projections of national interest – elevating short-term profits and short-term yields above all else.

I would encourage anyone interested in this ongoing social and environmental catastrophe to donate their time and money to direct-action organisations that operate outside of 'the industry process' within a process of their own, on behalf of clients who lack a voice in the struggle to rein in the worst impulses of industry – namely affected workers and marine life itself, in all of its varied and wonderful forms.

As a small contribution of my own, it's my intention to donate a proportion of my earnings from sales of this book to such organisations.

Acknowledgements

This novel was conceived and written on the land and sea country of the Whadjuk Noongar people. I would like to acknowledge their ongoing custodianship of this country, as well as the specific importance of Noongar friendships and perspectives in shaping my own understanding of human responsibility and care.

There are many people to thank who helped make this novel possible. I'd like to thank my brother, Senator Peter Whish-Wilson, for his perspectives and contacts, as well as Sea Shepherd's Captain Pete Hammarstedt and Jeff Hansen, and also colleagues Matt Chrulew and Thor Kerr, and fellow writers Cass Lynch, Sara Foster, Portland Jones, Richard King, David Allan-Petale and Paul Hardisty. This book is partly dedicated to marine biologist Jeremy Prince and sculptor Simon Gilby for the conversation, fisheries background and the opportunity to dive on the old limestone reefs off the coast of Perth, accessible only by boat. Learning new things and sharing stories while dripping wet, drinking strong black coffee and eating cinnamon scrolls is good learning in my book.

Texts that provided useful background to the writing of this novel include Stephen Adolf's *Tuna Wars: Powers Around the Fish We Love to Conserve* (Springer, 2019), Joy McCann's *Wild Sea: A History of the Southern Ocean* (NewSouth, 2018), Guy Standing's

The Blue Commons: Rescuing the Economy of the Sea (Pelican, 2022), Ian Urbina's *The Outlaw Ocean: Journeys Across the Last Untamed Frontier* (Knopf, 2019), Vinciane Despret's *What Would Animals Say If We Asked the Right Questions?* (University of Minnesota Press, 2016), Richard Ellis's *The Empty Ocean* (Island Press, 2003), Jonathon Balcombe's *What a Fish Knows: The Inner Lives of Our Underwater Cousins* (Farrar, Straus & Giroux, 2016), Matt Chrulew and Jeffrey Bussolini's *Angelaki: Journal of the Theoretical Humanities* online special issue on philosophical ethology, the many terrific articles contained in the online *Hakai Magazine*, as well as the reports and databases of NGOs and organisations like Greenpeace, Oceana, Sea Shepherd, WWF, The Pew Charitable Trusts and many others.

The snatch of song that Captain O'Reardon sings in the novel is taken from the Alfred Noyes poem 'Song of the Wooden-Legged Fiddler'.

As always, I'd like to acknowledge the insights and efforts of the team at Fremantle Press – my wonderful publisher and editor Georgia Richter, tireless publicity team of Claire Miller, Chloe Walton and Adam Matthews, as well as CEO Alex Allan. It's a privilege to work with you all.

Lastly, thanks to my family: Bella, Max, Fairlie and Luka, for the laughs, encouragement and regular mood corrections, as well as my parents, Tony and Rosemary, who taught me not only to swim but also to put my head under and look.

More crime from David Whish-Wilson

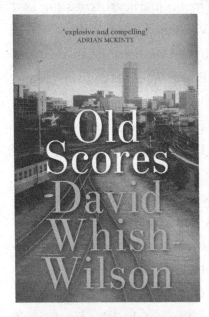

'explosive and compelling'
ADRIAN MCKINTY

Old Scores
David Whish-Wilson

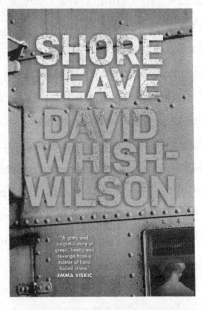

SHORE LEAVE
DAVID WHISH-WILSON

'A gritty and insightful story of greed, family and revenge from a master of hard-boiled crime'
EMMA VISKIC

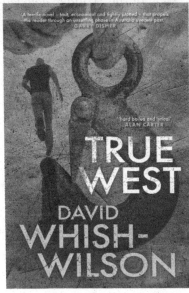

'A terrific novel – taut, economical and tightly plotted – that propels the reader through an unsettling phase in Australia's recent past.'
GARRY DISHER

'hard boiled and lyrical'
ALAN CARTER

TRUE WEST
DAVID WHISH-WILSON

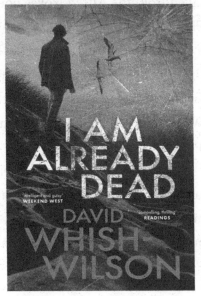

I AM ALREADY DEAD
'intelligent and gutsy'
WEEKEND WEST
'compelling, thrilling'
READINGS
DAVID WHISH-WILSON

available from fremantlepress.com.au

Historical fiction from David Whish-Wilson

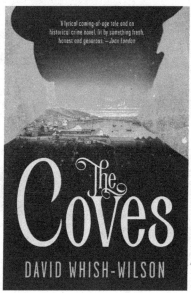

and all good bookstores

More great crime

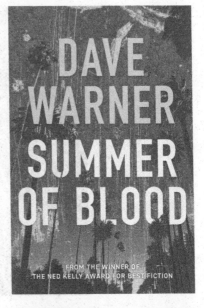

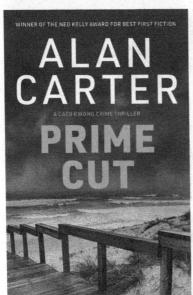

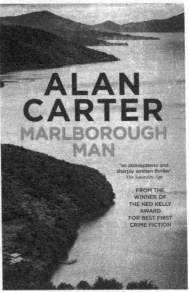

available from fremantlepress.com.au

from Fremantle Press

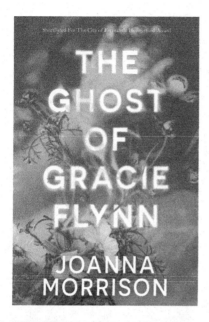

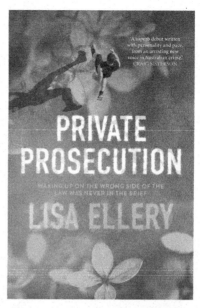

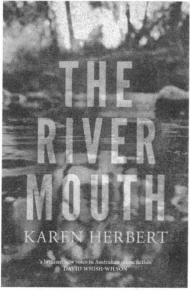

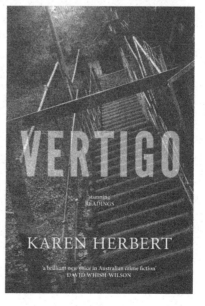

and all good bookstores